Readers love the Bronco's Boys series by ANDREW GREY

Inside Out

"I knew I had to read this as soon as I saw the cover, and I was not disappointed."

—Hearts on Fire

"Ready, Set, Go… Mr. Grey did it again! What a story! I completely absolutely loved it."

—Love Bytes

"Three reasons to grab a copy of *Inside Out*. 1/ it's Andrew Grey 2/ that glorious cover 3/ it's Andrew Grey!"

—MM Good Book Reviews

Upside Down

"I loved this book."

—It's About The Book

Backward

"If you are a fan of Andrew Grey, and I know many of you are, you won't want to miss this installment in the Bronco's Boys series."

—Prism Book Alliance

"*Backward* is a well-crafted addition to this series… I do believe this is my favorite Andrew Grey series now…"

—The Novel Approach

By ANDREW GREY (CONT.)

CHEMISTRY
Organic Chemistry • Biochemistry • Electrochemistry

GOOD FIGHT
The Good Fight • The Fight Within • The Fight for Identity • Takoda and Horse

LAS VEGAS ESCORTS
The Price • The Gift

LOVE MEANS…
Love Means… No Shame • Love Means… Courage
Love Means… No Boundaries
Love Means… Freedom • Love Means … No Fear
Love Means… Healing
Love Means… Family • Love Means… Renewal • Love Means… No Limits
Love Means… Patience • Love Means… Endurance

SENSES
Love Comes Silently • Love Comes in Darkness
Love Comes Home • Love Comes Around
Love Comes Unheard

SEVEN DAYS
Seven Days • Unconditional Love

STORIES FROM THE RANGE
A Shared Range • A Troubled Range • An Unsettled Range
A Foreign Range • An Isolated Range • A Volatile Range • A Chaotic Range

TALES FROM KANSAS
Dumped in Oz • Stuck in Oz • Trapped in Oz

TASTE OF LOVE
A Taste of Love • A Serving of Love • A Helping of Love
A Slice of Love

WITHOUT BORDERS
A Heart Without Borders • A Spirit Without Borders

WORK OUT
Spot Me • Pump Me Up • Core Training • Crunch Time
Positive Resistance • Personal Training • Cardio Conditioning
Work Me Out (Anthology)

Published by DREAMSPINNER PRESS
www.dreamspinnerpress.com

ROUND
AND
ROUND

ANDREW GREY

Published by
DREAMSPINNER PRESS

5032 Capital Circle SW, Suite 2, PMB# 279, Tallahassee, FL 32305-7886 USA
www.dreamspinnerpress.com

Round and Round
© 2015 Andrew Grey.

Cover Art
© 2015 L.C. Chase.
http://www.lcchase.com
Cover content is for illustrative purposes only and any person depicted on the cover is a model.

ISBN: 978-1-63476-846-7
Digital ISBN: 978-1-63476-847-4
Library of Congress Control Number: 2015952959
First Edition December 2015

Printed in the United States of America
∞
This paper meets the requirements of
ANSI/NISO Z39.48-1992 (Permanence of Paper).

Love always to Dominic

CHAPTER ONE

THE BASS beat started at his feet, working its vibrating way up his legs to his hips. Normally that would be enough to get Kevin Foster to dance. It sure had that effect on everyone else. But instead he stood next to the table in Bronco's and watched as the club went wild. Everyone had already been whipped into an erotic frenzy by the strippers, who were showing off almost everything the good Lord gave them, and they hinted at what they couldn't put on display. Kevin had watched, and of course he'd enjoyed himself. After all, he didn't have a boyfriend, and as it turned out, he was the only guy in the club tonight who no one seemed to be interested in.

"Come dance with us," Zach shouted as he reached for Kevin's hand.

Kevin shook his head, and Zach turned and was engulfed in his lover's arms. Bull was a great guy, and Kevin thought the world of him. But truth be told, he was jealous as hell. One by one, each of his friends had paired off, leaving him the odd guy out. Zach had Bull, and Jeremy had paired up with Lowell, a guy they affectionately called Spook. Kevin hadn't been too keen on him to begin with, but he'd saved both Jeremy and their friend Tristan, so the guy was okay in Kevin's book. Besides, Jeremy loved Lowell, so what was he going to do? Tristan had captured Harry's attention and heart. Harry was Bull's partner in the club, and that had grated because Kevin had liked Harry as well, but then Ken had come along and Kevin's attention had been captured by the sexy police officer and….

His wandering thoughts stilled as a small flash of light in the far corner caught his eye. Kevin didn't even know why it got his attention.

1

It had to have been Bull telling all of them over and over to be aware of what was going on around them. He watched that area but didn't see anything more for a few seconds—until the light began to build. A chill ran up his spine and everything else was forgotten. Kevin raced to Bull, parting dancers and pushing people aside. He patted Bull's shoulder, and when he didn't respond right away, Kevin slapped him on the arm. Bull turned and Kevin pointed. He knew Bull had seen what he saw. Bull stopped dancing and pulled Zach along with him toward the DJ booth.

Kevin raced to the door to the office area and put in the code Bull had told them to use in case of an emergency.

The music suddenly stopped. "Everyone please exit the building," Bull said into the microphone that connected to the sound system. "Don't delay, just make for the nearest exit immediately. Security, open all the doors right away."

Kevin pulled open the door as light burst from the back corner and flames began licking up the wall. Every time he'd entered the office corridor, he'd passed the fire hose on the wall, though he hadn't really noticed it until now.

"Fire!" someone cried, and screams rent the air. Kevin propped the door open and grabbed the hose. He yanked it out behind him as he raced back into the club. "Turn on the water," he yelled to a man who passed him. "Just follow the hose and turn it on now." He hadn't seen anyone he knew and just had to hope the kid did as he asked. He continued racing through the club, and the hose got heavier as it filled with water.

He stumbled and swore at the top of his lungs, pointing the hose in the direction of the fire. Water sprayed everywhere, and he was damn lucky he didn't take anyone out with the force of the spray. He continued moving toward the flames, spraying water on the walls. Instantly he was soaked. Walls of steam rose from where the heat met the water. The flames had reached the ceiling, but they died down fast. Kevin remembered being told in school that when using a fire extinguisher to point it at the base of the flame, so he did that here.

He coughed and angled his face away from the black smoke that came off the fire, rolling along the ceiling of the club.

The flames flared up for a few seconds, and Kevin worried that he'd done something wrong, but then they died pretty quickly, steam mixing with the acrid smoke. It burned his eyes, but he blinked and continued spraying the water.

Someone grabbed the hose and muscled him out of the way. "Get out of here," the guard, who Kevin recognized after a second, told him.

"I got this. You make sure everyone is safe." Kevin wrenched back the hose and continued what he was doing. He kept spraying water until it ran over his feet, soaking his shoes, and the last of the fire was out. The smoke was lessening and he could see better, even as the dampness soaked him to the skin. When he saw no more fire activity, he turned off the nozzle and breathed a sigh of relief, his heart still pounding in his ears.

"Is everybody out?" Bull's voice boomed in the empty space. Kevin turned, and the huge man took the hose from him. "Quick thinking," Bull told him. "I'll go shut off the water, and then we all need to get out of here."

"Bull!" Harry called from across the room.

"We all need to get out of here now!" Bull cried. He guided Kevin through the office corridor, where he shut off the water, and ushered him out through the club's back door to where everyone gathered on the street. Traffic was being cordoned off by the police, and firefighters passed them on their way inside, with ambulance personnel right behind.

"Did everyone get out?" Bull asked as Harry hurried up to him. Kevin could tell by the way Harry's face was drained of all color that something worse than the fire had happened. Firefighters exited the building, hurrying right to the police, where they conferred for a few seconds. Then they all rushed back inside. "What happened?"

"I'm not sure," Harry said. "But there was a man on the floor maybe twenty feet from the door. I don't know what happened, but he wasn't moving. I tried to get him out, but…." Harry shook his head.

"He was dead?"

"Oh yeah. I don't know if he was trampled or what, but…." Harry turned away. He walked toward the parking area next to the club and bent over. Retching sounds filled the air, and one of the EMTs hurried over to Harry.

Kevin rushed to his friend, comforting him as he helped Harry stand up, and the EMT gently took him over to one of the ambulances.

Harry was basically okay, and there wasn't much more to be done other than wait around. The police fanned out and talked to all of the people in the club, letting some go and asking others to remain. Slowly, as people were questioned and released, the crowd thinned.

"Can we talk to you?" a firefighter asked Kevin, and he nodded. Jeremy hovered around Harry, and since there was nothing further Kevin could do for him, he followed the firefighter to where other firefighters and a police officer waited.

"We understand you saw the beginning of the fire?" the police officer asked. Kevin tried not to let his mind flash on Ken; that was over and he needed to move on.

"Yes. I saw a flash of light and then a few seconds later the actual flames."

"You were the one who got the hose and actually extinguished the fire?" the policeman asked.

"Yes," he answered, nodding. Kevin didn't like him. His questions sounded like accusations.

"How did you know where the hose was?" the firefighter who'd first approached him asked in a light accent that Kevin thought was Scottish, now that he got a chance to hear it again. Wow, their own personal MacDreamy, right there in Harrisburg.

"I'll conduct the interview," the policeman interrupted.

Kevin turned to him. "He can ask the questions," he said, smiling at the fireman. In the light now, he could see the man was gorgeous, with olive skin and the shadow of a beard. The firefighter smiled and his face lit up. "I'm friends with Zach, Tristan, and Jeremy." He pointed out each of them. "Zach's partner owns the club with Tristan's partner, Harry. So I've been in the back room area plenty of times. Bull gave us each a code so we could get in if we needed to. He's very protective of Zach, and by extension the rest of us." He smiled because, well, he couldn't help it. This guy was firefighter hotness to the extreme.

"So after you saw the flames…," MacDreamy Hotness said.

"Yeah. I grabbed the hose and hurried back into the club. I told a guy running past me to turn on the water. I wasn't sure if he would, but he did, and I started spraying the wall. The smoke from the fire was really black, and it rolled up onto the ceiling. I stayed as low as I could and sprayed the water at the base and then up the walls."

"You did really well," MacDreamy Hotness said, and Kevin grinned. "Your quick thinking probably saved the club and kept quite a few people from getting hurt."

"Can you tell us anything else you remember about when the fire started?" the policeman asked.

"Only that I thought at first someone was lighting a cigarette. I figured one of the bouncers would take care of it. They're pretty good about that sort of thing."

"Where were Mr. Klinger and Mr. Krebbs when all this was happening?"

Kevin figured they probably had to ask stuff like that, but it pissed him off nonetheless. "Bull was dancing with Zach."

"Does he do that a lot?" the officer pressed.

"Usually just once or twice a night. He has a job to do, but Zach loves to dance, and Bull loves it when Zach dances. Harry doesn't dance much at all, but Tristan managed to get Harry out of his office and onto the floor for a quick dance."

"So they weren't near the area where the fire started?"

"No. I couldn't see who was nearby. I only saw the light. I told Bull, and I heard him on the sound system, getting people out of the club, while I was getting the hose. Then someone yelled fire, and people must have stampeded to get out. Bull was trying to keep people calm and just get them to exit. I heard him."

"No one is accusing your friends of doing anything wrong," MacDreamy Hotness said. "He has to know what happened even if he's being kind of a jerk about it." MacDreamy Hotness looked at the officer and then back at him. Kevin wondered if there was some history there. "Is there anything else you can remember?"

"Not that I can think of. Did everyone get out?" he asked, pretending he hadn't overheard what Harry had told Bull.

"No. We're still trying to piece together what happened. But without your quick thinking, things could have been much worse." MacDreamy Hotness took a step closer. "You showed courage under pressure, and that's rare." He turned to the police officer, and Kevin was sure he saw a challenge in his expression. "Is there anything else you need, Reyes?"

5

Officer Reyes walked away, and MacDreamy Hotness turned back to Kevin. "Don't let him bother you. The guy's a hothead and a pain in the ass." He leaned closer. "I ought to know—I dated him for a while. What a piece of work." He winked, then turned and went back inside the club. Kevin watched him go, mouth hanging open a little. He hoped he wasn't drooling as he thought of MacDreamy Hotness and what he might look like under all the fire equipment.

Almost instantly he chastised himself for having lusty thoughts about the firefighter when someone had died trying to get out of the club.

"Is everything okay?" Jeremy asked as he came up and put an arm around him.

"Yeah. They wanted to know what happened, that's all. Where's Spook?"

"You know him. There are way too many police officers around, so he made himself scarce. He's probably somewhere nearby, watching everything that's going on. Before he left he said to keep an eye out because the guy who started the fire is probably hanging around to see the aftermath of his handiwork."

"I didn't think it could be an accident. Not with what I saw."

"Spook said it wasn't, but he didn't know any more. He told me to keep my eyes open, and that he'd be watching."

Kevin nodded but didn't look to see if he could spot Spook. He'd learned long ago that when Jeremy's partner didn't want to be seen, he wouldn't be. Being able to blend into a crowd and be noticed by nobody was one of his talents. His real name was Lowell, but only Jeremy called him that. To everyone else he was Spook. "Okay." That made him feel better.

Kevin watched the front of the club and saw MacDreamy Hotness come out. This time he took off his jacket and walked around in fire pants, boots, and a T-shirt. Man, Kevin's imagination must have been going faulty because the real thing was so much better than what he'd conjured up.

"I see you watching," Jeremy teased.

"I can watch all I want."

"What about you and Officer Ken?" Jeremy asked.

"He moved to Pittsburgh a while ago," Kevin said.

"I thought you were doing the long-distance thing."

Kevin kept watching the firefighter and wondered how he could get a peek to see just what he had in those yellow pants. "We were, but it wasn't working out. I made plans for last weekend to go over and spent three hours in the car to get there, and he got called in to work. I spent the weekend in his apartment waiting for him to come home. It sucked, and after that we both realized the whole thing wasn't fair to either of us. So we broke it off."

"I'm sorry."

"It was over long before that. I think we both knew it but weren't ready to admit defeat. He's happy being closer to his family, and they love him on the force there. He's going to get promoted and stuff...."

"Are you really okay?" Jeremy asked and hugged him.

"I am. It's better for both of us, and I was tired of sitting around waiting for him to call. Then he would call and I'd be at the club or something. It's okay. I guess there's no breakup easier than the one with hundreds of miles between you. Absence doesn't make the heart grow fonder, just lonely as hell."

"Feel sorry for yourself much?" Jeremy teased.

Kevin glowered at him. He really wasn't in the mood.

"I'm just picking on you," Jeremy said.

They wandered off so they wouldn't be in the way, watching as a stretcher with a covered figure was wheeled out of the club and loaded into an ambulance. Kevin lowered his gaze to the ground.

"Poor guy," he whispered. "I'm only grateful it wasn't someone I know."

Jeremy pointed across to where a lone figure stood, nervously shifting from foot to foot. "Is that... God, what's his name?"

"Bradley, and my guess is that he's missing someone."

"Oh God," Kevin groaned softly. "Wasn't he dating Mario Vitelli?"

"Yeah. They were dating, and I think we just got a pretty good idea who was on that gurney," Jeremy whispered, but Kevin was already on his way over. He didn't know Bradley very well, but as soon as he got close enough he grabbed him in a hug, and Bradley fell apart in his arms.

"They need me to wait. Since I'm not family, they said I can't ride with him. Not that there's anything I can do." He broke down on Kevin's shoulder, holding him tight. "They said they would notify his family. I don't have their number, and they wouldn't give me his cell phone, so I don't know what else to do right now."

"Just hold yourself together and answer any questions they have."

"He was right behind me. As soon as someone yelled fire, it was pandemonium, and everyone in back was pushing those in front. I stayed on my feet but lost Mario's hand. When I got out, I looked and looked for him, but…. That guy who first said to leave did things right. It was the morons who panicked that should be strung up!" Bradley yelled and then broke down once again.

"Can I help?" It was MacDreamy Hotness.

"This is Bradley. He was the boyfriend of the man—" What could he say? "The guy they just took out."

"They've spoken to you, right?" MacDreamy asked, and Bradley nodded. "They're taking him to the medical examiner. They need to find the exact cause of death. I know it's hard, but the best thing you can do is go home. Call your family and make sure someone can be with you. Sitting alone at a time like this is not good."

"Do you have anyone?" Kevin asked.

"My sister," Bradley answered.

"Then call her. We'll stay with you until you know."

"She has kids."

"I'm sure they would love to see their uncle, no matter what the circumstances," Kevin said. He stayed with Bradley while he made a call.

Apparently Bradley's sister told him to come right over. "She's going to wait up," he said.

"Then I'll go check and make sure they're done with you." MacDreamy hurried away, and Kevin couldn't help watching him leave.

"You're going to be okay." Kevin stayed with Bradley until the police said he could leave. Then he and Jeremy walked Bradley to his car and made sure he got on the road okay before rejoining the ever-dwindling groups of people. Of course, the news vans showed up a few minutes later, adding even more excitement as they set up cameras and lights to do their stories.

"You might as well go home," Bull said to both Kevin and Jeremy. "Harry and I need to stay, but if you could get Zach and Tristan home too, I'd appreciate it."

Kevin had had a few drinks, but that had been hours ago now. He offered to drive, so they all piled in his old Taurus and he made the rounds, getting everyone home before going to his own small, crappy place.

For the past few years, Kevin had lived with one of his friends, but when Tristan paired off with Harry, that had left Kevin on his own, so he'd moved from the place they'd shared to a small one-bedroom apartment he could afford on his own. For Kevin, there were things more important than his apartment, and those were his computers. Once he arrived home, he went to the bedroom, which doubled as his office and work space. He logged in and checked his e-mail for anything urgent. Thankfully there was nothing other than a note from his father, which could wait until morning.

Knowing everything was okay in his little world, he undressed, putting his stinky clothes in a plastic bag and getting them out of the room. Then he hopped in the shower to get the smell of smoke off him before climbing into his twin bed. There hadn't been a need for anything bigger with Ken gone, and this way he had more room for his electronics. Kevin turned out the lights and tried to go to sleep, but it was hours before he was able to drop off.

KEVIN WOKE to knocking on his front door. He got out of bed and had the presence of mind to put on a robe before opening the door partway to see who was banging at this hour of the morning. "Mrs. Vertebedian."

"I heard you come in late last night, and since I made baklava, I thought I'd give you some." She offered him a plate, and he took it gratefully.

"I love you," he whispered, and the old lady giggled. "That's so thoughtful."

"You know, you shouldn't stay out till all hours. I know it's what you kids do, but did you see there was a fire at one of those places? I know you like to go out dancing and hunting for boys, but you should be careful."

"I was there," he said and stepped back from the door, letting her in. Kevin had met her the day he'd moved in, and she was sweet, but very lonely. "How about I put on a pot of coffee and get dressed? Then we can sit down and eat ourselves into a delightful sugar coma, and I'll tell

9

you all about it." He started the coffee and then padded to his bedroom and closed the door before pulling on clothes. When he returned, the apartment smelled of coffee, the scent enough to revive him a little. Kevin got two mugs, filled them, and handed one to his guest.

"Was it as bad as they said on the television?" she asked. Kevin placed milk and sugar on the table, and she began adding what she wanted. Lord, the amount of sugar she added was enough to turn *him* diabetic.

"I don't know. I haven't watched. The fire itself wasn't a big deal. I put it out with the hose at the club. But someone was trampled in the panic, sort of a friend of a friend."

"I suppose you would know him." Kevin didn't correct her. She didn't need to know that there wasn't a secret gayboy handshake or that every gay man didn't know every other one. It wasn't worth the explaining, and she hadn't meant anything by it.

"It was really sad. His boyfriend was there and lost track of him during the crush." He sipped from his mug and closed his eyes briefly, letting the caffeine start to work its magic.

"I'm sorry, dear." She sipped loudly and added some more milk before tasting again. Apparently it was to her liking now. "Did you say you put the fire out? Then you're a hero."

He shook his head. "I did what anyone would have done. The fireman said I did a good job, though." Kevin didn't mean to sigh, but he did. He leaned closer. "He was really cute and Scottish, I'd guess. His accent...." He rolled his eyes and held his breath, then blew it out. "Like buttah...."

"What's his name?"

"I don't know. In my mind I'm calling him MacDreamy Hotness, and let me tell you I'd love to see what he has under his kilt." He cackled and Mrs. Vertebedian did the same. From her stories, she'd been a high-stepper in her youth. "But I got to see him in his fireman's pants and a Tshirt. That was enough to start a fire." He reached for one of the pieces of baklava and bit into it, humming at the numminess. "No one can make these like you."

"Thank you, dear," she said, beaming, and then she ate one herself. "I used to have lots of people to bake for, but now they're gone."

He knew. In the time he'd lived here, he'd only seen her have visitors a few times.

"Have you been to the senior center lately?" Kevin knew she went like clockwork, but it gave her something to talk about. He reached for another pastry, then curled his nose. He sniffed and followed the smell to the door of his apartment. When he opened it, smoke wafted in. "Call 911," he told his guest and raced down the stairs. He found Mrs. V's door open with smoke billowing out. It was white, and he didn't see any flames or black smoke. He thought about going in but pulled the fire alarm in the hall instead and raced back upstairs.

"We need to get out."

"They're coming," she said. "Where is the fire?"

Kevin didn't answer. He hustled her out of the door and down the stairs. She didn't move quickly, stopping to gasp when she realized the smoke was coming from her apartment. Others hurried past them, carrying bags and other small things in their hands.

Sirens rang out as he stepped from the building. Mrs. V coughed and Kevin gasped for air. Being in a fire twice in less than a day was apparently more than his lungs could take. He managed to make it to the grass before his legs collapsed and he gasped for breath.

The sirens screamed and people rushed around him. A mask was placed over his mouth, and he looked up into a familiar face.

"You again?" MacDreamy Hotness said with a smile. "Just keep that in place. It'll help you breathe."

Kevin nodded. "What happened?"

"An oven fire. It's all right, just smoke. The fire was only in the oven."

Kevin pointed to Mrs. V, who wandered around a little helplessly. MacDreamy got someone to help her, and that was a relief. "She must have forgotten. She came up to see me and must have forgotten she had something in the oven." He felt bad.

MacDreamy put the mask over his mouth again. "Just breathe and get the smoke out of your lungs."

"All right." If MacDreamy kept looking at him with those kind eyes, he'd sit still the entire dang day.

"They're clearing out the building and opening the windows to get the smoke out." There was a breeze, and it wasn't long before smoke puffed out the front windows of the building, driven by the wind. "Feeling better?"

Kevin nodded again. "I'm okay."

"Just breathe and stay quiet. You gave us a scare."

"My head is clear and I feel much better," he said, removing the mask. "Thank you."

"I certainly hope this isn't going to be a habit—you showing up at all my fire calls."

"To be precise, you're showing up to all my calls, and I think I like it. Hopefully I won't have to be in a fire to see you again," Kevin said and blushed something fierce. He hadn't meant to be that provocative or forward. His mouth had engaged before his brain. But he liked it when MacDreamy Hotness smiled at him.

"Let's get this area cleared of people," another firefighter said. "The building should be safe to reenter soon, but the apartment where it started is going to need to be cleaned."

"I better go," MacDreamy said and turned away to help control the gawkers.

After a few hours they were all allowed back inside. To his surprise, even Mrs. Vertebedian was able to go. She didn't have a stove. That seemed to have been carted off, which was probably just as well, but at least she still had her home.

Kevin kept his windows open all day, and the landlord put fans in the hallways to get the smell out of the rugs and things. After all the excitement and the fact that he'd been up late and hadn't slept much, he tried resting in the afternoon.

"Okay, Mrs. V," he called when he heard a knock and went over to open the door. He had expected her to ask to use his stove. The woman cooked all the time. It was her thing, and being without a stove must be driving her crazy, so he'd figured she'd wander up. He pulled open the door, but it wasn't Mrs. Vertebedian.

It was MacDreamy Hotness, and this time he was in jeans and a Tshirt that left much less to the imagination than those baggy fire pants had.

"Did I do something wrong?" Kevin asked, looking around. After the past couple of days, he half expected his apartment to burst into flames.

"Of course not. I wanted to make sure you were breathing okay. You looked pretty wiped out when we found you on the grass." He smiled, and what a smile it was: perfect teeth, a glint in his eyes, and dimples, even.

"I'm okay. I was going to lie down for a while." He covered a yawn. "Sorry. I'm a little tired." He wondered why MacDreamy was here. "Was there some other information you needed?"

"No. I didn't come by to talk to you about the fire." He stepped a little closer. "It isn't very often that I get to meet a guy who's a hero twice in two days. Well, not one as cute as you are."

Kevin giggled and covered his mouth again. "I'm not a hero," he said. The cute comment he wasn't going to dispute because it was really nice to hear. "I just did what I was supposed to do. I only hope that part of my day isn't always going to include a call to the fire department." Although if MacDreamy was the one to show up, Kevin just might. "So you came here to see me? Was it to ask me questions or something?"

"Actually, it was. I was wondering if it would be all right if I took you out sometime." He flashed a smile that would stop traffic, and for a brief moment Kevin wondered if this was happening to him. Before his friends settled down, they were always getting asked out. They were outgoing and good-looking. Kevin wasn't. His features were average at best.

"Me?" Kevin asked, instantly feeling stupid. There was no one else here, after all. "MacDreamy Hotness is asking me out." Kevin slapped his hand over his face and hoped like hell the ground under his feet would open up and swallow him whole.

"What did you call me?" he asked with a grin.

"I only made that up because I didn't know your name, and with your accent and all, it just came to mind." Kevin's cheeks heated. He wondered how much longer he was going to have to endure this before MacDreamy Hotness decided he was crazy and turned to leave. At this point, Kevin gave him thirty seconds, tops.

"I think that's the nicest thing anyone has said to me in a long time." He continued smiling. "I'm Angus MacTavish. At least that's my real name, but I'll have it changed to MacDreamy Hotness for you."

Kevin's cheeks heated even more. But at least Angus wasn't upset. "I'm Kevin Foster," he stammered.

"So how about it, Kevin Foster?"

Dang, he loved the way Angus said his name. "Okay." He wanted to giggle, but that wouldn't give the impression he wanted, so he managed to stifle it and ended up smiling like some sort of idiot. "Ummm, do you want some coffee or something?"

"That would be nice," Angus said.

Kevin backed up so Angus could come in. Kevin immediately began fluttering around the apartment, touching pillows and wishing he'd thought about what the place looked like before inviting MacDreamy inside. *Angus. His name is Angus.* He offered him a chair and then fluttered into the kitchen. He started the coffee and put the plate of baklava on the table. "Mrs. Vertebedian made them for me. She's the lady who set her stove on fire earlier. Poor thing, she came up here to give these to me, and I asked her to stay, and she forgot what she was cooking. So the fire earlier is partly my fault, and I feel really bad for her because now she doesn't have a stove, and all the people in the building are going to blame her because everything smells like smoke, and it wasn't her fault." Had he really just said all of that without taking a breath? He needed to get a grip or Angus would think he was some twink version of the Energizer Bunny. *Breathe. Take a minute and breathe,* he reminded himself.

"Do I make you nervous?" Angus asked.

Kevin stared at him for two seconds and was off again. "Of course you do. How can you not? MacDreamy Hotness is in my apartment. I mean, I only saw you the first time last night, but…." He fanned himself. "Those fire pants aren't very flattering, but they do leave a lot to the imagination, and then you took off your jacket—" He found himself staring at Angus's chest and completely lost his train of thought, which was probably good because at least now he wasn't rambling on like a complete fool. He abruptly turned away and went back into the kitchen. He needed to shut the hell up. This was embarrassing. He'd only just met the guy and he was already making a total fool of himself. He willed the coffee to hurry up. When he turned around, Angus was just biting into one of the sweet pastries.

"Dang," Angus muttered.

"Mrs. V is awesome. She's pretty much alone now, so when she cooks, I tend to be the recipient of part of the amazingness. That's why the fire started, I guess. She needs someone to talk to, and we were having coffee." He felt terrible.

"Things like that happen. What's really important is that no one was hurt and everyone got out of the building safely."

Kevin's mind went immediately to Mario and Bradley.

Thankfully the coffee finished, and he poured two cups and handed one to Angus. "I never know what to say at times like this," Kevin said as he sat down. "I mean, I sort of knew the guy who died last night, and I'm sorry that he's gone and all, but would it be awful to ask how badly the club was damaged? Bull and Harry are friends, and…."

"Thanks to you, things are mostly just wet and smoke-damaged. The fire itself didn't get much of a chance to get going. We gave them the name of a fire recovery company. They'll come in and clean, and they have the equipment to get the smoke smell out of everything. They can even help with some of the building repairs."

"I should call them," Kevin said.

"They'll need all the help they can get, I'm sure," Angus said as he sipped from his mug. Kevin could feel him watching, and at first he shifted nervously, but then he started getting warm and tingly. It was nice being the object of Angus's intense gaze.

"Do you know what actually happened?" Kevin wanted to lift the mug, but he was mesmerized by Angus's stare. He turned away and began to fuss with the edge of the place mat on the table.

"Someone set the fire—that much is pretty clear. We're not sure if it's connected to any other incidents yet."

Kevin's phone rang and he started. He jumped up and snatched it off the coffee table. "Hi, Zach, how's Bull?"

"He got home early this morning and went right to bed. It was bad, but not near as awful as it could have been. We're all going down there in an hour or so to help start cleaning things up. There's a company in there now, but I know Bull and Harry are going to need help."

"I can meet you there," he said, turning back toward the table. "What about insurance and stuff?"

"That's who Bull was waiting on before he got home. So he's all set there."

"Is Bull still asleep?"

"Yeah. Harry called and he was going to the club to meet the restoration people. Bull sent him home last night." Zach sighed. "They've been through this drill before. Remember when Eddie's people smashed the place up?"

"Yeah. Just call me when you're ready to go, and I'll get over there. I have company at the moment, and then I can tell you about my morning. You aren't going to believe this… or who's sitting at my table right now," he added in a whisper. "I'll see you soon."

"Thanks."

"Does Bull know you're doing this?" Kevin asked.

"You know how he is. Every time anything happens, he gets all big and puffy, telling me to stay home. He only wants to protect me, the big lug. But he and Harry need help, and we're going to be there the way we have in the past. Bull and Harry may own Bronco's, but we're its heart and soul. They just haven't figured that out yet." Kevin could almost see the mischief on Zach's face.

"Okay, but if he gets mad…."

"I'll handle him."

Kevin chuckled. "I bet you will." They signed off, and he put his phone in his pocket. "The guys and I are going to the club to help clean up in an hour. There are four of us, and we've been friends a long time. The others are all married. I'm the last one." He didn't say he felt like the one nobody wanted. That wasn't exactly true—Ken had been interested, but not enough for him to stay. It really sucked.

"What happened to put such a sad expression on your cute face?" Angus asked.

"I'm not cute. I've never been cute. The other guys are adorable. I'm just normal."

Angus reached across the table and lightly caressed Kevin's cheek with his fingertips. The touch was almost ghostly, and it sent a ripple of heat through him. "Why don't you let me decide what I think is cute?" Angus withdrew his hand, and Kevin immediately missed it. Angus glanced at his watch and then stood. "I need to get to the station or I'll be late for my shift. Please try not to get involved in any more fires today."

"Okay," Kevin whispered. He walked Angus to the door and said good-bye. He closed the door with a wide grin on his face until he realized Angus didn't have his phone number. Kevin burst out the door and down the stairs, then ran down the walk. He got to the parking area just in time to hear the throaty roar of a motorcycle and see Angus, bent over the handlebars, zooming away.

AN HOUR later Kevin pulled into the small parking area next to the club, near a group of familiar cars. The acrid scent of smoke and damp assaulted his senses and made his eyes water as he walked inside. Men in coveralls were cleaning the walls and floors. Fans hummed everywhere, sucking air in through the front door and blowing it out the others.

Zach hurried over and gave Kevin a big hug. "We're over at the bar. Everything has to be washed, including all the bottles. We don't want to rub off the labels, but everything is covered in a film. Bull said we should just throw everything out and get new, but that's a huge expense, so we're going to clean everything up. The insurance people are being dicks because of the last incident with Eddie. Harry thinks they're going to raise their rates sky high, and Bull thinks they may need to find someone else because the company is going to dump them the next time the policy comes up for renewal, so…."

"Where do you want me to start?" Kevin asked.

"Tristan and Jeremy are washing all the glasses and wiping down the bar and refrigerators. You and I can start on the bottles. We have to take them all down and wash the mirrors, shelves, and everything. They gave us some stuff that will cut through the grime, but you have to wear gloves because it's strong."

"Okay," Kevin agreed, and Zach handed him a pair of gloves. "I'm going to get some tables from the back. That way we can put the clean bottles on them while we wash the rest." He hurried to the office area and the smoke smell lessened quite a bit. He hefted one of the folding tables and brought it out to where they were working. He set it up, and Zach began placing the bottles he'd already cleaned onto it. Kevin pulled on his gloves and got to work.

"So what's this big news you alluded to on the phone?" Zach asked.

"Well, Mrs. V baked again and brought me up some baklava. We were having coffee when I smelled smoke. At first I thought it was the stuff I'd been wearing from last night, but then when I opened the door, the hallway was full of smoke. Mrs. V left something in her oven and forgot about it, burning the thing up. She called the fire department, and I got her out, but I got too much smoke and the next thing I know MacDreamy Hotness, from last night, was giving me oxygen."

Tristan stopped to listen, pausing with his hands in the dishwater. Jeremy remained bent low where he'd been washing the refrigerator doors.

"His name is Angus, and he stopped by this afternoon to make sure I was okay, and he asked me out."

"The hunk running around last night in the fire pants and T-shirt? He was hot," Tristan said and started working again.

"Yeah, the thing is, he said he wanted to ask me out, but he had to go back to the station, and I forgot to give him my number." He'd been kicking himself about that since Angus left.

"Don't worry. If he came to your house to find you, he'll find you again," Zach said. Jeremy made a humphing noise, and Tristan smacked him on the shoulder and glowered. "Stop being an ass," Zach chastised, and Jeremy went back to work.

Kevin began lifting bottles down from the shelves, then carefully cleaned them and put them on the table. Zach removed the register and hauled it away. It needed to be cleaned as well, but had to be done carefully, and one of the restoration contractors took it from him.

"What's this?" Kevin asked as he plucked a strange-feeling envelope from behind a couple of bottles. "It feels weird."

"Set it down and don't touch anything more," Spook said gently from the other side the bar. It was creepy how he always appeared when Kevin wasn't looking. Kevin did as he said, and Spook leaned forward, sniffing it. "Stop what you're doing and get out from behind there."

"What is it?"

"The reason it feels weird and smells funny is it's been sprayed with fire retardant. This was meant to survive the fire." Spook turned and waved Bull over. They spoke quietly while the rest of them stood nearby, wondering what to do.

"I'll call the police and fire department. They both need to know about this."

"What about us?" Zach asked.

"You might as well continue. They cleared the place for us to be here, and you've already moved most of the bottles. Just be careful and don't touch anything that seems out of place," Bull told them.

Spook left the area, and Kevin followed him with his gaze.

Zach tapped him on the shoulder, and he turned away. "Let's finish up," Zach said.

Kevin nodded, and when he turned back around, he couldn't see Spook anywhere. "I hate it when he does that," he grumbled.

"Lowell does have his advantages," Jeremy said with what Kevin thought was supposed to be his naughtiest grin, but it came across as silly.

"I know. He just startles me all the time," Kevin said. He couldn't be angry at the guy. He'd rescued Tristan a few months ago, when Tris's psycho ex-boyfriend had kidnapped him, and he'd helped all of them at one point or other. Spook was a good guy; it was just that maybe he should wear a bell or something.

Kevin returned to the task and didn't find anything else. The last of the bottles were clean and lined up on the table when Reyes, the police officer from the night before, strode in.

"What have you got?" Reyes asked.

Bull met the officer and guided him to the bar. "We were cleaning up and found this. We think it has flame retardant sprayed on it. One of the guys touched it with his gloves, but it hasn't been opened or touched otherwise."

"I found it behind the first row of bottles," Kevin explained.

"So it could have been placed there by one of the bartenders?" the officer asked.

"I suppose," Kevin told him. "Except when the fire started, none of the bartenders were in that part of the club. They were all working, and it started in that corner way over there, away from the bar area. I was the one who saw it, so I doubt it was the bartenders."

"Remind me who you are again?" Officer Reyes asked in a tone that shot cold up Kevin's spine.

"Kevin Foster."

"He's the one who put out the fire last night," Bull said.

Reyes checked his notes. "Right. He's also the one who sees what's going on, and then this morning he finds this with flame retardant on it."

The mockery in his voice was clear. "This kid seems to be in the thick of everything."

"You can go!" Bull bellowed, and the officer flinched. "This is private property, and we called for help. I think my next call will be to the local news media, and we'll see what they think of your harassment. You don't get to treat people like this in my place."

"No, he doesn't," a commanding voice said, and Kevin smiled as MacDreamy Hotness… err, Angus, walked in. "I heard all of it." He strode over. "Is this what you found?" He looked at the envelope without touching it, sniffing slightly. "Do you know what's inside?"

"We haven't touched it since we found it," Bull said.

"Then we need to see what's inside." Angus turned to the police officer. "That okay?"

He shrugged, and Angus pulled out some gloves. Then he carefully opened the envelope and placed it in a plastic evidence bag. Holding a corner, he opened the note and showed it to the officer. "This is what I was afraid of."

"Is this the arsonist we've heard about on the news?" Kevin asked.

"Yes," Angus answered as he placed the note in another evidence bag. He handed both to the officer. "We'll need a copy of the crime-scene forensic results sent to the office." Angus seemed to ignore the officer after that, and Kevin smiled as Reyes seethed.

"I was trying to ascertain the facts," Reyes finally said.

"No. You were causing trouble." Angus stepped up to him. "I know what you're up to, and when I get back to my office, I'll lodge a complaint with my department that will most definitely get passed on to yours. I definitely see sensitivity training in your future… again." Angus grinned, and the officer stomped off.

"You dated him?" Kevin said quietly as he watched.

Angus shrugged, then said, "The guy's a dick. He's got a real attitude problem. Every time I deal with him, he acts like an ass. When we first met, I thought it might be because I'm gay, but now I just think he's like that with everybody."

"So we really do have a serial arsonist?" Bull asked.

"I'm afraid so. Last night I thought it could be an isolated incident, but now I don't think so. He always leaves a note of some kind. This one was about the evils of sodomy and the gay agenda. Whatever that is. Unfortunately, the police haven't been especially helpful up until now. But the good thing is that the arsonist hasn't struck the same place twice."

"So what do we do?" Bull asked.

"Take precautions. The last time he struck, it was a women's clinic. They didn't perform abortions, but he thought they did."

"Do you know it's a guy?" Kevin asked.

"We believe so, yes," Angus said. "I'll follow up with the police regarding the note. They are in charge of the investigation."

Bull stepped closer. "Do you think they'll do anything? That guy was a piece of work."

"Yes, they will. He's an ass, but he's also a good investigator, and he wants to catch this guy pretty badly," Angus said.

"You could have fooled me." Bull put his arms across his chest in one of his signature poses.

"I know. He'd get better results if he wasn't a jerk, but we're stuck with him." Angus reached into his pocket. "Call me if I can be of any help." He handed Bull a card.

Kevin waited until they were done talking and then followed Angus to the door. "Do you think he really thought I did this?" Kevin's mouth went dry. "I tried to put it out."

"I know you didn't have anything to do with the fire." Angus stopped in the doorway. "Believe it or not, some arsonists set fires so they can help put them out. Others set them just so they can watch them burn. A lot of the time an arsonist is in the milling crowd outside their fires."

"Oh," Kevin said. That tracked with what Spook had told Jeremy the night before.

"I have to go, but I will call you." Angus hurried away, and Kevin watched him for a few seconds before racing after him. "Is something wrong?" Angus asked when Kevin caught up with him.

"Yeah. You don't have my number," Kevin said. "You didn't ask for it earlier."

Angus grinned. "I got it off the fire report, cutie." He grinned. "I looked you up and put you in my phone." Kevin's phone rang, and he pulled it out. "Now you have mine. I'm on shift a lot this week, but I'll call you as soon as I can. I promise." He smiled, and Kevin nodded, figuring if he tried to talk, he'd only stammer. He watched as Angus drove away and then went back inside to get back to work, a grin plastered to his face.

He saw Tristan elbow Zach lightly, and they all circled around.

"Did you get his number?" Zach asked.

"Yeah." Kevin waved his phone. "He said he's on shift this week, but that he'll call me." Even Jeremy's earlier skepticism seemed to have vanished. "He keeps calling me cutie." Why he felt the need to tell them that, he didn't know.

"You are a cutie," Bull said, and Kevin blushed. He hadn't known Bull was right there behind him. "You've had a tough time of it, but you'll find someone special."

"Thanks, Bull," Kevin whispered and once again put Ken out of his mind. He hated that Ken kept intruding into his thoughts. That was over, and a gorgeous fireman was now calling him cutie. "Let's get this finished up," he said with as much enthusiasm as he could muster and got back to work.

CHAPTER TWO

"GOD, ANTONIO, there was no need to behave that way with Kevin," Angus said as he strode into the arson investigator's office at the police department on Monday morning. "The guy is a hero. He grabbed the hose and may well have saved lives in that fire."

"So it's Kevin, is it?" Antonio Reyes looked up from the papers on his desk as Angus closed the door. The rest of the department didn't need to hear their conversation. The guys were gossipy as hell.

"Is that what this is about? I thought you were just being your usual dickhead self, but you're jealous." He stepped closer to the desk. "We've been through for a long time, and the crap you pulled today was over the top. They found something they thought might help, and they called it in. Jesus."

"I saw you with him yesterday. You two looked pretty cozy."

"I thought he was cute, and he knew the partner of the guy who died and consoled him. He was only a friend of a friend, and yet he was right there." Angus sat down in a once familiar chair, one he hadn't seen much of recently. "I haven't met someone open and caring in a while. I'm sure you can see the attraction." His relationship with Antonio had started hot but burned out pretty quickly. Antonio was deeply in the closet, and Angus hadn't been willing to live a lie. He still wasn't. Some of the guys in the department gave him shit, and a few had asked for transfers so they didn't have to work with him, but all that was better than pretending.

Antonio blinked at him. "All right, I was kind of sharp with him."

"Kind of sharp? You pretty much accused him of starting the fire. That was harsh, and if you'd read the report, you'd know that he's already been cleared. He was nowhere near where the fire started." Angus settled down. "Were we able to get anything off the note?"

"Just like the others, it was clean. There were a few smudged fingerprints, and the lab is trying to see if they can get anything through enhancement. It seems our boy was in a hurry to leave this time and may have actually touched the envelope."

"What about DNA?"

"They're trying that too, but there were so many chemicals on the paper they aren't sure they can get anything."

Angus didn't see why this one should be any different from the others. "I wonder if there's any security video in the club that we can use."

"I pulled the tapes, but the actual start of the fire was just off camera."

Sometimes Antonio could be so unimaginative. "We don't have to have the guy on tape starting the fire. All we need is a picture of him that we can put out there. Figure out who this guy is so we can get a lead on him. Now if he was just off camera when the fire started, then he had to leave the area just before. So let's take a look and see if there's anything we can use."

"Don't you think I already did that? There's nothing to suggest who the guy is." He opened his desk and handed Angus a thumb drive. "Here's a copy of the footage. If you want to take a look and see if you see anything, great. But we came up with a whole lot of nothing." The frustration rang in the room. Antonio was a good investigator and wanted to solve his cases. This particular one had gone on long enough that it was starting to get to him. On top of that, Angus knew his workload was piling up to the ceiling. It wasn't like on television, where the case happened and all they worked on was that one thing. There were always multiple cases and assignments pulling on his time. Sometimes Angus wondered how Antonio kept from going crazy.

"Did you lodge a complaint with your department about me?" Antonio asked, trying not to appear as though he cared.

"No. Because I know you were doing your job. But you need to get it together. Those people might have been able to help you, but you alienated them within seconds. Those guys you were picking on don't work at the club—they're the owners' partners and like family. A real family." Antonio's was so screwed up that it was a wonder if he had any concept of family at all. "Just relax. They want to help you."

"Yeah, I know," Antonio admitted, which was a shock and out of character. Fight and argue until blue in the face, but never take a step back—that was how Antonio usually operated. "It just seemed so damned convenient."

"If you'd looked at the facts, you would have known it was nothing of the kind," Angus told him, not giving any ground. "So when you go back, do you think you can be civil?" His accent crept in, and he saw Antonio pause.

"Yes." He put his hands on the desk, sighing. "God, when you sound like that."

"What?"

"Sometimes your accent comes through, and it reminds me what drew me to you in the first place," Antonio said, a smile ghosting over his face. But it didn't last long. They never did.

"You're an unhappy man, Tony, and you need to find something to add some joy to yer life. That's not me anymore, but find something or someone or yer going to explode." Angus stood, holding up the thumb drive. "Thanks fer this. I appreciate it." He let his accent really come forward. He'd been in the States long enough that it wasn't too heavy, but sometimes it crept in, and like now, he let it show for Antonio's benefit. "I'll see you 'round." He left the office and strode through the station and out to his car. He began driving back to the firehouse and for the millionth time thought about Kevin.

There was something about him that stuck with Angus, and not many guys did that. His mother would say he was flighty, and she would probably be right. Angus noticed guys and knew guys saw him. But he'd really seen Kevin, and seeking a guy out was something he never did, let alone hunt up his phone number and put it in his phone just so he'd have it. He'd thought of calling him a number of times, but his shifts would keep him busy for a few more days yet.

"Hello," he answered when a call rang in through the car.

"Did you get the video of the club?" his captain asked.

"Told you I would."

"You're the only one who can get anything out of that guy," the captain said gruffly. These arsons were weighing on the department big-time. Natural fires were one thing, but intentionally set ones were a totally different matter. Sometimes there were traps built in so the firefighters got caught. Those increased the media attention on the fire and gave the arsonist a boost of some kind. "What do you have on him?"

"Do you really want to know?" Angus asked. He heard the chief groan. "Didn't think so."

"We'll look at it when you get here. The guys have been watching crowds outside the fires. So maybe they saw something. It's a long shot, but at this point it's what we have."

"I'm less than ten minutes away with traffic. I'll see you soon." He disconnected and continued the drive to the fire station.

The building was old, but they did their best to keep it maintained. The equipment inside, however, was new, and that was because they raised the money themselves to buy and take care of it. The city itself was in terrible financial shape, as their last set of raises had attested, which had left a lot of the men grumbling… loudly. Promotions had been put on hold, and everything had been done to squeeze the budgets. It really sucked.

He walked inside, passing Clark, who had a paint roller in hand, like he usually did. It was his thing, and all the interior walls were clean and bright because of it. Of course that also meant the building smelled of paint nearly all the damn time. "How's it going?"

"Almost done here. Then I'm going to give it a rest. The place looks good." Clark looked at his handiwork with pride in his eyes.

"It looks great," Angus said with a smile. "The captain is waiting for me." He hurried on past and up to the office. He knocked and went in. "Antonio said there wasn't anything useful. I think that's the only reason he gave me a copy."

"He's probably right," Captain Justinian said, taking the thumb drive. "But it isn't going to hurt in case anyone sees a familiar face in the crowd. This has the entire department on edge, so whatever we can do to get this guy off our backs, the better." He looked the drive over. "I'll gather the men and let them know what's going on. If it stays quiet, we'll get together in half an hour."

Angus left the office and wandered down to the equipment garage. It was sunny and warm outside, so one of the trucks had been pulled out and was being washed. Fire calls always left the trucks covered in soot and film, and everyone had worked so hard to get the money to buy the equipment that they all took pride in its care and maintenance.

"Did you get it?" Roy asked. He was as big as a house and liked to use his size to intimidate, but most of the guys knew he was really a big softie and paid him little attention. The guy was also hairy as hell, and with his shirt off looked as though he had a bath mat on his chest.

"He gave me a copy," I told him.

"That guy is a pain in the ass. How come you can get through to him?" He narrowed his gaze as though he thought he knew the answer. "He one of your *friends*?" Roy had a problem with him; everyone in the station knew it.

"Jealous? Because you aren't my type," Angus retorted. He loved watching Roy turn red.

"Too manly?" He posed, flexing his arms and jutting out his chest.

"Too dumb," Angus said, and the other guys all snickered. "I can do this all day and you're never going to win, so give it up." He disguised it as teasing, but he wasn't going to back down with anyone. Being strong and giving as good as he got was how he'd earned their respect, and that was what ensured his brother firefighters would have his back. Not that he had a doubt about any of them, even Roy. "The truck is looking good," he said, both to change the subject and to try to ease the tension that was building.

"We're almost done," Roy said. He began walking around it, pointing out areas that had been missed or needed a little extra polishing.

"Excuse me," someone said from behind him, and Angus turned around. Kevin stood on the sidewalk, carrying two white boxes in his arms.

"Cutie" was out of his mouth before he remembered where he was. He heard Roy growl in the background.

"Knock it off, ya big lug," Angus scolded and turned back to Kevin. "What are you doing here?"

"Mrs. V was really grateful for your help on Saturday, and the landlord has replaced her stove. She got a new one—well, a new old one, anyway—and she started baking and then asked me when I got home to bring these to you to say thank you."

"Whatcha got there?" Roy demanded.

"Baklava. Mrs. V, the lady with the oven fire, she made them for you," Kevin said with a squeak, and Angus wanted to punch Roy right there for being mean. Roy came over and lifted the lid on one of the boxes.

"Man, those look good."

"So the way to a man's heart and past his prejudices is through his stomach, then." Angus couldn't resist, and even Roy gave him a small smile for that one.

"Where should I put them?" Kevin asked.

"Come with me," Angus said, taking the top box before Roy reached in and began grazing. "We'll go inside and up to the station kitchen."

"Okay. I hope I didn't cause any trouble," Kevin said, turning back to where Roy watched them.

"He's harmless. All bark and no bite." Angus held the door and motioned Kevin up the stairs. He followed behind him and knew he shouldn't be watching, but he couldn't take his gaze off Kevin's jeans-encased butt as it swung back and forth like a metronome, ramping up the heat with each movement.

"Who's this?" the captain said as they reached the kitchen.

"This is Kevin. He was the hero at the club fire, and the one who got everyone out of the apartment building with the stove fire on Saturday."

"The lady with the stove fire, Mrs. Vertebedian, sent these over as a thank-you. She's getting older and forgets things sometimes, but she loves to cook and doesn't have anyone left to cook for." Kevin set the box on the table, and Angus put the one he was carrying next to it. "I didn't want to interrupt."

"Bringing food to this crew is never an interruption." Just as the captain finished, the guys began making their way in. "See? Food will call them every time." The captain smiled. "We'll run the security video, then you can get something to eat. This is going to be pretty dull, especially since we're looking for someone we've seen hanging out at fires. You all know the drill and how some arsonists behave. Let's hope this one follows the pattern."

"I should go," Kevin said. "You all have work to do."

"You could stay if you want. You were there and might see something. Do you have to go back to work?" Angus asked.

"I work early at the call center, so I'm done for the day," Kevin answered, and Angus shooed one of the guys off the sofa so they could sit together.

"No hand-holding," Roy grumbled.

Angus made a face. "Don't want to hold your moldy hand anyway." The guys chuckled, and Roy crossed his arms over his chest. Angus made sure to sit between Roy and Kevin as the captain started the video.

"That's way before the fire started," Kevin said as an image of part of the dance floor and tables played on the screen. "Maybe an hour or so."

"How do you know, other than the time signature?" the captain asked.

"Because Zach isn't dancing, and the strippers just ended. Zach loves to dance, and most of the time he dances with one of us because Bull doesn't dance much. He does his security thing." The captain fast-forwarded the video until Kevin said to stop. "Okay, see, that's Bull and Zach. I think they only danced for maybe two songs. It was during the second one that the fire started." Kevin got up off the sofa. "Watch right there." He pointed at the screen, and a flash appeared in the corner. "I was over here, but I saw that."

The captain slowed the playback as the light returned and got brighter. Flames showed on the screen, and then Kevin rushed into the frame, spraying water as people hurried around him, the floor emptying in the rush to get out.

"Stop," Kevin said. "Can you go back?"

"What do you see?" the captain asked as everyone in the room leaned forward.

"Those shoes. They're Nike Air Max in fluorescent yellow. See? Watch as you move forward."

The captain started the video, and Kevin pointed out the shoes. "I'll be damned."

"Yeah, even in the rush to get out, he takes the long way around to avoid the camera. Now maybe he doesn't want to get his expensive shoes wet, or he simply wants to stay off camera."

"Good eyes," the captain said with a smile. "But it doesn't get us further in getting a look at the guy."

"Maybe not, but the club is near the capital complex, and there are cameras there. Maybe one of them caught the scene outside. We know what shoes he was wearing, and they aren't exactly dark. They would show up if he was standing alone or something. I can ask if Bull has video set up outside, but I don't think he's allowed."

"I wouldn't think so."

"It gives us a place to start, and that helps a lot." The captain was smiling, and Angus grinned at Kevin. "You just keep coming to the rescue."

"Nah, you would have figured it out." Kevin was too modest, in Angus's opinion. "I was there so I knew what not to look at."

"That doesn't make sense," Roy said.

"Sure it does," Kevin countered. "I work in computers, and sometimes in order to make a program work, you have to devise the logic so you get what's left. You have a list of things you know your answer isn't, so you reverse the logic. That's what I did here. I knew it wasn't me or the guys running toward the exit, so I looked for something different." He flashed a smile and stood up. "I should let you all get back to what you were doing."

Kevin left the room, and Angus followed him to the stairs. "It was really nice of you to bring by the desserts. The guys will love them." Now that the show was over, they were most likely already gathering in the kitchen area.

"Of course. Mrs. V felt bad getting everyone out because she forgot she had things in the oven. She's very sweet, and getting old alone is hard on her. Her circle keeps shrinking, and she doesn't know what to do about it." He descended the stairs and Angus went with him.

"Did you drive?"

Kevin pointed out where he'd parked. "I'm glad I could help." He began walking to the car, and Angus realized this was the third time they'd parted without him actually making a move.

"How about Sunday afternoon? My last shift is Saturday, but I'm off Sunday and we could do something."

Kevin paused. "That would be nice. Bull is hoping to be able to reopen the club on Friday, and I usually go with the guys. So Sunday would be perfect."

"Let's hope there's no repeat of last week," Angus said, and Kevin waved as he took advantage in a lull in traffic to cross the street. "I'll call soon." He watched as Kevin got in his car and waited until he pulled away from the curb and had joined the flow of traffic before turning to go back inside.

He met a number of the guys, baklava in hand, as they came down the stairs heading back to truck-washing duty. Angus had just decided he'd lend a hand when the siren went off. Guys shoved food into their mouths. Angus raced to his gear, stepped into his pants and boots, and grabbed his coat and hat before jumping into the driver's seat of the hook and ladder. Within seconds his heart was racing, adrenaline pumping, and they were pulling out of the station, lights and sirens blazing. Traffic stopped as they made the turn and raced to the address that flashed on the GPS built into the dash. This was what he lived for: the excitement. It was what they all loved. There was an excitement to being a fireman that was lacking in any other job Angus had held, and this was what he longed to do for the rest of his life.

He went as fast as he dared, screaming through the city streets. He saw smoke rising in the distance, and it got closer as he followed the directions. This was no oven fire, but an old house converted to apartments that hadn't been in the best of condition, and it was now getting worse, judging by the flames already shooting out of the upper-floor windows. Angus pulled to a stop, and the men jumped off, already working to secure hoses to hydrants as he lowered the jacks that would support the engine. By the time it was secure, hoses were run from the hydrants and water was gushing at the fire.

THAT SEEMED to be the routine for the rest of his shift. Every time anyone got started on a project, a call came in and they were off and running. "It's fire season," said Harold, the old-timer and self-proclaimed source of general wisdom of the group. He was semiretired after a lifetime of fighting fires and manned the station when the team went out. "Happens this time every year. It gets dry, and people get careless."

Angus wondered what the heat had to do with their last call, a house fire. A man got drunk, lit his cigarette, and went to bed. Burned the place to the ground around him. Fires with a death were bad. He was only grateful there weren't children involved—those were the worst.

He looked at the clock and kept quiet, not wanting to jinx anything. He would be off shift in two hours and silently willed it to remain calm until then. He was exhausted. He never slept well at the station with other men around, especially with Roy doing his imitation of a chainsaw.

"MacTavish," Captain Justinian called down the stairs to where everyone was hurrying to clean and ready the equipment for the next call.

Angus handed his cloth to Frankie, who took it with a flash of concern. They all knew that tone of voice. Angus wondered what he'd done as he climbed the stairs and went into the captain's office. "There was another one last night."

"Arson?"

"Yeah. Cameron United took the call. It was at a halfway house for former gang kids. The entire building went up, and three people didn't get out—one of the counselors and two of the kids. This guy's body count is starting to stack up."

"Are there any leads?"

"No, and cameras in that part of town are nonexistent. You've been involved in this since the beginning, so I wanted to let you know. I told their captain to make sure your best friend in the police department was involved. He probably was anyway, but you know how organizations work. Right hand and left hand, and all that." Justinian stopped. "You look like hell."

"It's been a long week." Angus resisted the urge to look at the clock yet again.

"The guys will start to arrive in a few minutes. You get out of here as soon as turnover's done."

"Thanks," Angus said, though some of the joy in going home had been sucked away. "I really want to get this guy."

"I know. We all do."

Angus shook his head and took a deep breath. "There's something more, isn't there?"

Justinian paused, giving Angus one of those steely stares that was supposed to get him to open up. Angus had become immune long ago. "You're a gifted firefighter. Sometimes I think you understand what the fire is going to do before it does."

"It's like a living being to me," Angus said. He stopped there. There was more, so much more, but he wasn't in the mood to tell the story. He hadn't in quite a long time, and he thought he'd buried the ache deep down where it would never show its head again. "Is there anything else?"

"No. But I talked to the chief today, and he's asked in his own way"—which meant he'd told him and Justinian was softening the blow—"that you be the point man for the department on this. You're the only one who can get squat out of Reyes."

"We have a history," Angus explained, but that was as far as he was willing to go.

"I don't want to know. The two of you fight like cats and dogs when you're together, yet you always get the goods."

"He isn't a bad guy. I just know how to get around his pain-in-the-assness." He made light of it. Antonio's life in the closet was his business. It was no longer Angus's.

Voices rose and overlapped as people gathered outside the office. The station was filling with men and women from his shift and the next one. Angus allowed himself a look at the clock and waited for Justinian to nod before leaving the office. He joined the others as he wondered just what being the department point of contact for this arsonist would involve... and the toll it would take on him.

After turnover, he left right away. He wished he'd ridden his motorcycle, but the weather report that morning had been iffy. He was in his Mustang and pulling away from the station when he heard the rumble of the alarm, and a minute later the trucks started pulling out. He pulled to the side of the road and silently wished for all of them to be safe as they whirred past, honking the horn as they went. When he'd first joined the department, he would have followed and checked to see if he was needed. At the moment, he was too tired to be of any use to anyone, so he continued to his house in the historic Shipoke area of town, pulled into his garage, and then went up to his living quarters.

The house was newer construction. This part of town had a tendency to flood every few years, so having the garage on the first level meant his living space and possessions remained high and dry. He left his gear in the garage and made a note to clean it soon. He carried his laundry up with him and started the machine right away. Then he wandered through the house, checking every room, glad to be home once again.

He spent the afternoon on the sofa, doing very little but watching television and dozing off. He made something from the freezer for dinner, ate, and went to bed, sleeping soundly in his own bed in his quiet room.

When he woke the next morning, he felt human again, rested, and was filled with excitement. He had a date—a real date, not one of the hookups he usually ended up with. Angus checked the clock. It was well after ten, so he snatched up his phone to call Kevin. The guy had to be wondering about him. He'd forgotten to plug the phone in, so he found the cord, waited for it to power up, and hoped like hell there were no messages from work. When it finally came up, the phone remained quiet, no message chimes or anything, which was just plain lucky. He located Kevin's number in his contacts and dialed.

"Are we still on for this afternoon?" he asked when Kevin answered.

"Yeah. I was wondering since I hadn't heard from you," Kevin said with a jittery voice.

"Sorry. When I'm on shift, things are so busy I usually don't get much time, and when I got home yesterday, I slept. Just woke up, as a matter of fact."

"Me too," Kevin said, and Angus wondered exactly what kind of fun Kevin had been up to. He'd said he was going out with his friends. "We went dancing. Well, they did most of the dancing, since they are the ones with boyfriends. Zach and I danced together, though, because after the fire, Bull won't take any time away from his security duties." There was such energetic joy in the way Kevin told him about his night. "Not that I blame him, but it makes it hard on Zach. Bull is a great guy, but Zach loves to dance… and he really loves to do it with Bull." Kevin giggled when he realized what he'd said. The guy was so cute sometimes. "So what did you have planned?"

"Is it okay if I pick you up at two?"

"That would be great," Kevin said. "I'll be sure to be ready. Mrs. V should be up in a few minutes for coffee, and this time I'll make sure she doesn't leave anything in the oven." Kevin chuckled a little. "Do you get calls on your day off or anything?"

"Not unless there's something really bad." And he hoped like hell that didn't happen. "So I'll pick you up at two, and we can have some fun."

ANGUS PULLED up in front of Kevin's building just before two and parked. He strode up to the door in time to see Kevin come out and stare at his motorcycle.

"Are we going to ride that?" Kevin asked, and Angus wasn't sure if the reaction was good or bad.

"I hoped you would ride with me," Angus explained. "I brought some extra gear for you." He was still unsure of what Kevin thought until he broke into a grin and raced down the walk to the bike.

"That's so cool. I never got to ride on one of these. My mother had a friend who was in an accident when she was young, so she would never let me ride on one for any reason." Kevin patted the seat lightly, running his hand over the black leather. "Do I need to get anything?"

Angus looked over his tight jeans and a T-shirt that seemed painted on. Kevin wasn't bulky, but he was otter sleek, and Angus wondered if that analogy applied to the rest of him. The thought went to his groin and suddenly there wasn't a great deal of room in his jeans. "No, you're just fine. I brought a light jacket for you. It might be little big, but it'll be good." He checked him out once again and turned away. He'd worn jeans and chaps, which he'd been told accentuated his package, but if he didn't cool down, his entire package was going to be on vivid display.

He got a jacket from the compartment on the back and handed it to Kevin. It was indeed too big, but Kevin still looked good, and Angus liked him wearing his clothes. Angus handed him a helmet as well and helped him adjust it to fit.

"Ready?" Kevin asked with a grin. "I'm ready for some air. This is getting warm."

Hot was more like it. "Sure. Let's go." Angus got on and started the engine. Then he helped Kevin on, showing him where to put his feet. "Put your arms around my waist and stay close to me. Just move with me and we'll be fine." He released the clutch and they moved forward.

Kevin tightened his grip, and Angus felt his nervousness as he moved closer, right up against his hips and butt. He turned on the street and picked up speed. He made it to the first light, and it turned red just ahead of them. "This is cool," Kevin said, and when the light changed, Angus took off. Kevin tightened his grip again as they picked up speed. When he reached the freeway, Angus accelerated and joined traffic. When he got to cruising speed, Angus patted Kevin's leg and got a pat on his belly in return.

"Jesus!" Kevin yelled in his ear. "This is awesome!"

Angus grinned, knowing he'd made the right decision. Talking was difficult, but that didn't matter. He watched the road and did his best to keep his attention where it should be, rather than on the fact that Kevin was hard against him, combined with his own arousal, which Kevin was going to discover for himself if his hands drifted any lower. Man, he was a firecracker of the highest magnitude.

They roared past Carlisle on 81 and got off a few miles later, taking the country roads up into the mountains to one of the state parks. Trees stretched across the road, and away from the highway and the sun the temperature dropped and the air freshened. Angus came here often. It reminded him of home, and he felt he could breathe and clear the cobwebs.

"Where are we going?" Kevin asked.

"I brought a picnic," Angus said, patting Kevin's denim-encased leg once again before pulling through an intersection. A short way along, he made the turn into the park and drove around until he found a parking spot. He pulled in and silenced the engine.

"Wow."

Angus waited for Kevin to get off and then followed. They removed their helmets and jackets. Angus opened the case on the back of the bike, pulling out a small cooler before stowing the jackets.

"That was something else. I can still feel the engine vibrating." He took a few steps away and then returned. "It went right up my legs to my butt." Kevin chuckled as he took high steps to work the kinks out of his legs.

"I've always loved the feel of a bike."

Kevin glanced downward and then looked away, but not for long. "I think everyone can see that." He giggled again and then stepped closer.

"What are you doing?"

"Shielding you from little children." He continued his laughter. "Besides, we might get mobbed, and we're on a date, so you're mine and they can all eat their hearts out." His laughter died away and slowly his smile fell away as well, his gaze becoming more and more heated. "That ride was amazing and… well. It did the same thing to me."

Angus's excitement had diminished, and he'd felt Kevin's arousal, but having him admit to the excitement had him hard once again.

"Are you going to wear those chaps all day?" Kevin asked, and Angus set down the cooler and removed them. He locked the case and secured the bike before leading Kevin into the park.

"Do you want to walk around or eat first?"

"Let's walk, if that's okay," Kevin said.

Angus grabbed the cooler, and they headed off to the lake. As they got closer, the happy yells and screams of children mixed with overlapping voices and splashing, a sound that meant joy the world over. Kevin stopped where the path approached the lake. Kids jumped off a floating raft, calling out to friends before hitting the water.

"I used to love swimming," Kevin said softly.

"Not anymore?"

"I drowned when I was six. I was at a lake and dove in. I remember shooting under the water and then everything went dark. My mom told me that when I didn't come up, she started yelling, and all kinds of people jumped in. One of the men found me. I guess I was lucky. He knew CPR and brought me back around." Kevin stared out over the water. "I coughed and spat up. When I opened my eyes, Mama was crying, and then I did too. They made me lie still and just breathe for a while."

"Do you know what happened?"

Kevin shook his head. "No. They said they thought I might have bumped my head, but I never felt anything, and it didn't hurt when I came out. Of course if I had, I could have forgotten or something. But I don't go in the water. It took weeks and a lot of pleading from my mom before I'd even take a bath." Kevin shuddered. "I hate the water."

"You don't even wade?" Angus asked.

"Sometimes, but I'm always nervous, and after a while I just get out." Kevin turned back to him. "I went to summer camp for years and sat on the beach watching the other kids play. I used to take a book and sit in the shade. This one counselor decided he was going to help me get over my fear. So he picked me up, carried me to the water, and was going to throw me in."

A chill ran up his spine. "Oh God. That must have been terrifying."

"It was. I threw up all over him just as he reached the dock. After that he left me alone." Kevin grinned. "The kids called me Pukey after that, but no one tried to force me into the water again." Kevin began walking down the path. The farther he got from the water, the less rigid his posture became. "Sorry if I'm spoiling things."

Angus caught up with him and took Kevin's hand. "You aren't. I wasn't planning on swimming or anything." Actually, he had thought about wading, but they could forego that. "It's just really nice here. There's a dam right over there that makes the lake. It isn't very big, but it's great for playing in." Angus led them away. Some other walkers looked at them askance, but Angus ignored them. A few looked like they might say something, but his glare kept them quiet.

"What do you like to do besides fight fires?" Kevin asked. "Oh, and ride motorcycles?"

"That's about it, really. I have a house with a small backyard, so I keep it clean and have a few plants. There isn't a lot. I guess I'm someone who doesn't need much. How about you? What do you do?"

"I got moved to the company help desk a while ago, after this whole office shake-up. Stores call us with problems and stuff. I like it, but now it's getting pretty boring. I want to be a programmer, but no one at work thinks I can do it. I've asked but never get anywhere. So as a hobby I do things I like. I created my own video game, sort of. Zach draws comic books, and he has a superhero named Bull who was inspired by his husband. When they go to comic events, Bull dresses up. It's really cool. I made a video game to go with the comics. I think it's pretty good."

"Have you shown it to anyone at work so they know what you can do?"

"No. They would think it's dumb or something," Kevin said. "I did it for fun and as a favor to Zach. I still have some work to do on it, and once it's done, Zach said I could go with him to, like, Comic-Con or something, and we could try it out and see what people think." Kevin's excitement leaped with each step they took.

"That's pretty neat. I'd like to see it sometime," Angus said. "I used to play video games a lot, but I haven't in a while. I used to be pretty good."

"Then I'll have to play you. Not at my game, because you'd lose—I know all the secrets. But we can play Mario Kart or something like that. There are characters who ride motorcycles." Kevin squeezed his hand as they approached the second lake. This one was quiet.

"The path goes around it," Angus told him.

"I know it's stupid, and I hate that I'm such a baby that I get nervous just being around a lake. I know the water isn't going to jump out and grab me, and there isn't some monster under the water. For me the monster is the water."

"I'm not going to try to make you get any closer." They followed the path around the lake, sun sparkling on the water. Angus tried to see it as Kevin saw it and really couldn't. Most fears weren't rational, but Kevin had a basis for his.

"My dad sent me to a doctor who was supposed to cure me, and the same thing happened that did with the camp counselor, only all over his office."

Angus chuckled. Served them right. "Some people think they know best."

"They do. I'm mostly happy staying away from water. It isn't like I miss swimming and long for it but can't go near the water. It's something that has bad memories for me."

"Let's talk about something happier," Angus said as they left the lake behind and entered the deep words.

"Like what?" Kevin asked.

"Your video game. It really seems cool. How did you get interested in creating them? I mean, there aren't any video game companies around here."

"I've always been interested in computers. I'm really good with them. I understand them almost better than I do people. I'm a geek through and through." Kevin stopped walking and Angus did the same. The air under the trees was still and moist. "I used to love video games as a teenager, but I was never very good at them. My hand-eye coordination really sucks. I'd put quarter after quarter in the machines and be dead in a few minutes. I got a Wii one year for Christmas. My dad got his hands on one by sheer luck, and he gave it to me. It was really nice of him. He got it because it was the hot toy that year, and he thought I'd really like it. But I wasn't very good. I played a lot, hoping I'd get better, but it didn't really happen. Eventually it sat there most of the time unless company came over, and then they'd kick my butt."

"Okay. I can understand that. But something obviously changed." Angus took Kevin's hand again.

Kevin looked down at their clasped hands. "You don't have to do that, you know. We are out in public."

"I'm not ashamed of you," Angus said. "If people have a problem with me holding hands with you, that's their problem. It was hard for me to come to grips with who I am, but once I did, I decided I wouldn't hide. I figure if we don't make a huge deal out of holding hands, then no one else will either." Angus met Kevin's gaze with a smile. "So tell me what made you decide to try making games."

"I started playing again with the guys. Jeremy is really good, and so is Tristan. They showed me some of their tricks and what exactly to concentrate on and what to ignore. Once I knew that, they started to make sense and we played a lot. Sometimes against each other, but always for fun. Then I started playing around with different graphics packages and found I could come up with some interesting things. When Zach's *Bull* comic books started to take off, he and I sat down and developed the game. It turned out really well."

"So this is your first one?" Angus asked, his mind beginning to churn.

"Yeah. But I have ideas for others. Why?"

"How about a video game based on fires?" Angus said. "Say you're in the building, it catches fire, and you need to get out. Or you can play the fireman, and he needs to get in and rescue the family. But what happens when they don't get out is they all die and you get no points. Then you have to replay the same fire to move on."

"Where the player could be the firefighter?"

"Sort of. What if you developed the program to act as a fire simulator, to help with decision making? Instead of doing it as a game, you make it a training tool. I've heard of a few of them, but in this area we have a few types of buildings that are particularly prone to fires that quickly grow out of control. State Street is block after block of old row houses. If one catches, they could all go up… and so on. We could build in weak, old floors, weakened even more by fire. The player would need to make decisions about where to enter, step, maybe jump out a window because it's the only option. Sure, they might get hurt and we could have a potential injury, but if they make it out alive, they win."

"Are you serious?" Kevin asked. "Because to build something like that would be really cool. We could come up with a bunch of buildings, houses, offices, hotels, even the state capitol or the archives. Each would pose unique challenges." The enthusiasm in Kevin's voice was contagious. "You'd need to come up with building layouts and things like that, including windows, fire escapes, and other variables. The cool thing could be that the controller decides if the place has sprinklers or not. Variables could be set so the same building could be used with a lot of different scenarios."

There was no way Angus could keep from smiling at Kevin's enthusiasm and the way his mind seemed to churn out ideas. Hell, he practically skipped down the path he had so much energy. Even as the path curved and opened up near another small lake, Kevin barely seemed to notice it.

"I could build in fire-intensity indicators, so you could… say… program in if there were chemicals or something that would make the fire burn hotter or faster. I remember there was that factory fire a while ago, and no one knew there were chemicals in the building. There are smoke factors, closed windows, open windows, stuff like that. You'd need to tell me what they are and what the effect is, but I could come up with something that should be interesting. That would be so awesome."

Angus hated to interrupt him, but he seemed to be winding down. "Are you hungry?"

"Thirsty, I guess," Kevin answered. "You should have told me to shut up, because once I get going, I can talk for hours, and this could be cool."

"Yes, it could, and you talk all you want. I like your energy and your ideas," Angus said. He motioned Kevin over to where he knew there was a secondary picnic area off the trail ahead. They walked a little farther and took the path to a small glade with four picnic tables. It was completely empty, with only the creek running over stones and birds chirping in the trees as accompaniment. Occasionally a car engine could be heard as a low rumble in the distance, but other than that, it was as if civilization had left them behind.

Kevin shrugged.

"What was that for?"

"Nothing. Just that my dad says I can not talk for three days and then the dam will burst and I won't be able to shut up again."

"Like I said, you talk all you want." Angus put the cooler down on a table in the shade and sat down, patting the bench next to him. Kevin sat as well, and Angus began pulling things from the cooler. It was only some light snacky things, fruit and some cheese and crackers, along with drinks, but as soon as Kevin started eating, he didn't stop. "Where do you put it?"

"Don't know. I didn't realize I was hungry until I ate something." He'd already eaten half the mixed fruit and was going for more. "You know, maybe we could program into the game how far the ladders will run and even the distance to the nearest water source. There have to be places where hydrants don't work or won't open. Stuff like that." He was getting up a good head of steam again, and Angus touched Kevin's jaw. Kevin turned toward him, and Angus leaned close to kiss him.

Kevin hummed and seemed to forget about food. He released his fork and within seconds wound his arms around Angus's neck, sliding closer until he was practically sitting on Angus's lap. He was like a live wire, radiating energy in every direction. Angus held him tighter, deepening the kiss as Kevin made little moans, and that went right to his dick. He wanted Kevin, badly. Never had he tasted anyone as sweet as Kevin or felt such a huge amount of energy in such a small, compact package.

"We shouldn't do this here," Angus whispered when they came up for air.

"We're just kissing," Kevin said with a slight pout to his lower lip.

"Maybe. But if we keep that up, it's quickly going to go beyond kissing. And that we definitely shouldn't do here." He held Kevin still, breathing deeply to calm his racing heart. Fuck, Kevin felt good, and as soon as the word entered his mind, that was exactly what he wanted to do: lay Kevin on the grass behind the table and fuck him so hard and deep that it caused an earthquake. Because Kevin was already rocking his world and he hadn't even realized it. "I haven't been on a date in a very long time."

"Oh. Then what do you do? Are you the meet 'em, fuck 'em, and leave 'em kind?" Kevin shifted away and sat back on the bench. "I've dated way too many of those kinds of guys."

"I don't know if I'm a kind, but the easy fuck and then go our separate ways does describe most of the relationships I've had. Sometimes they last for a few weeks, but they stay casual with lots of sex, some fun, and then we move on."

Kevin grinned. "I like the lots of sex part." He giggled. "But I'm not so keen on the leaving part. Ken, my last boyfriend, left for Pittsburgh, and my mom left my dad and me one day. Dad said he came home from work—I was at the neighbors—and Mom was gone and never came back. They found her in Ohio somewhere. She couldn't take being a mother, so she left and went to live somewhere else. My dad raised me on his own." Kevin didn't pick up his fork again, just stared at the can of Coke he cradled in his hands. "I always figured that I must have done something wrong or wasn't a good enough son for her to run away." Kevin set down the can and pushed it away. "I mean, mothers are supposed to love their children, so I always thought I was either really bad or too stupid for her to want me." Kevin stared at the woods. "I used to think that if I was good all the time and did what I should, then my mom would hear about it and she'd come back."

"Oh God."

"Yeah, so I was seven and accidentally rode my bike into Daddy's car. I scratched it a little. Daddy didn't even get mad, but I burst into tears because Mommy wasn't going to come back if I was naughty. He held me and said that Mommy leaving wasn't my fault. He said it was his, and that Mommy loved me wherever she was." The break in Kevin's voice told Angus that the wound was still there. It might have largely scarred over, but the kernel at the core was still raw. Angus ached to hold him and try to make things feel better, but voices on the trail got louder, and then a group of kids burst into the picnic area. They looked rough, with long, scraggly hair and dirty, ripped T-shirts and jeans.

"Why don't you finish eating and we'll head out." Angus kept an eye on the kids. They watched the two of them suspiciously, and Angus tensed, ready for trouble. Kevin nodded and went back to his plate. Angus stayed where he was, not willing to turn his back on the kids as they jumped on one of the other tables before doing flips off it, basically being stupid kids.

Once Kevin was done, Angus packed up everything and they left the area, turning back the way they'd come on the path. Some of the spring had left Kevin's step when they started out, but it slowly returned the closer they got to the motorcycle. "I'm sorry," Kevin eventually said as Angus put the cooler away and got out the riding gear. "I didn't mean to kill the mood."

"You didn't," Angus said as he closed the lid. "Sometimes things lead where we don't expect." He handed Kevin the jacket and got into his gear. Then he climbed on and waited for Kevin to get on and slide his arms around his waist. Angus started the bike and slowly backed it out of the space and rode out of the lot and out to the road.

He wasn't sure what to do now. Angus had planned to spend the afternoon in the park, but it didn't seem like a good idea any longer. When he got to the freeway, he cranked up the speed, and Kevin shifted closer. "I like riding," he said into his ear, and Angus nodded, hoping for some sign as to what they would do next. Maybe it would be best if he just took Kevin home.

CHAPTER THREE

KEVIN FELT like complete shit. He hadn't meant to dredge up all those old hurts. It was a first date, after all, and he'd managed to suck all the fun out of it. Angus picked up speed on the freeway, and the energy from the bike ramped up, zinging up Kevin's ass and thighs until it reached his head. He tightened his grip around Angus's waist, closed his eyes, and enjoyed the ride.

At first he'd been too nervous to move his hands, but Angus's granite abs drew him in, and he wondered how anyone could be so firm. He began exploring a little, sliding his hands lower, not realizing how far they'd wandered until Angus stiffened against him. Kevin grinned and stilled his hands, lightly sliding a finger along Angus's cock. Shivers ran through Angus, and Kevin pressed his hips to Angus's butt.

Kevin had never imagined how exciting riding a motorcycle could be, but this was the best thing ever. He actually wondered how he could get his hand around Angus's cock but figured that might be a little too dangerous, so he contented himself with his initial explorations as they zoomed back toward the city.

Angus turned off the freeway at the edge of Harrisburg, took the ramp to street level, and turned off into Shipoke. They slowed, and Angus stopped in front of a house and raised the garage door. He pulled in and came to a stop. The door slid down behind them, and Angus turned off the engine. Instant silence surrounded them. Kevin pulled his hands away in order to get off the bike. His legs wobbled slightly, and he adjusted himself in his jeans, watching as Angus took off his helmet. Kevin did the same and got out of the rest of the gear, handing it to Angus, and then followed him to the stairs and up into the house.

"This is really nice," Kevin said as they walked through the living room with its overstuffed leather furniture. The kitchen looked like it had been recently remodeled, with granite counters and gleaming appliances.

"Would you like to have a seat?" Angus offered. Kevin sat on the sofa, and Angus sat right next to him. "I hope you knew what you were doing on the bike."

Kevin giggled slowly and blushed. "I'm not usually that forward."

Angus leaned forward, and Kevin closed the gap between them, capturing Angus's lips in a kiss that deepened quickly. Angus pushed against him, and Kevin lay back on the sofa cushions, Angus's solid weight comforting as he pressed down on him. Kevin held on to Angus, pushing upward with his hips, moaning softly at first and then louder as Angus continued kissing him. Each of Angus's touches left him wanting more. When Angus pulled away, Kevin groaned until Angus pulled his shirt up above his nipples. He ran his rough cheeks over Kevin's chest and belly, and Kevin shivered with anticipation.

Kevin thrust his hips forward, but Angus made shushing sounds.

"Just take it easy." Angus licked one of Kevin's nipples, and Kevin whimpered softly as ripples of excitement raced through him. "I'll take really good care of you, cutie." Angus sucked at his chest and then down his belly. Kevin pulled at Angus's shirt, sliding it up his back, and as soon as he could, he grasped for skin.

Angus climbed off the sofa and stood up. Kevin blinked, wondering what had just happened. Angus grabbed his hands, and before Kevin could let out a squeak in surprise, Angus had him up and over his shoulder in a fireman's carry. "What...."

"We're going to continue the tour with the bedroom." Angus carried him up the stairs and into a large room with a huge bed. Kevin giggled as he bounced on the mattress and then looked up into Angus's eyes. They were deep, dark, and filled with something he hoped was passion, but Kevin was afraid to look too deeply, as though they might swallow him up. Angus's words about leaving rang in his ears. Maybe being up here with him was a bad idea, but if it was, so be it. Whatever he saw in Angus's eyes shot heat through him. He tried to turn away, but

Angus caught him under the chin, his touch hot and gentle, as though he were crooking his little finger, telling him to come closer.

Kevin did, going with what he wanted and leaving reason and common sense behind. As Angus leaned closer, Kevin's giggles, which had turned nervous, faded away. Angus's lips touched his, guiding him back onto the huge bed that dwarfed him completely. Angus didn't seem to care. He was already tugging at Kevin's shirt. He pulled it over his head, stopping his lip feast just long enough to get the fabric out of the way. Then Angus returned, pummeling him with lips and tongue, sucking on both, taking possession of Kevin's mouth. Like the heroine in one of those old Harlequin novels from the seventies, Kevin surrendered to the sexy fireman and let him have him. Angus's heat and intensity had his head swimming.

Angus splayed his hands against his chest, feeling him, taking him in like he wanted to get to know every inch of him. Angus worked his hands under him, stroking down his back, then broke the kiss and licked down Kevin's neck. Kevin put his arms over his head to give Angus better access, and Angus took advantage, working his exploring tongue down to a nipple as he slipped his hand inside Kevin's pants, cupping one of his cheeks in his huge, strong hand.

Kevin whimpered. He wasn't sure if it was because of the hand or the mouth, and he didn't much care—he just hoped like hell he wouldn't stop. He whimpered softly and stretched to give Angus access to whatever he wanted.

Angus worked open his belt and pants, tugging the denim apart. Then he licked harder, scraping his teeth over Kevin's nipple, working the second hand down his pants to hold his ass. Kevin wasn't sure where to concentrate and gave up, letting the sensations simply wash over him. When Angus tugged his pants down past his hips, he moaned softly, his cock bobbing free.

"Yes," Angus groaned softly under his breath, just loudly enough for Kevin to hear. He sucked a trail down Kevin's belly, pushing his ass up off the bed. It was like Angus held him in his hands, and when he encircled the head of Kevin's cock with his lips, he did. Angus could have anything he wanted.

"Oh God...." Kevin's head was going to explode any second. It had been weeks since he'd been with Ken, and he was ready to burst.

Instead of sucking him deeper, Angus lifted him higher, bringing him to his lips as though he were the star dish at a buffet. He took him deep, pressing his nose to Kevin's skin, and Kevin trembled with excitement.

"Fuck, you taste good," Angus whispered when he came up for air, kissing Kevin hard once again.

Kevin used the momentary reprieve from Angus's mind-melting excitement to pull at his shirt. Angus tugged his hands away and sat back so Kevin could get his shirt off.

"Damn," Kevin moaned before leaning in to lick one of Angus's large, pink nipples. He was all hard muscle, wide shoulders, and narrow waist, a body built from hard work and conditioning—all to do a difficult job that required a lot of physical strength and stamina.

"You like?" Angus asked with a smile.

"Hell yes," Kevin answered, pressing against Angus and reveling in the energetic sensation that zinged through him each place their bodies met.

When Angus pulled away, he tugged off Kevin's shoes and then pulled off his pants all the way, leaving him naked. "Scoot up on the bed," Angus told him as he worked open his own pants. Kevin watched as the clothing disappeared and Angus did a little back and forth dance to get his shoes off. Kevin spread his legs, cock throbbing. He wanted to stroke himself and figured he could come in a matter of seconds just by looking. Angus was stunning: muscled, tall, his brown hair tinged with red and echoed on the planes of his chest and down the center of his belly. His whipcorded legs flexed as he shifted slightly, and Angus's cock pointed right at him, jutting out. Everything about him was perfectly put together, and Angus obviously cared how he looked, especially naked.

"Manscaped and everything," Kevin said as he licked his lips. "Damn." He had to stop his hand or it was going to be over.

Angus crawled up onto the bed, slowly coming closer until he hovered over Kevin, who held his breath with nervous anticipation, wondering just what Angus had in mind. "Dang, you're stunning." Before Kevin could argue, Angus cut off his ability to speak with a kiss that sent heat shooting through him. Angus slowly lowered himself until their bodies met in a frenzy of heat. "I want you so bad," Angus whispered into his ear after breaking the kiss. "I'm going to suck you until your brain melts and then just when you can't take it any longer, I'm going to rim that tight, pretty ass of yours before sliding my cock deep inside you until you scream for me."

Kevin shivered.

"I take it you like that idea." Angus slid down him, pressing Kevin's legs apart. Knowing what Angus had in mind only heightened the anticipation. He held his breath and waited, eyes wide as Angus licked from his balls to the tip of his cock, then sucked him between his lips.

"Jesus," Kevin groaned as Angus took him all the way. "Damn, you're good at that." He wished he'd kept his mouth shut because Angus slid back off his cock.

"I'm good at lots of things," he replied with a wry grin. Kevin nodded; after all, this was not the time for a conversation. Angus grinned and opened his mouth, taking him in once again. Kevin moaned softly, thrusting his hips forward slightly. Angus was a natural, and Kevin was almost instantly on edge. But Angus had said he wasn't going to come yet, and Kevin did his best to hold back, to the point that stars formed behind his eyelids.

When Angus backed off, he breathed deeply, sucking in air as Angus lifted his legs off the bed. "Damn, you're amazing," Angus whispered to him, and Kevin shook his head on the pillow. He was normal, not particularly special. "Yes, you are," Angus said definitively, lightly moving his hands up and down Kevin's thighs, making him quiver gently. "Now isn't the time to argue." Angus licked down his crease and then blew on his wet skin.

"God," Kevin whined, gripping the bedding in his fists, anticipation growing by the second. "I'm really not."

Angus zeroed on his opening, teasing him, swirling his tongue before probing him. "Yes, you are." Angus licked and sucked, patting his ass, running his fingers down his crease and around and away, giving just enough sensation to leave him wanting more.

Kevin seemed to balance on the edge for a long time. Angus really knew how to play him, to give just enough that he couldn't think straight, yet not enough to allow him to tumble over the edge. When Angus came up for air, he was grinning, eyes shining. Kevin smiled back, and Angus leaned over him, kissing Kevin hard, their tongues dancing and sparring with each other. It was beyond hot, and Kevin tasted a hint of his own muskiness on Angus's lips. They continued kissing until Angus reached to the side table. Kevin heard a drawer slide open and followed the sound.

Angus pulled out the lube and a condom, nearly dropping the drawer on the floor. Kevin laughed, and Angus glared at him.

"Sex is fun, and sometimes it's goofy," Kevin explained.

"Am I goofy?" Angus asked, his lips still curling upward.

"No," Kevin breathed and placed his hands on Angus's broad chest. "You're hot, strong, and yet gentle." Ken pushed at the edges of his mind, but Kevin shoved back those memories. He lifted his head, placing his mouth over Angus's. "You make me feel wonderful."

Angus's eyes shone, and it occurred to Kevin that Angus might have a few insecurities of his own. "And you are stunning."

Kevin pushed Angus back on his haunches, working down his chest to a pink nipple that he licked, making small circles with his tongue. Angus's thick cock poled up from his lap, and Kevin curled his fingers around it, stroking slowly, enjoying the heft. "Lean back," Kevin groaned with excitement. Angus put his hands on the bed behind him, and Kevin stretched out on his belly until he was eye level with Angus's cock.

It was a thing of beauty, long and really thick, and Kevin shivered in anticipation. He stuck out his tongue and licked along the length. Angus parted his legs, and Kevin stroked his hairy inner thighs as he took the head in his mouth.

"Fuck yeah," Angus mumbled.

Kevin took more of him, and Angus lifted his hips. Kevin relaxed his throat and pressed forward, taking all of Angus, tightening his lips, and pulling as he retreated. He raised his gaze and would have smiled— if his mouth wasn't full of Angus's glorious cock—at the sight of this huge man with his mouth hanging open in wonder. "I'm talented," he whispered when he paused for air.

"You're amazing," Angus breathed. He guided Kevin to his lips, cutting off his protest before it could fully form. Heat zinged through him as Kevin returned the kiss. When their lips parted, he gazed into Angus's eyes for a few seconds and then trailed his lips and tongue down Angus's chest and rippling belly to his cock once more.

He bobbed his head, listening to Angus's groans. They were like music. "Sweetheart, stop," Angus said. "I'm going to come if you continue." He tugged Kevin into a kiss. "I want to come buried inside you."

Kevin's cock jumped at the thought, and he nodded. Angus shifted, kissing him back on the bed. Kevin held Angus around the neck, clamping his legs on his waist, shivering when Angus stroked up his thighs, teasing his opening.

The snick of the lube bottle echoed through the room. Kevin waited in anticipation until Angus pressed a slicked finger to his opening and then slid it inside him. "Damn, even your fingers are thick."

"Just wait for my cock," Angus said softly. "I'm going to fill you and then ride you slowly until you scream for me at the top of your lungs."

"Oh God," Kevin groaned, then became shrill when Angus touched that spot inside him, rubbing softly as he quivered like a leaf about to fall.

"See? You are beautiful with your eyes closed and your mouth open." Angus kissed him gently, tugging on his lower lip. "You're glowing." A second finger joined the first, and Kevin rocked slightly to get Angus's digits deeper inside. He wanted more and whimpered when Angus pulled his fingers away, though he knew the main event was coming. He breathed shallowly to relax while Angus put on the condom. Kevin grabbed the lube, slicked his hands, and stroked up and down Angus's cock before guiding it to his opening. He inhaled as Angus pressed forward, entering him.

The stretch was eye-rolling. Kevin gasped, his mouth dropping open as the initial jolt of pain morphed into a nearly overwhelming sensation that dang near overloaded his brain. Angus sank deeper, and Kevin patted his leg, silently asking him to pause. "Too much... just stop," Kevin said between pants and closed his eyes. Once his heart rate slowed a little and the spasms of excitement passed through his muscles, Angus pushed deeper, and damn if Kevin wasn't fuller than he could ever remember once Angus's hips pressed to his ass.

Angus leaned forward and pressed a gentle kiss to his lips. "You feel so hot." Kevin clenched his muscles, and Angus trembled. "Good God, you're so tight." Kevin did it again, smiled, and Angus gently pulled out, moving slowly, his gaze locked on Kevin's. "I love your eyes," Angus said, his accent becoming more pronounced. "They darken when I pull away," Angus nearly pulled out of him and then slowly pressed back into him. "They sparkle when I fill you." Angus rolled his hips, slow and steady.

"Oh yes!" Kevin loved that. Angus scraped his cock over that spot, and Kevin shook like hell. "More."

"I want to take my time," Angus said as he rolled his hips.

"Screw that," Kevin said, reaching for Angus's hips and pulling him close. Then he wrapped his arms around Angus's neck and pulled him closer. "I'm not going to break, so I want you to fuck me like you mean it."

"But...."

"Fuck me, dammit!"

Angus pulled away and then rammed back into him, vibrating his entire body.

"Yes!"

"That better?" Angus asked and withdrew before snapping his cock back inside him.

"Hell yeah," Kevin yelled, shaking as erotic energy filled both him and the room. The air grew close and filled with the scent of sweat and testosterone. It was heady and only added to the excitement. Kevin breathed in deep, taking it all in, especially the way Angus's stomach muscles rippled as he snapped his hips.

Most of the time during anal sex, Kevin tended to lose his erection. The sensation was so overwhelming that he would concentrate on that and forget about his dick. Angus took him in hand, stroking him slowly, and Kevin's dick roared back to life. Within seconds he was on the edge once again, trying not to tumble over too quickly. "So close," he groaned, arching his back.

"Put your hands over your head for me," Angus told him, and Kevin grabbed the headboard, gripping the wood hard, arms corded with tension as he stayed just this side of nirvana. "You gonna scream for me?"

"Oh yeah, wanna come so bad. Got to," Kevin gritted as Angus paused in his stroking. He groaned as his release slipped further away. All he needed was a little bit more. Angus thrust deep, stilling, cock bobbing slightly inside him. Tiny thrusts followed, and Kevin's head swam as Angus sent waves of heat through him.

"You ready?"

"Yeah," Kevin said, his voice trembling. He couldn't take much more of this erotic torture. His vision began to tunnel, and then Angus gripped his cock hard, stroking like hell. "I'm right there!" Kevin stretched and clamped his eyes closed as his release began at the base of his balls and raced through him. "Fuck!" he yelled as the pressure built and built, and then he erupted, shooting onto his chest and belly. He even felt his release on his chin.

Kevin vibrated with excitement as Angus came inside him. He felt Angus's cock swell slightly, throbbing. He opened his eyes, and the sight of Angus in climax stole his breath away. Sweat glistened on Angus's chest, his eyes shone, his mouth open just a little.

"God!"

"Yeah, you're so fucking sexy," Kevin told him and held on to Angus, tugging him down as afterglow began to settle in. His weight on top of him was glorious.

"I'm so sweaty," Angus whispered.

Kevin chuckled. "Your sweet talk needs work."

"Probably," Angus said. "You really don't mind?"

Kevin stilled, realizing Angus was being serious. "Why would I?" He shivered when Angus slipped from inside him. He continued holding him, only letting Angus move away to take care of the condom. When he returned to the bed, Kevin tugged Angus back into place. "I take it someone told you sweat wasn't attractive."

"Well, I had a boyfriend for a while, maybe a few weeks, and he always raced for the shower after sex so he could get clean. Granted, we had fun in the shower most of the time, but he had to get clean right away. And a few other guys have said that I sweat too much, so…."

"You're a big man, and you were doing all the work," Kevin said with a grin and then sucked at the base of Angus's neck. "Never apologize for being who you are. I learned that a long time ago." Kevin lay back on the pillow. "I wouldn't stay with someone who expected me to be who I wasn't."

"Is that what happened to you?"

"It has, I guess," Kevin said. "Some people are never happy with who anyone is, and they always want to try to turn them into what they want." Kevin sighed. "Sometimes I feel left out since all my friends have partners. So I let myself feel desperate and went out with a few guys I should have told to take a hike. They weren't abusive, but they were a little dumb and only interested in sex."

"I guess that was me," Angus said.

"Why?" Kevin asked. Angus shrugged, and Kevin looked deep into his eyes and saw a well of pain that nearly made him gasp. "Not everyone will leave." He hoped he wasn't jumping to the wrong conclusion.

Angus shook his head. "Everyone leaves," he said in response, and Kevin gaped. "In one way or the other, people leave you, and you need to get used to it." The vehemence in Angus's voice had Kevin doing a double take.

"That's not true. I know plenty of couples who will be together for a long time." He knew that was true in his heart. Bull and Zach were, like, the perfect couple. Sure, he supposed they fought about things, but they also loved each other more than air. The same was true for Jeremy and Spook, and Tristan and Harry. Though if he were truthful, Kevin was a little jealous of Tristan, because at one time he'd crushed on Harry. But in retrospect, Harry and Tristan were great together, so he couldn't be really upset.

Angus rolled away and lay on his back on the mattress. Where Kevin had felt so close to him a few minutes earlier, it seemed a gulf had suddenly opened up, and he wasn't sure what to do to bridge it. He found Angus really hot and all, but he didn't know him that well and wasn't sure what to say.

"Some people are lucky in that way, but I'm not," Angus said.

"How do you know?" Kevin decided he wasn't going to let this go. So he climbed on top of Angus with a grin and wriggled his hips against his. "Have you met everyone? Or taken some sort of poll?" He giggled softly when Angus huffed. "I got it. You're psychic and know everything before it's going to happen. If that's true, then I want to know the Powerball numbers so I can buy a ticket."

"You're being silly."

"So are you," Kevin retorted. "I don't know who left you, but not everyone does that."

"How can you say that? Your mom left you."

Angus's words stung, and for a second he pulled into himself. Kevin glared at him and then smacked him on the shoulder. "Don't be an ass. It's not cute or funny. If you wanted to be a real dick, you succeeded. But you didn't hurt me, if that's what you were trying to do. I'm an adult now, and I can choose how I want to feel and what I'm going to react to." Kevin moved closer, glaring at Angus. "Maybe it's time I go home. I thought you were a good guy, but I can see now that you're just an ass. I certainly don't need any more assholes in my life. There have been more than enough." Kevin rolled off Angus and got off the bed, searching around on the floor for his clothes.

"I…," Angus started.

"You what? Have some explanation of childhood trauma to explain why you were a jerk?" Kevin shook his head. "Just save it."

"I shouldn't have said that."

Kevin found his underwear and pulled them on. "No, you shouldn't. I trusted you with something difficult that happened to me, and you threw it back in my face." He turned and stepped back to where Angus sat naked on the side of the bed. He picked up his pants and fished in his pocket, coming up with a quarter. He handed it to Angus. "Use this to call someone who can teach you some manners." He pulled on his jeans and had just fastened them when Angus touched his shoulder.

"Sometimes I don't know when to keep quiet."

"Bullshit. I was treading into territory you didn't want to go, and instead of saying you didn't want to talk about it, you lashed out hurtfully, and I won't stand for that crap. But I have news for you. My mom left when I was a kid, and she never got to know me. But that's her loss, not mine. I'm an amazing person, and she's the one who lost out on knowing me. I can deal with that—in fact I did a long time ago. So whatever it is that's bothering you, figure out how to deal with it or whatever it is will dog you for the rest of your life." Kevin turned away and grabbed his shirt, pulling it over his head before yanking on his socks and stepping into his shoes. Then he marched to the bedroom door, refusing to turn around. "I'll see you around. And don't bother giving me a ride home. I'll call a friend." He pulled open the bedroom door and hurried out into the hall, closing the door behind him with more force than was necessary. Then he hurried down the stairs and out of the house. He pulled out his phone and pressed a number.

"Zach, can you please pick me up?"

"Where are you?" Zach asked right away.

"Shipoke." He kept his voice as steady as he could even though he was quickly alternating between anger and hurt.

"I take it your date didn't go well."

"Prince Charming turned out to be a frog with huge warts," he answered. He turned around when he heard the door open behind him.

Angus strode toward him, and Kevin stared daggers at him. "He's coming this way."

"Do you want me to call the police? I can have them there in a few minutes."

"No," he said when Angus stopped a few feet away. "I'll call you back."

"Fine, but if I don't hear from you in five minutes, I'm going to call in the cavalry and everyone is going to descend on him."

Kevin agreed and then hung up. "You have exactly five minutes," he said as he glared at Angus, slipping his phone into his pocket.

"Five minutes for what?"

"To properly apologize and stop acting like a complete fucking pain in the ass." He put his hands on his hips. "I'm waiting."

Angus broke eye contact. "I didn't mean to hurt you. It's just that the subject is closer to an open wound than I want to admit." He raised his gaze from the sidewalk. "I'd like to think I'm over what happened, but every time anyone gets close to it, I lash out."

"You know that isn't an excuse for hurting me… or trying to hurt me. See, in order to truly get to me, you have to be someone I'm willing to care about, and as of this moment, the jury is out on that. Right now I can take or leave you. Sure, you're hot and all, but if you can't treat me right, you can hit the road." Kevin's phone rang, and he pulled it out of his pocket. "Hi, Zach."

"Are you okay?"

"Yes, I'm fine. I'm here with Angus and we're talking for a moment."

"Do you need a ride home? I can be there in a few minutes, we can kick his ass, and you can come here. We'll have ice cream and watch old crappy movies, and you can roast this Angus guy on a spit."

Kevin tried not to smile, but he couldn't help it. He knew his friends would be there for him. They always were.

"My friend Zach wants to know if I need a ride home," Kevin told Angus. "He's offering ice cream and a chance for the two of us to discuss all your character flaws." He was starting to have fun with this, especially as Angus got more and more nervous.

"I have ice cream, and we can talk about all my character flaws all you want. I'm sure I have more than a few."

"Did you hear that?" Kevin asked Zach. He heard him laughing on the other end of the phone.

"Yeah. And if you ask me, I think you better keep him. I've been trying to get Bull to debate his character flaws for years, but he always distracts me with sex and then I forget all about them." He continued laughing. "Go ahead and talk things out, but call me if you need me." Zach hung up, and Kevin put his phone back in his pocket.

"He says I should kick your ass if you ever do that again," Kevin told Angus, who folded his arms over his chest. "You think I can't do it?" Kevin mimicked Angus's stance and expression. "Bull taught all four of us some basic self-defense moves after Tristan was kidnapped last year. And the one lesson I learned very well is that the bigger they are, the harder they fall."

"Geez, I thought you were a sweet, rather quiet guy, but you're a real badass."

Kevin knew he was teasing, and he lured Angus onto the grass. He motioned forward with his finger, and Angus smiled, humoring him, Kevin was sure. When Angus came at him, he grabbed his hand, used his body as leverage, and flipped Angus onto his back, leaving him lying on the grass, staring up at the sky. "Do you believe me now?" he asked, leaning over him. "See? I'm a real badass."

Angus blinked and slowly got to his feet. "I guess so," he said with much more respect.

"Just because I'm smaller than you doesn't mean I can't take care of myself or that I'm helpless." Kevin put his hands on his hips once again, tapping his foot on the grass. "I'm still waiting for my apology."

Angus got to his feet. "I'm sorry I lashed out at you. It was my own wounds and nothing you did." He stepped closer and gently touched Kevin's chin. "I'll try not to do it again."

"You better not, because next time I won't be as nice."

Angus chuckled and shook his head. "You really are something else."

"Do you make a habit of being mean to people?" Kevin asked. "I don't want to be around you if you act like that all the time."

Angus shook his head and took his hand. "I'm not usually like that."

Kevin allowed Angus to lead him back into the house. He wasn't sure he was fully convinced, but he was willing to give him a second chance. "What happened to you? Because you got this 'everyone leaves' thing going, and then you pushed me away."

Angus's steps faltered for a second, and then he pulled open the front door. "I really hate talking about it."

"Yeah, I get that, and I won't press you if you don't want to talk about it." Kevin sat on the sofa in Angus's living room, watching as he left the room and wondering if he was being a complete fool. After that whole 'lashing out' thing in the bedroom, it would probably be smarter to walk away and go home. He'd seen abusers before and knew how Tristan had behaved with Eddie. Whatever happened wasn't Eddie's fault. Tristan was always to blame and had a million excuses. He wasn't doing that, but it did make him pause.

When Angus returned, he had two glasses of iced tea and handed Kevin one. "I spent time when I was a child with friends of my parents in York. They already had four kids, and I was the fifth. All of them fought all the time and were nasty to each other. I mean, really nasty." Angus sat next to him. "It was a very bad time, and I ended up like a tennis ball between family members. Whenever their daughter Mary got mad at her brother Mick, she'd say the meanest things, and then she'd try to get me on her side, and Mick would do the same thing. And I guess I learned to do the same thing just to survive. It was pretty miserable, and I don't think I've acted like that in a long time, but…."

"I pushed a button?" Kevin asked.

"Yeah. One I didn't really know was there," Angus said, clearly upset. He put his arm around Kevin, and Kevin leaned against him. The last few hours seemed like a strange dream, and he tried to figure out what he wanted to do. "Should I take you home?"

"I don't know," Kevin said. "Things seem strange now. I'm not a baby, and I understand being upset."

Angus kissed his forehead. "Then I'm going to have to show you I'm not a monster."

"I don't think that. And what you said wasn't untruthful, just a little hurtful. My mother did leave, and it fit your point. But not everyone leaves. You have to believe that or else you'll push people away."

"If you say so," Angus said.

"I do," Kevin said firmly. "Just give folks a chance."

Angus sighed. "Most of the guys I've been with were fine with keeping things casual and quick."

"Well, I'm not most guys, and if that's what you want, then you're welcome to it. But it's not what I want." Kevin reached for the glass of tea and drank some of it. "That's what you have to decide." He glanced around. "Now I think we can have some of that ice cream and then talk about those character flaws you mentioned earlier." Kevin smiled, figuring it was time to try to lighten the mood. "What kind do you have?"

"What? Ice cream?"

"No, character flaws. You need to tell me all about them."

"Jesus," Angus groaned and got to his feet, tugging Kevin to his. "I've got chocolate and mint chocolate chip."

"Character flaws? Those are some pretty weird names," Kevin teased.

"Ice cream," Angus said, laughing. "Man, you can be really goofy."

"I'm not the one naming my character flaws after ice cream flavors," Kevin retorted. "Seriously, I want mint chocolate chip. It's my favorite. And let me guess, lack of attention span is one of your flaws."

Angus pulled open the freezer door and got out the carton. He set it on the counter and pulled out spoons and bowls. "You can tell a lot about a man by the kind of ice cream he likes. Vanilla guys are just that: they like things plain, but steady. Men who prefer chocolate want a little more richness but still don't stray far from the path." Angus scooped out the ice cream and handed him a bowl and spoon.

"What does mint chocolate chip say?" Kevin asked as he watched Angus get some for himself.

"Intelligent, smart, likes things a little different without going way out there," Angus told him.

"Okay. How about…." Kevin paused. "Rocky road?"

Angus dropped his spoon in his dish and began to laugh. "I dated a guy once, just once, who liked rocky road. He was adventurous and liked to have sex outdoors, which was fine. Except the idiot didn't know what poison ivy looked like and picked a shady spot near a beautiful creek. We went at it for a couple hours. He was pretty energetic, but let me tell you, there is nothing more annoying than poison ivy on your ass."

Kevin giggled and nearly dropped his bowl. "You're kidding."

"No. I had to go to the doctor and drop my pants to show him. Then I needed to explain how it got there."

"Oh God." Kevin's giggles picked up again. "What did he do?"

"He gave me a shot and unfortunately it had to be in my ass. So not only did the damn thing itch like hell, but it was sore from the dang shot too. It hurt to sit down for days, and God, work was hell. So there is no more rocky road in this house ever—either ice cream or the men who like it."

Kevin giggled again and tried to pick up his bowl, but all he could envision was Angus squirming every time he tried to sit down. "Okay. No rocky road. Definitely not. I like your butt."

"You do, huh?"

"Yeah." Kevin took a bite of ice cream and stared hard at Angus.

"What?"

"Just imagining you with your butt in the air."

Angus stopped eating. "Ummm."

"Have you never bottomed?"

Angus set down his bowl. "I have. I really don't care for it, though." He shrugged, and Kevin figured he was trying not to make a big thing about it. But that well of pain was back in Angus's eyes, and Kevin couldn't help wondering what had happened to him.

"Well, I like it just fine, especially with you." There were so many things he was curious about, but Kevin wasn't going to steer the conversation in those directions if he could help it. Angus had obviously known pain, and if he wasn't willing to talk about it, that was his business.

"Good," Angus said with a huge grin, the darkness slipping away from his eyes. "Because I like being with you."

Kevin ate the last of his ice cream and set the bowl on the counter. "So tell me what you like."

"Huh?"

"Tell me what you like." Kevin stepped closer. "Did you like it when I sucked on your big cock, swirling my tongue around the pink head?" He saw Angus swallow. "Or did that not really work for you?"

"Jesus," Angus moaned, and he looked like he was going to snort ice cream out his nose. "Of course I liked it. You nearly had me coming in two seconds flat." Angus took his final bite and slid his bowl on the counter without taking his eyes off Kevin. The heat was instantaneous and would have melted the ice cream if there had been any left. "What did you like? The way I sucked you hard and deep, or the way I ate your tight little ass until you were ready to scream for me to fuck you… or maybe it was the way I was so deep in you it was hard to breathe." Angus stepped closer. "Two can play that game," he whispered.

"You know…." Kevin stroked his chin. "I can't really remember. Maybe you're going to have to jog my memory."

Angus grabbed the carton of ice cream and practically threw it in the freezer, then slammed the door. Then he grabbed Kevin around the waist and lifted him over his shoulder again. Kevin did squeak this time as Angus carried him up to the bedroom.

"You're a Neanderthal, you know that?" Kevin said. He initially squirmed to get down but found he had a great view and access to Angus's ass, so he made the very most of it, sliding his hands inside the back of Angus's jeans. "The view, on the other hand, is spectacular from here."

Angus started slightly when Kevin squeezed his cheeks, and then he half dumped Kevin on the bed. "I think it's time to get on to the memory refreshment." Angus had his shoes, pants, and shirt off practically before the bed stopped bouncing, and Kevin wasn't so sure about memory refreshment as Angus proceeded to turn his mind to mush.

CHAPTER FOUR

ANGUS SPENT the next few days doing all the things he'd put off while he'd been on shift: the piles of laundry, paying bills, and of course he had to clean the house. Kevin had stayed well into the evening the day of their date, and Angus had later taken him home. However, since then, Kevin hadn't called, and Angus figured he'd really blown things with him. He had a few more days before he was back on shift and decided he might as well man up and call him.

Kevin's phone rang and then went to voice mail. Angus left a message for Kevin to call him and hung up before finishing up his chores around the house.

His phone rang an hour later, and he snatched it up, his pulse racing a little in anticipation. But it wasn't who he was expecting. "Hey, Marv," he said to his friend.

"Well, don't sound too damned disappointed. I can always hang up if you don't want to talk."

"What crawled up your butt?"

"Carolyn is on the warpath again," Marv said.

"What did you do now?" Marv was most definitely clueless, and Carolyn was one of the kindest and longest-suffering people he'd ever met. The two of them loved each other. But every now and then she couldn't take any more of Marv's crap and they had a huge, often loud fight that tended to get Marv's head screwed on straight, at least for a while.

"I had to go down to York with Steve after work, and I didn't call her. Dammit, she has a cell phone and she could have called. Instead, she was waiting at home."

Angus knew there was more to it than that and waited a few seconds. "I tried calling you yesterday, and you didn't answer."

"Well, I kind of lost my phone," Marv said.

"Where did you see it last?"

"Falling out of the truck into the creek near the house."

Marv had just officially graduated to moron status. "So you went to York and didn't call her because you lost your cell phone and didn't want Carolyn to know. How many phones have you lost?" Angus had to ask. "Is it eight?"

"Only six," Marv said indignantly.

"And you don't think Carolyn has a reason to be upset?" Angus knew that sometimes Marv needed to have things pointed out to him. "Go to the store and buy Carolyn some flowers and whatever else she's been asking for. She loves you—God knows why—and you need to treat her better, because what would you do without her?"

"Okay, point taken. I'll do that. But you haven't told me why you're all growly. You usually listen a little more before giving me hell." Maybe Marv wasn't totally clueless.

"It's not important," he answered.

"Uh-huh. This wouldn't have anything to do with that guy you went out with on Sunday."

"Maybe a little. I thought we had a good time, but he wanted to know about my past, and I got a little snippy and may have blown it. I left a message the other day and then today, but he hasn't called me back."

Marv snickered. "I take it you like this guy, because you've never obsessed over anyone before. If they don't like you, and all the guys like you—the girls do too, but you don't notice them at all—"

"Get to the point," Angus said.

"Fine. You go from guy to guy all the time, having a good time. But you've never wondered if a guy was going to call you back. So take your own advice and go get some flowers or something and go see him. You know where he lives, right?"

"Yeah. I picked him up on my bike."

"Then don't sit around like a pussy—go do something." Angus could see Marv rolling his eyes. He wondered when Marv had gotten a clue and figured that wasn't bad advice. His phone beeped that he had another call coming in. He checked the number.

"I have to go. It's work," he told Marv and took the other call. "This is Angus."

"MacTavish, grab your gear and get to the station. There's an apartment fire, and we need all available hands."

Angus was already moving through his house, grabbing the bag he kept packed next to his door. He hefted it. "I already have it. Do you just want me at the scene?"

"Do that. The address is 1245 Marshall Avenue," the captain said.

Angus nearly dropped his phone. He knew that address. "We were just there not long ago for an oven fire."

"This is a lot more than that. Part of the entire building is involved, and as fast as it's spreading, there's definitely accelerant."

Angus was already at his car and threw his gear in the trunk. "I'll be there as soon as I can." He hung up and got inside the Mustang, heart pumping. He raised the garage door and backed out of the garage, then headed back to Kevin's building, only this time it was for something potentially much more dire than a date.

Angus had worked as a firefighter for six years, but until this point he had never had to show up at the home of someone he cared about. The other guys told stories of arriving at the homes of family friends and even relatives, and all they could do was go to work, check that everyone was all right, and then comfort the ones they cared about after the fire had been extinguished. Angus had been spared that... until he pulled up in front of Kevin's apartment.

The rear of the building was fully involved. He stopped his car out of the way and raced out. Within seconds he had his trunk open and was pulling on his gear. "Cap," he called, and Justinian hurried over to him. "Is everyone out?"

"No. Get on breathing gear. An old lady and younger man are unaccounted for."

"Kevin and Mrs. V?" Angus asked.

The captain nodded. "They're most likely on the first or second floors. I have teams soaking the building, but we need someone to go in. I've assigned—"

Before the captain could say anything more, Angus pulled on the rest of his gear, checked it, and hurried toward the front door. Thankfully it was quiet and fire-free. Hoses had doused the area, and the firefighters pulled back briefly so he could get inside.

Smoke rolled everywhere, and Angus hurriedly kicked open the door to the first-floor apartment. The front was intact, but the rear was already on fire. He checked the first bedroom and bath before turning and trying the other. It was empty as well. Once he finished, the heat was building, but he didn't stop, hurrying up the stairs. The back of the hall was already in flames. One door stood open. He peered inside, saw no one, and then kicked open the other door. Heat and smoke rolled out of the door and flames burst through the rear door of the apartment as air fanned the fire. He found a woman with gray hair on the floor near the table and lifted her into his arms and carefully began the trek out of the building.

The smoke was increasing, along with the heat. He sighed as he reached the front door and handed the woman off to emergency personnel. Then he turned to go back inside. The captain grabbed his shoulder and shook his head, pointing toward the roof.

Angus shrugged him off and raced back into the building and up the stairs. The apartment was nearly fully engulfed. He found Kevin on the floor in front of the kitchen sink. He scooped him up, hoping like hell he was okay, and started for the exit. Angus reached the door as flames exploded behind him, pushing him out into the hall, and he nearly tumbled him down the stairs. Flames were shooting out of the first-floor doorways, and he steadied himself for a few seconds, cradled Kevin to him, and descended the stairs as fast as he could, leaping through the front door into a shower of water as sparks flew all around him.

He handed Kevin off in time to turn around as the roof collapsed, pancaking the other weakened floors. Everyone moved back as every hose dumped water on the old building, but it had most likely been weakened by years of improper maintenance and care. The side walls fell inward, and Angus raced back, grabbing coworkers as the front of the building broke away and began to crumble forward.

Thankfully, everyone got out of the way, and as soon as the rubble settled, the hose teams began dousing the pile of debris. Angus took off his breathing gear and helmet, coming face-to-face with his captain.

"If you ever do that again, so help me I will kick your ass from here to kingdom come and pull you in front of a review board. I know you got the missing man out, but we could have lost both him and you if you had taken twenty more seconds. You were damn lucky the roof lasted as long as it did."

Angus knew better than to argue, so he held his tongue, even though it was difficult. His defiance came out in his stare. There was no way he was going to back down, and if he had to remain silent, he wouldn't cower.

"Now, I don't know if you were just being stubborn, but what you did was as brave as hell, and you saved someone's life. That's what we're here for." Captain Justinian glared at him. "But next time you listen to me."

Angus nodded and turned away, pulling off his fire coat so he didn't completely sweat away. Then he went in search of the people he'd rescued.

He found Kevin on the ground with a mask over his mouth and nose. "How is he?" he asked the EMT.

"He roused for a few minutes but then lost consciousness again. We're transporting him to the hospital. He inhaled a lot of smoke, but we think he's going to be okay." The EMT turned to the ambulance, and Angus followed his gaze. A figure lay under a sheet, face covered. The door to the ambulance was closed, and then it pulled away. The simple glimpse gave him all the information he needed to know.

"She was a good friend of his," Angus said. He thanked the EMT, getting out of the way so Kevin could be looked at more closely. He watched as Kevin was transferred to the gurney and then loaded into the other ambulance. Once it had left, he returned to where the other firefighters were working.

"Did they both make it?" Clark asked.

"No. It looks like the woman didn't. She was the one who sent the sweets with Kevin to the station. I didn't know her, but she meant a lot to him."

"Do they have people to contact?" Clark asked.

"I don't know," he answered even as he started walking to his car. Clark walked with him, and Angus got his phone off the passenger seat and looked up the number for Bronco's. He remembered that Kevin talked a lot about a guy named Bull, so he asked for him when someone answered the phone. "I'm one of the firefighters who was at the club a week or so ago."

"Yeah," Bull said gruffly. "What can I do for you?"

"I'm calling because of Kevin."

"What happened?" the gruffness disappeared instantly, replaced by concern.

"I was called to his building, and it was nearly fully engulfed. I did get him out of the building, but he's been taken to Pinnacle Health Center. He was unconscious the last time I saw him, and I wasn't sure who else to call."

"Appreciate it. I'll call Zach, and he'll go up there to be with him."

"Thanks," Angus said, not sure what else he should do. They'd had one date, and he didn't have much of a claim on Kevin. "I didn't want him to be alone."

"No chance of that. Once Zach gets done there will be a steady stream of his friends looking out for him." Bull ended the call, and Angus threw his phone back on the seat and returned to the rest of the team. They continued pouring water on what was left of the apartment building, but the fire was out and now they were just making sure there wouldn't be a flare-up later.

The other tenants had gathered off to the side, where people from the Red Cross were already meeting with them to see to their immediate needs.

"Let's start to pack up," Captain Justinian said, and Angus got to work, putting away equipment as water was turned off and hoses retracted. It took some time to get everything packed back where it belonged, and one by one the trucks headed back to their stations. "Go on home," Justinian told him.

Angus got in his car and drove back to Shipoke. At least that was where he intended to go, but his car made the turn onto the bridge, and he zipped over to the west shore of the Susquehanna and into the Pinnacle parking lot. He parked his car and raced inside.

"I'm here to see Kevin Foster. He was brought in by ambulance from a fire. I was one of the responders on the scene, and I wanted to know how he was doing."

66

"I can't tell you much other than he is here." She motioned toward the waiting area.

"Is he okay?"

She shook her head. "I'm sorry. There isn't anything I can tell you."

Angus huffed and went to sit down. It was then that he remembered he was still in his fire pants and boots. He took off the boots and slipped out of the pants, draping them over one of the chairs before putting the boots back on. Then he sat down to wait, watching the doors as people came and went.

A small man raced in, coming to a skidding stop at the desk. "I'm here for Kevin Foster."

"Are you a relative?"

"I'm the one who has his health care power of attorney." He snapped the smug smile off her face as he showed her the paper. "Now show me where he is."

"If you'll have a seat, I'll have the doctor see you when he can."

"No, I won't. If he's being treated and can't speak for himself, then I need to speak for him." He was getting angry, and Angus stood and walked over.

"He's right," Angus said, and she blanched.

"Just a minute." The girl got up and left the desk.

"I'm Angus, and you must be Zach." The look he got was cold. "I was the one who pulled him out of the apartment building a little while ago." Zach nodded but said nothing. "I just want to know how he's doing."

"When they let me back to see him, I'll see that you know." Zach pursed his lips. "You didn't yell at him any more, did you?"

"No." Angus nervously rubbed the back of his neck. "I told him I was sorry, and we had a special day. At least I thought so, but he never called me back or answered my messages. I was about to go see him when I got the call about the fire."

"You can come with me," the girl said, and Zach followed her. Angus returned to his seat and hoped that Zach would keep his word. He read an old magazine and shifted in his chair. Finally, Zach came out and asked him to come with him.

"Is he awake?" Angus asked.

"Yes, but he can't talk much. They're still giving him oxygen, and they want to keep him a few days. The smoke really did a number on his lungs." They passed through the doors and walked down a hallway. Zach led him to a curtained-off area. They entered and Angus stopped just inside. Kevin blinked at him but otherwise lay still. He had a mask over his nose and mouth and was pale, almost ghostly. Angus wanted to rush up to him but settled for walking slowly and then taking one of his hands. Kevin was cold but curled his fingers slightly.

"You're going to be fine."

Kevin blinked at him and turned to Zach. "He wants to know about Mrs. V. Is she okay? Did you get her out?"

Angus swallowed hard. "I found her first and carried her out the building and then came back and found you in your kitchen. I carried you out as the place collapsed behind us." He didn't want to tell him about Mrs. V. She seemed to mean a lot to him, and Angus wanted Kevin to feel better, not go through additional pain. Kevin squeezed his hand slightly, eyes filling with tears. He blinked and then turned his gaze to Zach. "I'm sorry, Kevin," Angus whispered.

The curtain was pulled back and a doctor strode in as though he owned the world. "Mr. Foster, are you breathing any better?" He walked right up to them, and Angus knew the second his gaze fell on their clasped hands. The doctor said nothing, but his gaze lingered for longer than it should have. Kevin thankfully seemed oblivious and simply shrugged. "What we're going to do is schedule some tests and then move you up into a room. You inhaled a lot of smoke, and we need to give your lungs a chance to work it out. Thankfully, the heat didn't get to them, so they will recover on their own with little interference from us."

"There isn't something more you can do?" Zach asked.

"Not unless we have to. If his lungs can heal on their own, it's best to let them do so. We will need to check the extent of the damage." He turned back to Kevin. "You're likely to have difficulty doing anything that requires strenuous breathing for a while." The doctor's gaze shifted to Angus. He nodded, understanding what the doctor meant. "Just lie there and be as still as you can. Rest is the best thing for you now. Someone will be in to take you down for the tests and then move you to a room."

"Thank you," Kevin rasped from under the mask. If Angus hadn't already known what he was going to say, he wouldn't have understood him. Kevin closed his eyes, and Zach approached the bed, carefully touching the fingers of the hand with the IV.

"What do they have him on?"

"They said it was mostly fluids, but they also added an antibiotic just in case he picked up something from the smoke. They said old buildings can be filled with bacteria that become airborne or can hitch a ride in fumes or smoke, so they wanted to be cautious," Zach explained.

"Is there anything you want me to do for you?" Angus asked, realizing all of a sudden that not only was Kevin homeless but he'd most likely lost everything he owned. Kevin shook his head slowly and closed his eyes, tears rolling down his cheeks. "It's all right."

"Everything is gone," Kevin said.

"Things can be replaced, but you can't," Angus said, remembering how frantic he'd been racing back into the building to find him. "Are you going to stay with him?" he asked Zach, who nodded. "I need to get home and wash off all this smoke and sweat. Would you text me with his room number and I'll come back in a little while?" Angus gave Zach the number when he agreed and then said good-bye to Kevin before leaving the area.

As soon as he was outside, he inhaled a deep breath as a plan formed in his mind. He got into his car and raced home, where he showered and changed. Feeling clean again, he grabbed his phone and called a few contacts.

"Janice, it's Angus," he said when his friend answered. "I need a favor."

"What is it this time?" she asked playfully.

"A friend was one of the victims in that apartment fire. I'm sure it's been on the news. He lost everything and is in the hospital. Do you think you could work some of your magic to help find him a new place? He'll be there a day or so, but once he gets out, he's got nothing. Everything was in there when the place collapsed. He can't afford high rent, I suspect, but he isn't on assistance."

"Sure. That should be relatively easy. I'll compile a list of possible places that you can pass on to him. What else?"

"He needs everything," Angus said.

"Then stop by my office." Janice was a dear. She worked for a nonprofit that dealt with the homeless and people in times of stress or need. Their paths had crossed many times on the job, and the two of them had become friends.

"I'm already on the way," Angus said. He locked the house and descended the stairs to the garage. He unloaded his gear and pulled out, driving across town to park in the lot of a neighborhood church. He went inside and down the stairs.

"That was fast," Janice said when she saw him, a huge smile breaking out on her perfectly made-up face. Janice Kranz was an extraordinary woman. She and her husband owned a massive, fully restored house in one of the best neighborhoods in Harrisburg. She could have spent her time going to socials and charity events. Instead, she ran her organization in conjunction with the church that gave her the space, and she directly helped countless people.

"I was just leaving when I talked to you." He kissed her cheek and received a hug. "Like I said, he lost everything in the fire."

"I set aside one of our personal care kits for men. It's got the grooming basics. I take it he only has the clothes on his back." Janice motioned down a hall, and he followed her. She opened a door and motioned him inside. "Take what you need. These are good, solid clothes for men." She handed him a bag, and Angus got a few packages of white underwear in what he thought was Kevin's size, a few undershirts, and a pair of jeans and several shirts. He also grabbed some socks and a pair of pajamas for the hospital.

"This should give him something to start with," Angus said. He didn't want to take too much, but he knew how important it was for people to have some of the basics after they'd lost everything.

"Take one of my cards to leave with him, and we'll be able to help him once he's out on his own."

"You're a sweetheart, you know that? Everyone in need in this town owes you a great deal."

"I wish more people thought that way. I'm going to have to look for a new space because the church is being sold to a new congregation, and they want to use this space for themselves. Not that I blame them, but it means more hassle and a move. That is, if I can find someplace. I don't pay much here, and the donations I get barely cover my costs as it is. I don't need any compensation for my time, but I have people who help me, and they need to make a living." She huffed a little as Angus stepped out of the room. "I'll figure it out. I always do."

"I know you will. But if there's something I can do, let me know." Angus carried the bag of things for Kevin back toward the door. "I can talk to the guys at the station and see if anyone knows of a place. You might also call one of the television stations and see if they'll help you get the word out."

"One of them did a story on us last year, and it helped bring in some donations, but only for a while." She pulled open the door. "I'll have to think on what I want to do, and I'll call you as soon as I have some possible apartments." She smiled. "Now go make sure your friend is okay." She checked her watch and smiled. Angus took that as a sign that she had an appointment. He leaned in to give her a hug. They remembered the kit, and she placed it in the bag. Angus left and went back to his car, then returned to the hospital.

Zach texted him the room number as he was driving, and Angus went right up to Kevin's floor and found his room. Zach sat next to his bed. Kevin had his eyes closed.

"What's all this?" Zach asked.

"A friend of mine runs a charity that helps people who need it. I picked up a few clothes and a kit." He pulled it out of the bag and set it on the counter in the bathroom, still talking to Zach. "I also have a pair of pajamas so he doesn't have to spend all his time in those hospital gowns that are open in the back."

Kevin nodded and seemed to smile. "Thank you."

He grinned with relief into Kevin's gorgeous eyes. "She also has contacts all over town and is going to try to help line up a few apartments that you can look at once you're feeling better."

"You did all that in the hour you were gone?" Zach asked.

"Janice did most of it," Angus said as he set the bag in the closet and closed the door. "It isn't a lot, but I got some underthings, jeans, and a few shirts so you'll have some clothes to wear when you need them."

Kevin didn't answer, but tears ran down his cheeks. Angus knew how hard this must be for him. He'd seen it multiple times, just not this close. Kevin had suffered plenty of loss—his friend, his home, and all his things. In one day, a good part of his life had disappeared. Angus's phone rang and he was going to ignore it, but he was on call. He fished his phone out of his pocket and recognized the number.

"Antonio, what's up?"

"At your fire today, they found a note," he said.

Angus turned toward the door and stepped out into the hall.

"He's struck again, and this time it seems he's attached himself to a person," Reyes said.

"What do you mean?"

"I knew there was something about that kid I was questioning, the one where you stepped in. The arsonist addressed this note to him. Well, I'm assuming it's him since he lived in the building and the note begins, 'Dear Kevin.'"

"Okay. Take it slow. We believe accelerants were involved in the fire."

"Yeah, and that's been confirmed. The note was found outside the building. With the way it came down, it must have been placed after the fire was under control, so he was definitely in the crowd. He used a kid. Gave him the envelope and a dollar and told him to give the envelope to a fireman. The kid was, like, six years old and all he can say was that he was a man. So the arsonist was there and watched the entire thing."

"So he knows that Kevin got out."

"I suspect so. Apparently you're a huge hero."

The sarcastic ass. "Can you tell me what the note says?"

"'You spoiled my fun at the club, so now I'm going to enjoy watching you and your home burn. This is going to be spectacular. I don't know if you'll get out or not, but if you do, the fun will continue. You seemed pretty handy with a hose, but this is going to be more than you can handle, I'm sure.' That part was typed, and then there is a printed section. 'The fire was amazing and I loved watching the building come down. It was glorious.'"

"Jesus," Angus breathed quietly. He peered into the room where Kevin lay resting. "He's in the hospital right now. You don't think this guy will try anything here, do you?" Angus hated the thought of the damage and potential loss of life if a fire started in the hospital.

"I have no idea. But we are going to have to try to protect Kevin as best we can. This wacko's violence is accelerating, and from the sounds of it, quite rapidly. I believe that since he's now focused his obsession on

Kevin, he isn't going to stop until he sees Kevin burn. I'm getting news-camera footage to compare to the footage outside the club. I hope to hell we get lucky, because so far I'm batting zero, and I fucking hate that."

"I know. Send over anything you want us to see or go by the station. Justinian will help you."

"He hates me," Antonio said.

"Yeah, but he hates arsonists and murderers more."

"I'm going to have to talk to Kevin," Antonio said. "Maybe he knows something."

"Well, he can't talk right now. He's on oxygen, and they need his lungs to rest. So give him a little time and try to remember that he's the victim, not the arsonist." Angus disconnected and put his phone in his pocket. He leaned against the hallway wall and tried to calm the thoughts racing through his mind. He already knew the fire was arson based upon the accelerants. But to find out it was their serial arsonist and that he had attached himself and his obsession to Kevin was nearly too much. Part of him said to distance himself. He had a job to do, and that was to put out fires and help catch this arsonist.

But he couldn't walk away. Yes, that had been the way he operated in the past, but just holding Kevin's hand was more exciting than being with other guys. Giving that up would be stupid. And Kevin was going to need someone to help keep him safe. This guy wasn't going to give up. He'd set at least six fires that they knew about, and there were more that could possibly have been his. The others were before the notes started. Now he had to figure out how to explain things to Kevin. If he didn't, Antonio would, and he would blurt it out for effect to try to get Kevin to tell him what he needed. Antonio wasn't a bad guy; he just went at each case like a charging bull.

Angus pushed away from the wall and went back into Kevin's room. Zach sat in the chair, and Kevin was asleep. He looked peaceful, almost angelic. Angus didn't want to disturb him, so he pulled up a chair and sat down, settling in for a while. After a few minutes, an orderly came in the room. "I'm going to take you down for some tests," he told Kevin, who slid his eyes open and nodded once. Most likely all he wanted to do was sleep.

The orderly unlocked the bed and moved around the cables, attaching the IV and oxygen to the bed. Then he wheeled him out of the room, and Angus stared at where he'd been and then looked at Zach.

"What is it you aren't telling him?" Zach asked. "I know there's something. You keep looking at him and opening your mouth and then closing it again, like you can't make up your mind about something."

Angus nodded. "The fire at his building was set by the same guy that burned the club." Angus didn't want to go into any more.

"And you don't think it's a coincidence."

"It's not. That's the problem."

"You think he's after Kevin?" Zach whispered with fear in his voice, as though the arsonist might hear.

Angus nodded. "I know he is. Kevin is in his sights."

Zach gasped and put his hand over his mouth. "I won't ask how you know because you probably can't talk about it." That seemed to be a concept Zach was familiar with, and Angus wondered why, but he didn't ask for the same reason Zach hadn't. "But you're sure."

"Yeah. The police are going to want to talk to Kevin, but I think I put them off. He isn't going to be able to talk for a while and…."

"If it's that asshole who went after Kevin at the club, he won't have anything to do with him anyway." Zach sounded positive. "I can call Bull and we'll get Kevin lawyered up really fast. They can send someone else if they want, but not him."

Angus chuckled; he couldn't help it. "Antonio can be a pain in the ass, there's no doubt about that. But he's a good cop, and he always tries to get to the bottom of what is truly going on. He usually does it like a wrecking ball, but he gets results."

Zach humphed. "He's an asshole."

"Yes, he is, and it comes quite naturally to him."

Now Zach chuckled. "So is he one of those guys you need to worry about if he's being nice to you, because he's sharpening the knife and getting ready to plunge it in? I know guys like that. Some of the men at the club can be vicious. They say one thing to your face and are dissing you behind your back."

"With Antonio, if he's being nice, it's because he's got something on you and he's letting you hang yourself. Otherwise he's pretty much an ass." Angus sighed, realizing there was a pattern there. He'd dated a lot of guys who were asses, and he seemed to go from one ass to the next ass… and not in a good way. "I reminded him that Kevin was the victim here, not a suspect."

"Well…." Zach didn't seem convinced, and that was fine. Antonio had his own problems, and he was going to have to deal with them. "I won't leave Kevin alone with him if he shows up, and I'll call Bull if I need to." Angus had seen Bull, and he could intimidate anyone.

"Just get Kevin to help the police if he can so that they can catch this arsonist and keep him out of danger. That's what really matters here. As long as this guy is loose, Kevin is in danger." He needed to make Zach understand. "This guy was at the fire, watching what was happening as part of the crowd. He seems to like to do that, and we're all so busy we don't notice him." Angus made a note to check out the people watching the fire at his next call. It was something he needed to get better at. "I'll do what I can," Angus promised.

"Fine," Zach huffed. "I take it you intend to leave it to me to give him the bad news."

"No," Angus said, crossing his arms over his chest. "I'll be here to talk to him." He wasn't sure how to tell him yet, but he'd figure it out.

"Good," Zach said and his lips curled upward just a little. "Bull does that same thing when he thinks I'm being a pain." Zach stood and crossed his arms. "Though he does it better than you. The bald-head thing carries it off better. It also makes him sexier, and you know what they say about bald men…." Zach squinted and chuckled.

Angus rolled his eyes. There was definitely such a thing as too much information, and it seemed like Zach was getting close to it. They grew quiet for a while, and Angus wished he had something to read. After a few minutes he got up and left the room in search of coffee and something to do. To be nice, when he found a machine, he got two cups and brought one back to Zach.

"Thank God," Zach murmured. "The stuff here is terrible, but I needed some."

"Tell me about it," Angus breathed.

"Can I ask you something? You and Kevin had one date. So why are you here? It isn't like you've been together a long time or anything. You could just walk away." Zach sipped from his cup.

"You get right to the heart of things, don't you?"

"Why beat around the bush? I want to know, so I asked. What gives? He said your date was nice and all, but you already know I got the phone call because you were mean. So why are you here?"

"I wasn't mean. I was being defensive," Angus countered more sharply than he'd intended. "And we had a great time together." He felt his defenses rising once again. "He's a lot of fun to be with."

"That doesn't answer why you're here on your day off. I can sit with him just fine, and yet here you are."

Angus swallowed. "I like him, okay? He's special. And you're as nosy as they come."

"It's what I do. Kevin hasn't had a lot of luck with guys. As you said, he's really special and wonderful, but people don't tend to stick around, and it rips him up." Zach finished his coffee and dropped the cup in the trash. "I don't want to see him get hurt again." Zach's gaze was hard, and Angus had opened his mouth to tell him he needed to mind his own business and that he wasn't Kevin's father or something when the orderly rolled Kevin's bed back into the room and then fussed to get everything put back into place.

"How did it go?" Angus asked.

Kevin shrugged and lifted his mask. "It hurts to breathe sometimes."

"I know. I've gotten some smoke really bad more than once. You need to give things time to heal." Angus gently stroked Kevin's forehead. "I have some things to tell you, but you have to stay calm, okay?" Angus asked, and Kevin nodded. "The police are going to want to talk to you. I'm surprised they aren't here already. The fire at your building was set on purpose by the same man who tried to burn the club."

"How do you know?" Kevin asked, and then he lowered his mask back into place.

"He left a note. The thing is, he's fixated on you because of what you did at the club. You spoiled his fun… so that's why he said he set your building on fire."

Kevin blinked and tears welled in his eyes. He lifted the mask. "So Mrs. Vertebedian is dead because of me? All of this is because of me."

"Put the mask back in place," Zach said gently and glared at Angus.

"Of course not," Angus said, staring right back. He turned his attention back to Kevin "This isn't your fault, and Mrs. V isn't dead because of you. She died because of the arsonist, and we're going to find him. But the police need your help. Do you think you can do that?"

"I'll try," Kevin said. "I should have been able to protect her," he mumbled and then clamped his eyes closed.

Angus took his hand and stroked his fingers. "You did all you could," he said. "It wasn't your fault. None of this is your fault. You have to know that."

"Mrs. V doesn't have any family. I was as close to family as she had," Kevin said. "I need to help make the arrangements for her."

"Bull and I will find out what needs to be done," Zach said. "Don't worry about that. Just concentrate on getting better for now. You need to make your lungs stronger."

Kevin nodded, but Angus could feel the tension in the hand he was holding. "Just relax and try to get some rest. Everything will still be there. Zach will make sure Mrs. V is taken care of." In essence she was a murder victim, so he figured it would be some time before the body would be released anyway. Eventually Kevin calmed down and fell back to sleep. Once he was resting, Angus allowed himself a chance to relax a little.

Until Antonio stomped into the room like a herd of cattle. Kevin started awake, and Angus glared at the intruder.

"Subtlety was never your strong suit," Angus said.

"I'm going to call Bull," Zach said and pulled out his phone. He made the call and then hung up. "You don't have to talk to him if you don't want to," Zach told Kevin. "Bull said if he can't be civil, then he can talk to the lawyer."

"Your reputation precedes you," Angus said. "Now have a seat and try not to act like a complete jerk. Kevin has had a difficult time of it, so be gentle." Angus leaned closer. "Remember, he isn't a suspect." He got up and pulled the chair next to the bed, glaring at Antonio until he sat down.

"I'm Officer Antonio Reyes. I'm investigating the fire at your apartment building, which we believe is related to the fire at Bronco's. At the fire at your building, we discovered a note from the man we believe set the fire, and I'm afraid he's attached himself to you."

Angus watched Kevin's reaction, even though he already knew the information presented so far. Sometimes the second time, or hearing it from a police officer, made things feel more real. "What do you want from me?" Kevin was clearly suspicious.

"Any help you can provide would be appreciated. Have you seen anyone hanging around outside your building that you don't know? Or have you noticed anyone who might be following you?"

"No," Kevin answered and lifted his mask a little. "But I wasn't looking for anyone, either." He put the mask back down.

"Have you had any strange phone calls?" Antonio asked, and Kevin shook his head.

"Kevin," Angus said. "I know you looked at the video at the station and saw how the arsonist evaded the cameras. Did you happen to notice anyone behaving strangely over the last few days? It may have been at the grocery store or when you were getting gas. Someone who was trying not to be seen."

Kevin stared back at him, blinking, then shook his head. "I wasn't looking for anyone." He seemed seconds away from breaking down. Angus took his hand, and Zach held the other one.

"That's okay," Antonio said. "I know you wouldn't be looking, and we don't know how closely he's been watching you, but our arsonist did seem to know you were home." Antonio consulted his notes. "Can you tell me what happened when the fire started? Where were you?"

"I was having afternoon coffee with Mrs. V," he began and closed his eyes. "She comes over on the afternoons when I don't work, and we have tea, which is really coffee. She always brings something she baked, and we talk… or we used to. I worked early this morning and got home about two. She came up at three or so. I made coffee, and then we sat down together and were talking the way we usually did. I remember feeling really tired, and then I woke up outside on the ground finding it hard to breathe."

Antonio took notes, and Angus sent him a questioning look, but he gave nothing away. "Do you remember hitting your head?"

"No." He kept lifting his mask, and Angus helped him put it back into place.

"I think that's enough, Antonio," Angus said. "The oxygen is important, and talking will stress his lungs."

"Thank you, Kevin. You've been very helpful." Antonio lightly touched Kevin's arm and then stood and left the room. Angus squeezed

Kevin's fingers and then followed Antonio out into the hall. He was already on the phone. "I need a full toxicology report," he was saying. "It's possible she was drugged and traces could still be in her system." He hung up and then turned to Angus. "We may have caught a break."

"Yes, and remember you didn't have to beat anyone to get it. Kevin was calm, and you got information from him he didn't even know he had. Good things happen when you mind your manners."

Antonio's gaze burned with anger. "You aren't my fucking mother," he ground out between his teeth.

"Maybe not. But you need to let go of all this anger." Angus stepped closer and lowered his voice. "It's the main reason we didn't work." There were other reasons as well, but Antonio's hot head and constant state of agitation and anger at the world had been a huge reason Angus had decided that a long-term thing with Antonio wouldn't be a good idea. He looked back toward Kevin's room. "I need to get back."

"Tell him to call me if he remembers anything."

"I will."

Antonio hurried to the elevator and was already on the phone by the time the doors closed. Angus turned and went back into Kevin's room. He found Kevin asleep and Zach glaring at him once again.

"I went out in the hall and heard you," Zach said. "Are you and him…?"

"No," Angus answered. "Antonio and I had a thing once, but"—he grinned—"could you see yourself with him for the next twenty years?"

"I'd kick his ass," Zach said, and Angus didn't doubt that he would.

"That's what I wanted to do after a week or so. He's a good guy and very dedicated, but his people skills suck."

"I'm not your first?" Kevin asked sleepily. "I thought I popped your cherry." He began to laugh and then started coughing. Angus rubbed his arm and let the cough work its way through before settling him back on the bed.

"Take it easy. Laughing is not good for you right now."

Zach got the mask back in place, and a nurse came in to check that everything was okay. She scolded him for cracking jokes and lightly admonished Kevin to just relax. Then she checked his mask. "We can put you on oxygen only through your nose if you settle down, but not until we know you're getting enough air into your lungs."

79

"Sorry," Kevin said softly. He closed his eyes once again.

"Just be careful, honey, and you'll be fine." She fussed over Kevin, making sure he was comfortable, and then left the room.

"Do you want to go back with the cop?" Kevin asked. "He seems like he'd be more your type than me."

"You think pain in the ass is my type?" Angus said.

"No, but he is strong and handsome in a dreamy sort of way. Not as hot as you, but still nice-looking." The implication being that Kevin didn't think he was handsome. Angus didn't like that at all.

"I'm not interested in Antonio." Angus took Kevin's hand once again and hoped he'd go back to sleep. "I'm starting to understand that he isn't really my type."

"What is?"

Angus leaned close. "Cute heroes with fire hoses," Angus told him. He saw Kevin smile under the oxygen mask. "So don't you worry about anything."

"But I was nasty and didn't call you," Kevin said. "I should have but I was scared."

"I yelled at you, and I had no cause to do that. So you think about getting better. Before I got the fire call, I was going to come over and try to see you. Maybe bring some flowers and stuff. But then other things got in the way."

Two other guys about the same age as Kevin came into the room. Zach greeted each of them before introducing them to Angus. "This is Jeremy and Tristan."

"We got here as soon as we could," Jeremy said. "It was hard getting any information. Even Spook nosed around and didn't find out anything."

"Someone burned down my building," Kevin said. "He's after me and tried to kill me. He did kill Mrs. V." Kevin began to cry, and that set off more coughing.

The nurse came in right away, but this time she didn't scold him. "Honey, you need to try to give your lungs a rest." She removed the mask and ran a line that attached to his nose. At least Kevin would be able to talk more easily. "You boys all need to let him sleep, or I'll have to ask you to leave. He can only talk a little, and he needs his rest." Her steely gaze settled on each of them in turn, and then she left the room.

"You really think someone tried to kill you?" Tristan asked. "That's pretty dramatic, dude."

"It's true. The police were here a little while ago," Kevin explained.

"Tristan and I got together and talked, and when you get out of here, we'll take you shopping and get you new clothes and stuff. You can stay with one of us until you find a place to live, you know that," Jeremy said.

"Thanks. Angus has someone helping me find a place already, and he brought me some things to wear." Kevin smiled. "I'm not sure where I'll live, but the police think this guy is fixated on me, so I don't want to put anyone else in danger. I'm not sure that I'm really safe here, but I can't leave."

"You'll be fine," Angus said. "There are plenty of people around, and Antonio has things under control. It's what he's good at."

"If you say so," Kevin said. He reached for a cup of water. Zach helped him drink, and then Kevin closed his eyes and looked ready to drop off to sleep again.

Zach leaned over the bed. "I'm going to go and take one of the Boob-sey Twins with me. Jeremy and I can get anything you need, so just call us. Tristan is going to sit with you for a while." Zach hugged his friend and pulled Jeremy out of the room with him.

"Why?" Jeremy asked.

"Because he doesn't need all of us talking to him," Zach said, his voice getting softer as they left. "We'll be back in a little while."

Kevin sighed, and Tristan sat in the chair Zach had vacated.

"I should let you rest too, but I'll come up again later to see you." Angus leaned over the bed and kissed Kevin gently on his forehead. "I'll leave my number on the table here, and you can call if you need me."

"I will," Kevin said, and Angus left the room. He strode down the hallway to the elevators and saw Zack and Jeremy in one of the waiting rooms, talking together. Angus hadn't really thought they'd leave, but giving Kevin some quiet time was definitely a good idea. He was about to get into the elevator, but instead he walked over to where they were talking.

"You might want to see about getting Kevin a replacement phone. He lost his in the fire."

"We were just talking about that. Jeremy is going to stay here, and I'll get Kevin a phone and stuff." Zach stood and walked with Angus back to the elevator. "I don't want him to be alone."

"That's a good idea. You heard what Antonio said. This guy is out there and will be looking for him. Tell Jeremy and Tristan to keep their eyes open, including hospital personnel. And don't be afraid to ask questions."

"Where are you going?"

"To the station." The elevator doors opened, and the two of them stepped inside. "I'm going to see if I can arrange a safe place for Kevin once he can come home. Being alone in an apartment isn't going to help him, and staying with a friend is only going to put you all in danger. Remember, this guy has already set half a dozen fires at least, and now he's killed someone. He doesn't have much to lose now. Guys like him get a thrill, almost a sexual high, out of fire. They feed off it just like the flames feed off the wood. He isn't going to stop unless he's caught."

"Okay," Zach said, "but promise you'll let Kevin know about anything you find."

"I will." The doors slid open, and Angus walked toward the hospital exit. He got into his car, pulled out of the lot, and drove through traffic to the fire station.

"Your buddy was here stirring everyone up just a while ago," Captain Justinian said when Angus passed him as he was heading out of the station. "I'm going home to spend a few hours with my family before my wife decides to divorce me. Collins is on duty, and he can help with anything you need."

"Thanks." Angus went inside and up to the captain's office, knocking on the doorframe. "I've got some information you need to know."

Captain Collins looked up from his desk. He was one of those men who, when they were at work, were all business. Angus doubted he had ever been "one of the guys." "You do?"

"Yes, I was speaking with Antonio Reyes from the Harrisburg PD, and he said there was a note from our fire starter at the apartment-building fire."

"Yeah. It was delivered to me by a kid." Collins was impatient as all hell. "Get to the point."

"The arsonist has fixated on one of the tenants there, a man named Kevin Foster, and he's in the hospital and will need protection. What safer place could there be for him than a fire station?"

Collins laughed. "Rumor has it that the victim you're talking about is also the guy you've been dating. So instead of using the fire station as a witness protection safe house, you could take him in. You know the regulations, not to mention the liability of allowing a civilian to stay at the firehouse. If we allowed it for this guy, then I'd have guys requesting conjugal visits with their girlfriends in the dormitory." He rolled his eyes, and Angus was even happier than usual that he didn't have to work with Collins on a regular basis.

"He needs protection and might be able to help us capture this arsonist."

"If he needs help, then I suggest you put him up at your place. That way the two of you can play house and sew curtains together, or do whatever it is guys like you do." Collins looked up toward the door, telling Angus he was dismissed and that his presence was no longer welcome.

Angus turned and left the office. "Asshole," he muttered under his breath.

"What was that?" Collins demanded. Angus didn't answer and continued to the exit. "I heard that," Collins said, coming up behind him.

"And I heard what you said, loud and clear. I'll be bringing it up with the union, and I will request sensitivity training. The department has a clear antidiscrimination policy as well as an antiharassment policy, and your words violated both. I've played the games and been a team member for a long time, but I'm not going to take that from you or anyone. So I see sensitivity training in your future." Angus broke out in a grin at the way Captain Collins paled. The course was two days, taken during off-shift time. He'd had to take it once, as had most of the department, but sitting through it again would be painful.

"You know I can control your schedule," Collins said softly.

"Add more nails to your coffin," Angus told him plainly. He saw the other men pretending not to hear, but they all clearly had. "I have witnesses." How a simple question had gotten him into a test of wills with one of the captains was beyond him, but he wasn't going to back down. He'd done plenty of that in the name of getting along and team unity.

He turned to leave, needing to get out of the station before things escalated further. He was grateful when Collins didn't follow him out. He got to his car and drove home, gripping the wheel until his knuckles were white.

"Asshole," he breathed for the millionth time as he pulled into his garage next to his motorcycle. He went upstairs into the house and wandered aimlessly through the rooms. He wasn't sure exactly what he was angry about. He did know the regulations, but an exception could have been made, especially for someone who might help them catch the arsonist who'd been keeping them so busy lately.

He pulled open the door to the guest room and sighed. He hadn't had anyone use the room since a friend stayed over last year. He'd set it up when he'd bought the house, but he had very few guests, and this was the least used room in the house. There was dust on the top of the dresser and the bedding. Angus pulled off the spread and carried it outside, where he shook it out good. When he returned, he dumped the spread on the bed and got some Swiffer cloths and began wiping down everything in the room. He was halfway through his chore when he realized what he was doing. Collins might be an asshole, but some of what he said had struck a chord, and Angus figured he could offer his guest room to Kevin if he wanted it.

He finished dusting and then got the vacuum and ran it over the carpet. When he was done, Angus put everything away and remade the bed. He also opened the window to let in some fresh air.

The sun was setting by the time he was done. Angus ate a quick dinner and then left again, closing the windows and locking up the house before returning to the hospital.

Kevin was alone when he walked into the room. He opened his eyes and gave him a small smile.

"Where are your friends?" Angus asked.

"Most of them left a little while ago. Zach said he needed something to eat and that he'd be right back."

Angus nodded. "How is the breathing?"

"Okay as long as I don't laugh, swallow too hard, sneeze, chuckle, or inhale too deeply. Basically it sucks." Kevin exhaled slowly. "I need to stop making jokes about it or I'll make myself laugh and cough. Then I'll have

Nurse Adolph come in and yell at me again. The last time she did, she glared at me for almost half an hour and fluffed my pillows half to death."

"Okay...." Angus sat in the comfortable chair on the far side of the bed.

"Have you heard anything from the police guy?"

"No. I probably won't unless he needs something from me. It's likely you'll hear from him first."

Kevin grew quiet and lay in bed, staring straight ahead. "I keep thinking about when I can go home, but I don't have one. It's gone. Everything is gone."

"It will be okay. You have lots of friends to help you. I cleaned out my guest room in case you'd like to use it. I figured the safest place for you to stay was with a firefighter."

"Do you know anything about the other people in the building? Is someone taking care of them? There were families with children."

"I'm sure there are. The Red Cross was working with them—at least that's what I saw at the scene." Angus took Kevin's hand. "You need to rest. Is there anyone you want to call? You can use my phone if you like."

"I called my dad, and he came over from Shippensburg. He went with Zach to the cafeteria. He should be back soon." Angus nodded, pleased that someone had alerted Kevin's dad.

"Just rest. I'll be here," Angus said, holding Kevin's hand as he closed his eyes once more. A few minutes later Zach returned with Kevin's father. He looked like an older version of Kevin. Angus stood and quietly walked around the bed.

"This is Angus. He rescued Kevin," Zach said.

"James," Kevin's father said. "I appreciate all you did." Judging by the confusion on his face, he didn't seem to understand why Angus was here.

"Angus and I are dating, Dad," Kevin said softly. "He was coming over to see me when he was called in to work. He apparently pulled me out just before the entire place collapsed."

James nodded and walked to Kevin's bed. "I'm glad you're okay, and when I get home, I'll clean out your room for you to use until you find a place."

Angus wasn't sure how Kevin felt about that idea, and Kevin didn't directly answer the question. "I'll be here a little longer, and people are already working to help me find a new place." Kevin's father looked disappointed. "You can't blame me for not wanting to move back home. I have my own life."

"You can do more," Kevin's dad insisted. "You know you're better than what they have you doing on that help desk."

"Kevin and I are working on a project," Angus said. "We have an idea that could be used to help us train firefighters. It's sort of a fire simulation video game. Kevin hasn't had time to work on it yet, but it could be a big help with training in the department." He and Kevin hadn't talked about it again since their date, but the glow in Kevin's eyes said that speaking up had been the right thing to do. "As I was saying, I have a guest room at my house, and if you want to stay with me, then you and I could get started on the requirements."

"That would be cool." For the first time since Angus had seen him in the hospital there was life and some excitement in Kevin's voice. "I already have some ideas, and as I was going around town, I started to make a list of the types of buildings that we could include. You said the capitol, and I was thinking the high-rise Hilton downtown as well. Also, we could include that paddle-wheel boat—the Pride of the Susquehanna—that goes out on the river. How would you fight a fire that happened offshore? Stuff like that."

Kevin's father sat in one of the other chairs, clearly defeated. "I'm just glad you're okay."

"I am."

"He's a hero," Zach said. "He saved the club in a fire."

"Good grief. Are these things following you? First everything is fine, and then there are three fires in a few weeks."

"Someone set the fires, Dad, and I'm fine," Kevin said. He reached for his dad, lightly stroking his arm. "Angus saved me and everything is cool."

James's eyes narrowed. "Zach told me someone was after you."

Kevin glared at his friend, who had the decency to appear ashamed. "I'm fine, Dad. The police are on it, and so is the fire department. So nothing is going to happen to me. But if it will make you feel better, I'll stay with Angus." It clearly didn't make James feel much better. And Angus couldn't blame him, but he understood why Kevin hadn't wanted to live at home with his dad. "I'll be perfectly safe with my own personal firefighter to watch over me."

Was that a hint of heat in Kevin's gaze, or mischief?

"Kevin," James began in a fatherly tone. "I think it would be better if you came home for a while."

"Dad, I'm old enough to make my own decisions. Besides, you have your life to live, and I don't want to cramp your style." Kevin turned to Angus with a huge smile. "My dad has turned out to be quite popular with the ladies in the neighborhood. A number of houses have sold recently, and they all seem to be to divorced women who have eyes for my dad."

"I'm not dating—" James said.

"Then you should be. Mom left a long time ago, and you need to find someone to make you happy. Even if it's just for a night."

"Kevin!" James exclaimed, but he was definitely blushing. Angus didn't think James was as lonely as he wanted his son to think. "I do have a life of my own."

"Outside work?"

"Yes." James nodded. "And that's enough shifting the conversation away from what you don't want to talk about. He's an expert at that," he said to Angus and Zach. "I remember when he used to bring home his report cards. I'd check over the grades and ask him about the C in gym, and of course he'd point out that he got an A in math."

"The math did me a lot more good than concentrating on archery and volleyball in PE class," Kevin observed. "Now who's the one changing the subject?" It took only a few minutes to see that these two were very much alike.

Kevin lay back and closed his eyes. The conversation died pretty much away as Kevin dozed off for a while. James turned on the television and found a movie that drew their attention until Kevin gasped, jerked awake, and began coughing before choking out, "He was there."

Angus felt a chill run up his spine even though he had no idea what Kevin meant.

CHAPTER FIVE

"What do you mean? Who was where?" his father asked.

Kevin turned to Angus. "He was outside the apartment building. I just remembered."

"Okay," Angus soothed, and Kevin smiled. He loved the sound of his voice. "Tell me what you remember."

"Well, things were really fuzzy, but a little while before the fire started a man came to the door. He said he was from the gas company and needed to read the meter for the building. I didn't think about it at the time, but now I remember the same guy was watching the fire. He stood back in the crowd, but was watching things. It had to be him."

"Can you remember what he looked like?"

"Yeah, he looked like the gas man. I didn't take a good look at him. I mean, who memorizes what the gas man looks like? He was a little older than me, I guess, and sort of plain-looking. I wouldn't have dated him unless I found out he had a really nice personality and made me laugh. He was the kind of guy you see and forget. Really ordinary."

"That isn't helping much, I'm afraid," Angus said, and Kevin huffed softly. He wasn't sure what else to tell him.

"I've never seen him before, but if there's footage of the scene, I can probably pick him out. Can you call Officer Grumpy and see if he can help? Things were hazy after the fire, but I remember him now because he kept watching me." Kevin shivered when he thought about him. "He was creepy."

"Okay. I'll call Officer Grumpy, otherwise known as Antonio, and tell him what you've remembered. He'll probably come down to see you tomorrow with some more questions." Angus squeezed his hand, and Kevin smiled. He liked Angus's hands, rough from work, and he tried not to think how those hands had felt when they'd roamed over his thighs and chest. He didn't need to be sporting wood with blankets this thin.

"Take it easy, and I'll pass along the information." Angus got up and left the room.

Kevin watched him go and then turned to Zach. "He has a better butt than Bull."

Zach play growled. "You aren't supposed to be looking at Bull's butt."

"Come on. You didn't look at Angus's?" Kevin challenged, and Zach smiled. "Of course you did, and you gotta admit Angus's is better. More bubbly."

"I really don't need to know this," Kevin's dad said. "Is this the kind of thing you guys do on a regular basis? Go around talking about and comparing people's butts?"

"No," Kevin said. "We only talk about guy's butts. Not girls." He rolled his eyes when his dad paled a little.

"It sounds like the kind of conversation two golden retrievers would have," his dad said.

"That's funny, Dad," Kevin said and turned back to Zach. "Angus still has the better butt."

"If all you're going to do is talk like that, I'm going to go home for the night," his dad said. "Zach got you a new phone, and you know my number, so call me if you need anything. If you can tease and make jokes, you're feeling better." His dad stood and leaned over the bed, kissing him on the forehead. "And for the record, Bull has a better butt." His dad straightened and left the room without another word. Kevin could have heard a pin drop until Zach started laughing. Kevin wasn't sure how comfortable he was with that pronouncement, and he did his best to keep from laughing, though it was hard.

Angus came back into the room. "What did you do to your dad? He looked shell-shocked."

"We were having a discussion about butts, and it got to be a little too much for him. We may have chased him off," Kevin explained and reached for his tray. "I got a new phone, thanks to Zach, so would you put your number in it for me?" Kevin handed it to Angus, who typed in his number and then set the phone back on the tray.

"Officer Grumpy will be here first thing in the morning." Angus smiled. "I'm going to have to be sure to use that to my best advantage someday. Now, it's getting late, and if you want to get better, you need to sleep." Angus walked to the door and turned out the overhead light. "Go ahead and rest. I can see you're tired, and fighting to stay awake isn't good."

"When did you go to medical school?"

"Smartass," Angus told him with a smile. "Zach is going to go home and get some rest so he can come back in the morning, and I'm going to stay here with you for now." Angus sat in the chair next to his bed. "If I can sleep in a firehouse dorm with half a dozen snoring men, I can sleep in a hospital chair."

Zach stood and said good night, hugging him carefully before leaving the room. Kevin lay back in the bed and tried to breathe evenly. He was having trouble because Angus was so close and that always got his heart going. "I'm not really sleepy."

"Yes, you are. You've been yawning since I got here, and sleep is the best thing for you. It's going to take time for your lungs to get better, but if you want to go home, you need to sleep." Angus leaned closer. "Besides, they're going to be in a few times during the night to check on you, so sleep while you can."

Kevin sighed and then coughed a little. He knew he wouldn't be able to sleep with Angus sitting in the chair next to his bed. But after a few minutes he didn't remember anything until a nurse woke him for breakfast.

KEVIN WAS sick of lying down by the time he was released from the hospital late the following day. Angus's friend had gotten him a line on a couple of places, and he was scheduled to see them in a few days, but until then, well, he'd been pulled in two different directions. His dad still wanted him to stay with him. The prospect wasn't a happy one. He loved his dad, but living with him again was not his idea of fun, so he'd decided to take Zach and Bull up on their offer of their guest room. The hospital staff insisted he leave in a wheelchair. Dad came to pick him up, and Kevin sighed as the orderly rolled him out of the hospital toward the curb.

As they exited the building, Angus strode toward him with a huge smile. "Hey, cutie," he called.

Kevin loved that he called him that sometimes. It made him feel special. "I thought you had to work," he said.

"I was able to trade shifts for a few days. One of the guys owed me a favor. So I came to get you, but I see you already got... sprung."

"Kevin, you need to rest," Dad said. "You could rest all you want at the house."

"I know. But you're an hour away from all my friends, and I will have to go back to work. I'm going to stay with Zach and Bull. They offered me their guest room. I told you that already. I'll be fine. Zach is at work right now, and Bull had some things to do at the club, so maybe Angus can take me to his place, and then Zach will pick me up after work." He sounded like a whining child even to his own ears. "I can make my own decisions, Dad. I know you're trying to help, but sometimes you don't listen."

"I'm worried about you," his dad said.

"I know. But you have your own life, and I'll be fine." They had told him he needed to take it easy and not do anything strenuous. Kevin hugged his dad hard. "I love you very much, you know that."

"I know." His dad hugged him in return. "You can't blame me for wanting to keep you safe." Kevin always felt like that in his dad's arms. For a long time it had been just the two of them, and it would be so easy to just go home and hide out from the world. "I hate the thought that someone is out to hurt you."

"I do too. But staying with you is only geography. If someone wants to find me, they will. Bull is a formidable protector, and he'll keep me safe. Angus is a fireman. He's the antiarsonist. So I'll be fine." He stepped away from his dad. He felt alone in some ways, and though his dad was an amazing guy, Kevin needed to work, and commuting from his dad's wasn't the most pleasant prospect. Not when Bull and Zach were ten minutes away.

"Like I said, you can't fault me for trying."

Kevin hugged his dad again. "Actually, I love you for it." He lifted the plastic bag that carried the few things he owned in the world. Most of them Angus had gotten for him. His dad had given him a check and some gift cards so he could buy things he needed. "I'll call you later today."

His dad smiled and walked out toward the parking lot. Kevin had to fight the urge to go with him. He waved, and then Angus directed the orderly to push Kevin's wheelchair to his car, which was parked in the first row, right in front. "One of the benefits of being emergency personnel."

Angus unlocked the trunk and car and put Kevin's bag in the back as Kevin stepped away from the wheelchair. He thanked the orderly for his help, and the orderly took the wheelchair back into the hospital.

"Do you want to go rest? I can take you back to the house," Angus said.

"God, no. If I lie around and do nothing for two seconds longer, my head is going to explode. I need to get some more clothes if I can, and then I have to call my insurance company. Bull had talked me into getting renter's insurance. I never thought I had anything worth insuring, but now I see the beauty of it. At least I'll be able to replace my things when I get another place. Not that I had all that much…." He got in the car, and Angus walked to the other side.

"I'll take you to Macy's. But we can't stay too long. I don't want you to get worn out." Angus started the car and drove to the mall. It felt good to breathe nonantiseptic air once again. Angus parked close, and they walked inside. Kevin knew the store by heart and went right to the men's department. He got two pairs of jeans and a pair of khaki pants, some shirts he could wear to work, and a few pullovers. He got a light jacket as well.

"Don't you need to try anything on?" Angus asked him.

"No. I know my sizes in these clothes." He grabbed a Nautica shirt in light blue that he knew would look good on him and then stopped by the shoe department. Kevin smiled when Angus took his latest purchase and added it to the growing pile he was carrying.

"Is this enough?" Angus asked.

"You don't like shopping?"

"No. I'd rather be doing something fun," Angus huffed.

Kevin took pity on him and motioned toward the register. He was already tiring, so he pulled out the gift card his dad had gotten him, paid for the clothes, and waited while they were bagged.

Angus took the bag and guided him out of the store. "I can tell you're tired."

"Yeah, I am." He got in the car and let Angus put everything away. Then they drove to Angus's house and unloaded the car. Well, Angus unloaded the car, but only after getting Kevin inside and seated on the sofa in front of the television. It was nice being cared for, and Kevin listened as Angus trooped back down the stairs to the car.

"Make yourself at home," Angus told him, and Kevin nodded and yawned. There was a blanket draped across the back of the sofa. It was light and soft. He tried not to yawn again, but ended up pulling the blanket over his shoulders to keep out the air-conditioned chill. He rested his head back, and soon his eyelids got too heavy to hold them open.

Eventually he felt Angus guide him down onto the sofa. He stretched out and curled up under the blanket, falling deeper into sleep when Angus turned down the volume of the television. Something about cooking hovered at the edge of his dreams, and he figured it must have been the television. Not that he really cared.

When he woke, Zach was sitting at Angus's table, and Kevin heard soft conversation. "How long have you been here?" Kevin asked Zach as he slowly sat up.

"Just a few minutes. We didn't want to disturb you."

"I was talking to Zach—he has some ideas for the simulator," Angus said.

Kevin yawned. "He's awesome with graphics and things." He stood, feeling a little wobbly for a few seconds and then steadying. He walked to the table and sat down. "I think I should eat."

Angus went to the refrigerator and got out various dishes. He set them on the table and opened the lids: chicken salad, macaroni salad, coleslaw…. "I sometimes cook when I'm worried." He got plates as well and passed them out. Kevin took a little of each dish and ate slowly. He figured if he didn't, Angus would try to feed him, from the way he was hovering.

"I'm fine," Kevin said with a smile.

Angus didn't sit down right away and excused himself.

"I really think he likes you," Zach said.

"I know."

"You could stay here with him and take advantage of his guest room. Maybe pretend to sleepwalk into his room?" Zach winked.

93

Kevin shook his head slightly. He was too tired at the moment even for those thoughts. "Don't you think about anything but sex?" he asked.

"Don't tell me you haven't thought about it. I see how you watch him and the way he looks at you." Zach smiled. "Think about it: the guy stayed at the hospital all that time and has tried to help you find a place to live."

"He's just being nice."

"I don't think so."

"He wants to catch the arsonist, and I'm the one who saw him."

"I forgot to ask how it went with the police," Zach said.

Kevin heard footsteps approach. "It was fine. Officer Grumpy said he was going to check on some video, but since he hasn't said any more, I'm assuming he didn't find anything useful." Kevin took a bite of chicken salad and set down his fork. "I want this to be over. Maybe I should have gone to stay with my dad." He shivered and pushed back his plate. "But then I keep thinking that if this guy shows up, he'll do to Dad what he did to Mrs. V." He hated feeling like a crybaby, but tears had been close for days. "I can't believe she's gone."

Angus gently held him. "It's okay to grieve."

Kevin turned to Angus and paused. "What aren't you telling me?"

"You and Mrs. V were drugged. That's why you felt so sleepy. They found traces of a tranquilizer in her system."

Kevin blinked as the implication of what Angus had just told him sank in. "So he truly meant to kill both of us. I kept hoping that it was some kind of accident, or that he just set the fire and left. But he was in my apartment." Kevin shivered.

"Yes, and whatever he used the start the fire, he probably planted it when he came in to check the meter. Then he must have gone up to your apartment, probably while you were at Mrs. V's."

"But he couldn't have known when I'd be back."

"They found the remains of a timer or maybe something that he activated by phone once he had everything ready. This guy didn't leave anything to chance."

"And the only thing he didn't count on was you," Kevin said and closed his eyes. Angus held him, and Kevin felt Zach gently touch his arm.

"There are a lot of things he could have done, and none of it is your fault."

"That's easy to say. But it feels like it is. It's my fault Mrs. V is dead." Kevin let the tears come. "She was like a grandmother and always had nice things to say. We used to talk and watch silly shows together. She liked those stupid reality shows, but only because she could make fun of how dumb and overly dramatic they were sometimes. She didn't have anyone else."

"Shhh." Angus rubbed his hand over Kevin's hair. "It will be all right. They aren't releasing her body yet, but when they do, I asked Antonio to have them contact you. At least we can make sure she's properly taken care of."

Kevin nodded and then sat back in his seat and pulled his plate closer once again. He didn't have much of an appetite and ate only a few more bites. Then he sighed and slowly got up, returning to the sofa. He watched TV while Angus and Zach finished eating. He expected Zach to take him back with him, but instead he joined him on the sofa with one of the sketch pads he carried with him.

"So how do you see this game working? Do you want the flames to be cartoony or real looking?"

Leave it to Zach to try to take his mind off things. "They need to be as real looking as possible," Kevin said. "We also need to work with Angus to come up with building types. We agreed to include the capitol, and I thought we should include my old apartment building. Angus was going to make a list."

"I have it here," Angus said and pushed back his chair. He got a pad and handed it to him. Kevin examined the list. "I included some basic interior layouts. And I was thinking you should definitely include traps like weak spots in the floors and things like that." Angus sat on the other side from Zach, and Kevin found his attention wandering.

Angus and Zach talked back and forth. Kevin tried to keep his mind on what they were saying, but with his belly full, he leaned against Angus and closed his eyes. He'd been sleeping quite a bit, but getting to use Angus as a pillow was an added bonus.

"I should take Kevin home so he can rest," Zach said. Kevin didn't want to move. Angus was warm, and the way he had his arm around his shoulders was comforting.

"You can stay here if you want, cutie," Angus whispered, and Kevin wrapped his arms around Angus's waist and held on, not opening his eyes.

"I'll come back in the morning," Zach said. Kevin thought he might have mumbled a good-bye, but he was too tired to really make much of an effort. He felt Angus spread the blanket over him, and then Kevin was definitely asleep.

HE WOKE with a start and blinked, shaking until he realized that the flames dancing around him like some demented Disney movie weren't real. He gasped and then coughed, wondering where he was as he attempted to calm his out-of-control lungs.

"It's all right," Angus said as he hurried into the room.

"Where am I?" Kevin slowly calmed his breathing. His throat hurt from the coughing.

"In the guest room. I'm going to make you some tea to try to calm you. I'll be right back." Angus left the room, but Kevin followed him with his gaze, realizing Angus was only wearing a pair of boxer briefs. That lifted his temperature and made him cough once again. Of course he was only in his underwear too, which meant Angus had undressed him and put him into bed. Granted, they had seen each other naked, but this seemed different, even more intimate in some way. Kevin had been completely vulnerable, and Angus had taken care of him.

A soft beep sounded, and then Kevin heard Angus on the stairs.

"It's hot, so be careful." Angus handed him a mug with a tea bag tab hanging out of it. Kevin took the mug as Angus sat on the edge of the bed. "Just relax."

Kevin leaned against the headboard, sipping from the mug, and Angus placed his hand on his belly, making slow, gentle circles. "Just close your eyes and take steady breaths."

Kevin hummed softly at Angus's gentle caresses. He knew that they couldn't do anything. Sex would definitely overtax his lungs, but he closed his eyes and enjoyed the attention. He sipped the tea, then set the mug on the bedside table. He was trying not to get excited, but it wasn't working. He closed his eyes and soaked in the soft caresses like a sponge. "I want you to touch me in other places. I know we can't do anything, but I want it."

Angus pushed the bedding away and carefully scooped Kevin up off the bed. Kevin rested his head against Angus's chest as he carried

Kevin across the hall to his room, then into his bed. Kevin curled under the covers, lying on his side, watching as Angus pushed down the briefs, standing naked and proud in front of him. "This is what you do to me. I've been like this all night, just from knowing you were right across the hall." Angus slid his hands down Kevin's chest, not stopping until he hooked his fingers under the waistband of his briefs and tugged them down his legs and off, dropping them onto the floor.

Then Angus got into bed and softly tugged Kevin to him, his cock nestling against Kevin's butt. Kevin moaned softly and wriggled his hips. "We can't…."

"As long as you stay calm," Angus whispered and ran his hands down Kevin's chest and belly, then closed his fingers around the base of his cock and balls. He squeezed a little, sending a jolt of pleasure through him that made him whine softly in the near darkness.

"What if I start coughing?"

"You won't. I'm going to take things nice and slow." He stroked up and down Kevin's cock just fast enough that Kevin moaned and whimpered softly. "Does that feel good?"

"Uh-huh. So does your cock." Kevin pressed back and plastered himself against Angus, who held him a little tighter.

"I love the way you feel against me." Angus flexed his hips slightly, sliding his dick against Kevin's cleft. The movement slipped Angus between his cheeks.

"God."

"That's it," Angus purred. "Just close your eyes and listen to me. I've missed you so much. I sat beside your bed wishing I could hold you and caress your flat little belly and down your side. Do you remember when I parted your cheeks before, licking you until you screamed, and then slid my cock inside you?"

Kevin closed his eyes, letting Angus's words take him on an erotic journey. "I want that too."

"That might be too strenuous, but I can hold you and use my hands." Angus gripped him tighter, stroking and twisting his hand, sending Kevin on a happy journey. His breathing rate increased, but Kevin kept the breaths as even as he could. He wanted this, and he didn't want it to end in a coughing fit of epic proportions. That was certain to kill the mood in a huge way.

Andrew Grey

Angus moved away and gently rolled Kevin onto his back. Then Angus reached over and switched on a light. It was dim, just enough light for Kevin to see how dark and deep Angus's eyes had become. "I want to watch you. When you come in my hands, I want to see you and gaze into your eyes and hear your breath hitch just a little." Angus sliding along him slowly, only varying how hard he gripped him.

Kevin stretched out on the bed, Angus pressed to him. He was almost afraid at how intently Angus watched him, and yet he couldn't look away. The attention was powerful. Every time his breath hitched and he thought he was going to cough, Angus backed off and let him catch his breath. Then he'd start again. "I don't know…. It's so hard."

"I'll stop as soon as you tell me to," Angus said. "Just breathe slowly and think about how good you feel. You're alive and feel so good in my hands. I don't want you to hold your breath." Angus didn't stop, and Kevin concentrated on his breathing. As excitement built, Kevin ran a hand down Angus's chest, and then his belly, following a trail in his mind until he wrapped his hand around Angus's cock, holding him strongly.

"I love how you feel."

"And I love it when you touch me. You make me excited just being here with you. Nobody has done that before."

"Not even Officer Grumpy?" Kevin asked, and Angus gripped him firmly, pumping a little faster. Kevin felt himself slide closer to release, but Angus was taking the slow road to get there. Kevin stroked Angus at the same speed, and damn if the energy between them didn't ramp up with each second.

"I'm not going to last," Kevin said.

"I don't want you to." Angus sped up slightly, and Kevin's entire body tingled. He refused to hold his breath.

"Don't close your eyes," Angus whispered, and the sensation became too much. "Stay with me. I need to see you."

Kevin nodded, and Angus brought him to the precipice. He kept his mouth open, breathing as deeply as he dared before tumbling off the edge. He came in Angus's hand, thrusting his hips slightly.

"God, you're so beautiful," Angus whispered. Kevin held Angus tightly and breathed through the pleasure. "Your eyes sparkle, and there are little beads of sweat all over you—you shine in the light." Angus leaned over him, and they lightly kissed. Angus kept it short and then gently, as though he were made of glass, rested Kevin's head back on the pillow. "Do you feel better?"

"Yeah. I'm a little warm."

"You'll cool off in a few minutes." Angus lay next to him and turned out the light. "How is your breathing?" he asked as he placed his hand on Kevin's. Kevin turned it over, and Angus wound their fingers together.

"It's good." The urge to cough that had been very strong a few seconds earlier was fading, and he could breathe easily now. Angus got out of bed and went to the bathroom. Kevin closed his eyes as fatigue and contentment rolled over him.

He started a little when Angus wiped his chest and belly with the warm cloth. Then he used a towel, and the water evaporating from his skin cooled him quickly. Kevin sighed and waited for Angus to come back to bed before settling into his embrace and letting it all go.

The next time he woke, it was because sunlight streamed through the bedroom windows. But he was alone in the bed. Kevin wondered if he'd done something wrong, and he was about to get out of the bed when Angus came in the room, still naked, with a tray in his hands. He set it down over Kevin's legs and then got into bed next to him.

"It's a simple breakfast, but one we can eat with our hands. A little fruit, some bacon, and english muffin bites."

Kevin smiled. "What are english muffin bites?"

"I toasted the muffin and then cut it into triangles so each piece is a bite." Angus picked up a piece and fed it to him. Kevin grinned and put one to Angus's lips. He sucked it in along with Kevin's fingers. He pulled his fingers away to let Angus eat and picked up a strawberry from the tray, taking a bite and then giving Angus the rest.

"I take it you like this," Angus said.

"What's not to like? A naked breakfast. It's perfect. Food… naked… the perfect combination." Angus fed him some bacon, and Kevin teased him, sucking on a finger, adding some of the saltiness from Angus's skin to the smoke of the bacon.

"What do you have to do today?" Angus asked.

"First thing, I need to call the insurance company, and then I need to call about apartments." It all seemed so daunting. Everything was gone.

Even the quilt he'd always had on his bed because his mother had given it to him was gone. He could replace the things in his apartment, but none of the new things would have a history. Everything he'd had was wrapped in some sort of memory, even if it was only because he'd gone with the guys to the flea market to find the quirky lamps that had sat on either side of his bed. "I want to stay in bed and not get up for days. I mean, I have to rebuild my entire life, and I don't know where to start."

"Pick something and concentrate on that. You don't have to try to do everything at once. I'll call Janice and see what she has. If she has leads, we can look at them. Or you can call the insurance company, and then we can work on the fire simulator. Whatever you want."

"I have to call Zach too," Kevin said and then yawned. "I feel like I've been in bed for weeks and I'm still tired."

Angus chewed a strawberry and swallowed. "That's because your lungs are mad at you right now. I've had smoke inhalation, and it really sucks. You feel like crap, and if you push it, you swear you're going to cough your lungs out. They will heal, but it takes time."

Kevin had figured that out. He was seconds from saying that he wanted to go home and curl up for a while, but home was gone, and so was Mrs. V. "I'll call the insurance company and try to start getting my life back together. Sitting here doing nothing isn't going to help." Kevin ate some, but his appetite had pretty much flown the coop. Angus ate a little more as well and then took the tray away. Kevin watched him go, then got out of the bed, heading to the bathroom with the kit Angus had given him in the hospital.

Everything he had felt like it belonged to someone else. It was stupid to think about, but the deodorant wasn't what he used, and neither was the toothpaste. He liked a special kind of toothbrush, the ones with the bendy handle, but this one wasn't right. He used them anyway. Even the shaving cream wasn't what he liked, and it smelled funny, but he spread it on his face because it was all he had. Kevin rinsed the shaving cream from his fingers and used one of the disposable razors to shave. When he was done, he threw the razor in the trash and stared at his face in the mirror.

He looked the same, but he didn't feel the same. His life had been pretty good before the fires. He'd had a place of his own, friends, Mrs.

V to spoil him. Now nothing felt right. Kevin sighed and then began coughing when he breathed too deeply. He swore and eventually got himself calmed down.

"Are you all right?" Angus asked through the door.

"Yes," Kevin answered, taking a drink to calm the roughness in his throat. "I'm gonna take a shower."

"Of course. There are towels in the cabinet. I'll bring the things you bought into the bedroom and meet you downstairs."

"Thanks," Kevin said. He was grateful that Angus hadn't offered to join him. He needed some time to try to figure all this shit out. Or maybe what he really wanted was a few minutes so he could cry like a baby without anyone seeing him. No. He was an adult, and he was going to solve his own problems. That meant dealing with insurance people, finding an apartment, and rebuilding that part of his life. He had friends. He wasn't alone. Kevin shook off the loneliness that threatened to wash over him. He got out some towels and started the water.

He didn't take too long to wash his hair and get clean. It felt good to leave the remnants of the hospital behind. He was alone when he left the bathroom. Angus had left his clothes on the made bed, and Kevin dressed. At least the clothes felt like his, even if they were new. Once presentable, he went downstairs.

"Antonio—Officer Grumpy," Angus clarified with a smile. "He called a few minutes ago and said they found some video footage. The news station didn't want to turn it over, but he says he convinced them. He asked if you'd be able to come to the police station."

"I guess," Kevin said. "I should also see about my car."

Angus shook his head. "You'll need to call the insurance on it too. When the building collapsed, it fell on the side lot. There wasn't anything left of any of the cars."

"Oh," Kevin said softly. "I guess I should have known there would be nothing at all left."

"Your computer was in the apartment too, wasn't it?"

"Yeah," Kevin groaned. "But I have cloud backup, so I shouldn't lose anything."

"Okay. Make the phone calls to your insurance agent and get them to handle what they can. The fire was news, so they should be able to help

Grumpy ran the video at normal speed and then slowed it down. "Do you recognize anyone?"

Kevin watched as frame after frame shifted on the screen. "Him." Kevin pointed. "That's the guy who said he was from the gas company. He's still wearing the same shirt. See? Like at the club, he isn't turning his face to the camera, but that's his shirt. It didn't fit very well when he came to the house, and I thought he might have lost weight or something. But now I'm wondering if the shirt was someone else's and he stole it or something."

"You have quite an imagination," Officer Grumpy said.

Kevin stood up. "Am I done now, Officer Grumpy?"

"Reyes," he corrected.

"You can call yourself whatever you want, but you'll always be Officer Grumpy to me. I think it's kind of cute, like a Disney character rather than a clueless jerk." Kevin walked to the door.

"I still have a few questions."

"Kevin," Angus said gently. "He's trying to help. Antonio comes across as gruff, but he's trying to find the man who burned down your building."

Kevin crossed his arms over his chest. "Fine, but be nice." He sat back down in the chair and heard Angus snicker. He swiveled the chair to glare at him and then realized the snicker was for Officer Grumpy. "It isn't going to kill you."

"Had you ever seen the man before he came to the door posing as an employee from the gas company?"

"No. In fact I thought it strange that they were there on a Saturday. I never let anyone in the building, but I heard the buzzer, and Mrs. Carter, who lives across the hall from Mrs. V, must have let him in. I questioned him as I was going down to see Mrs. V. I should have looked closer."

"Can you remember anything else about him?"

"Brown hair, maybe 180 pounds or so, I guess. He was a little taller than me. Baggy clothes, but that doesn't really matter because he won't be wearing them anymore. He couldn't have been very old, though, because he had acne on his cheeks. Yeah…." Kevin smiled as the memory became clearer. "The guy's cheeks and stuff were marked, maybe scarred, like from a bad case of acne or something."

"Okay, that helps. Did he wear glasses?"

"No," Kevin answered. "And he had a ball cap on from the gas company and his hair stuck out the sides."

"So his hair was longer?"

"Yeah, I think you can see it in the video," Kevin said and turned back to the monitor. "Advance it a few frames." Officer Grumpy did, and Kevin pointed. "See? He isn't wearing a hat, at least not then. You can see his hair. It goes to the shoulders. But if I were him, I'd get it cut, because then it would be harder to trace him. He has to know that there's video everywhere. You guys have cameras in your cars, and I bet there are cameras on the front of the fire engines. So he'd have to change his appearance." Kevin watched the screen as the video slowly advanced. "There, that's him. You can see part of his face really clearly." Kevin pointed excitedly. "That's definitely the guy."

"Okay. Now we're getting somewhere."

"Can you enhance it or blow it up to see anything more?"

"We'll try, of course," Officer Grumpy said. "You've been a huge help, and I appreciate you coming down. This may be the break we've all been hoping for."

"You're welcome," Kevin said.

"Have you had any luck finding a place to live?"

"I just got out of the hospital yesterday. I'm hoping to start the search for something I can afford in the next day or so. I guess I probably have to wait for the insurance company. Hopefully they'll come through and I can get another car and stuff."

"That's good. I just have one more question for you. Have you noticed anyone following you? Or has it seemed like you're being watched?"

"No. But I've been with Angus almost the entire time I've been out of the hospital." He turned to Angus. "Have you noticed anything?"

"I haven't, and I've been watching. Of course that doesn't mean someone isn't keeping tabs."

Officer Grumpy nodded. "Okay."

"That's good, right?" Kevin asked.

"To guys like this, fire is like a drug. He got his fix at the club and at your building. So the need will die down for a while, and maybe he'll find someone else to fixate on before he needs another jolt of whatever it is that makes him do this. Then again, he might start looking for you once more when the need gets to be too much. Keep an eye out and call if you see anything suspicious. I'd rather have a number of false alarms and have you safe than one real incident that you were afraid to call in. We all want this guy."

"Okay. I'm staying with friends until I get a new place. My dad made me promise that if I wasn't going to go home with him that I wouldn't stay alone until this guy was caught."

"That's a good idea, but you call if you see anything or anyone suspicious. Our arsonist knows the system and how to make himself look harmless. He got into your building and ultimately your apartment because he didn't look like a threat." If Office Grumpy was trying to scare Kevin, it was working.

"I will," Kevin promised. He wanted to get out of there as fast as he could.

Angus looked about ready to kill as he stared bullets at Officer Grumpy. "Let's go. We have things to do." He led Kevin to the door, and they had just stepped into the hall when Angus's phone rang. Angus answered it and listened. "We'll be right there. … Yeah, he's with me now. … I'll bring him too." Angus ended the call and stopped Officer Grumpy as he left his office. "We all need to go."

"What?" Officer Grumpy snapped.

"There's a fire in Camp Hill."

"That's out of our jurisdiction."

"Yes, but it's at Kevin's job. The captain heard it over the scanner and called me. It has to be him. We can't go officially, but what if he's there?"

"I'll drive," Officer Grumpy said.

"I'm not riding in the back where the criminals go," Kevin said. "If I get out of the back of a police car, rumors will go all around my office that I was arrested, and I'll never get off the help desk."

"My car is unmarked." He was already leading them through the station and out the back to the parking area. Officer Grumpy unlocked a car, and Kevin and Angus got in the back together. Kevin was about ready to crawl out of his skin with worry.

"My building is pretty secure, and they wouldn't let anyone in unless they were with an employee," Kevin explained as they pulled out of the parking lot. "There are also security cameras around the building."

"For an office?"

"It's got all the computers and accounting systems, as well as other departments. So proprietary information and confidential records are stored there. After the whole Enron mess years ago, and the resulting fallout about accounting records, they instituted a lot of additional security."

"Antonio will work with the local police to get whatever information he can. Maybe we can get a better image of our fire starter."

No one wanted that more than Kevin. It seemed no one in his life was safe. "We have to call my dad. What if after this he decides to go for him?" Kevin began to shake and then coughed when he started to panic and breathed too hard. He couldn't have his dad hurt or lose the home he'd grown up in. Everything else was being taken away piece by piece.

"Give me his address after we see what's going on, and I'll contact the local police there. They should be able to help. I'd also like the names and addresses of your friends. He may go for them next."

This was a nightmare. Kevin leaned back in the seat and tried not to breathe too deeply. He almost asked Officer Grumpy—Antonio. He needed to think of him with his proper name—to take him back to the hospital. They had given him an inhaler, and he pulled it out of his pocket and took a dose. He hated the thing because it tasted like crap, but he felt better as soon as he took it.

"It's all right. This isn't your fault," Angus said.

"It definitely is not," Antonio said. "This is all the arsonist's doing, not yours. So don't start feeling guilty. Abusers and criminals always try to justify their crimes by saying it's someone else's fault. It distances them from their deeds and makes what they know is wrong easier to do." Antonio drove like a bat out of hell, screaming down the freeway and then pulling off and exiting onto the surface street.

Lights by the dozens flashed outside Kevin's office, where everyone was gathered away from the building.

"Damn, this is going to be harder than I thought," Antonio said. "There are so many people."

Kevin saw the managers herding people away from the building. "They take roll to make sure everyone is out. They would know if anyone's there who shouldn't be," he said as Antonio pulled in and parked.

"Both of you stay here." Antonio got out and strode up to the people in charge. Kevin watched through the window as Antonio spoke to others in uniform and then to a small group of the vice presidents before returning to the car. "He was here, but all the security protocols probably scared him off. It seems he couldn't get very far into the building so he tried to set a fire in one of the lobbies. It was discovered and put out almost immediately by one of your coworkers. They're going to send copies of the video once it's retrieved."

Kevin sighed. "Do they know the fire was set because of me?"

"No. I saw no reason to inform them of that. I only told them that I believed it was set by an arsonist we were looking for, and Camp Hill police have agreed to work with us." Antonio sat back down and closed the car door. "I'm not as big a dick as everyone thinks I am."

"You're not a dick, I guess. Just grumpy," Kevin said, and Angus started laughing.

"He has your number," Angus said.

"I did hear that Officer Grumpy remark earlier."

"There are worse things he could have nicknamed you," Angus commented and then started laughing again.

"I am a police officer," Antonio snapped.

"And I've seen you naked. Once that happens, you can be as grumpy as you like, but it doesn't have the same effect." Angus was teasing, but Kevin wasn't sure how he felt about knowing that they'd been together. His hands clenched and he had to consciously keep his breath from hitching. He had no cause to be jealous of Antonio; things were clearly over between them.

"How long are we staying?" Kevin asked as he slid down the seat.

"The fire seems to be out, with little actual damage, from what you said," Angus said.

"Yeah." Antonio put the car in gear and slowly pulled away. "There isn't anything else we can learn right now. You didn't see the guy from the video, did you?"

"No. And if I got out, I'd be in a lot of trouble. The doctors said I should take it easy for a few days."

"I need to get him home," Angus said.

"All right. I'll take you back to the station."

107

The ride back to Harrisburg was quiet, and Kevin sat in the back with Angus, wondering how his life could have fallen apart in just a few weeks. Someone had tried to burn the club, then they'd set his home on fire and killed his friend. Now where he worked had been attacked. This had to stop. Kevin yawned and leaned against Angus. When they arrived at the station, they got into Angus's car and went back to his house.

Kevin lay down on the sofa when they got upstairs and fell asleep quickly. He woke under a blanket with Angus in the nearby chair watching television with the volume turned low. Kevin rolled over, stretched, and curled under the blanket once again.

"Zach called. He said he'll be here in a few hours. Apparently he and the guys are going to the club tonight." Angus furrowed his brow. "I think he was asking if you'd like to go along, but I told him that wasn't a good idea."

"No. I need to rest, and going to the club wasn't what the doctor had in mind for resting."

"That's what I thought, so I invited them here. Zach is bringing a video-game console of some sort, and he said he'd ask Jeremy to grab some snacks and stuff."

Kevin smiled. "You don't have to do that."

Angus shrugged. "Get some rest."

Kevin shifted his legs back on the sofa, and Angus came over. Before he sat, Kevin lifted his feet, and Angus settled them on his lap, then rubbed them. "That's really nice."

"Just relax and rest."

Kevin closed his eyes and let himself wonder how in the hell he'd gotten so lucky. Sure, he'd lost a lot, but Angus had been there through it all—a guy he hadn't known until that first fire at the club just a couple weeks earlier. "Why?" Kevin asked sleepily. "Why are you doing all this? It isn't like I'm some great catch, and with all the drama surrounding me lately, I have to be more trouble than I'm worth." He swallowed. "What if he decides to try to burn down your house? If whoever this guy is has been following me, then he knows I'm here, and he's already tried to burn down all the important places in my life."

"He'd be a fool to try," Angus said. "I built this house a few years ago, and there are fire-suppression systems everywhere, including sprinklers and smoke alarms. I have a fire extinguisher on every floor, and a special alarm in the garage, since it's on the first floor and I live above it. You're as safe here as you can be anywhere." Angus rubbed his feet and then up his leg, sending a shiver through him.

Kevin closed his eyes once again. "You still didn't answer my real question."

"Maybe because it doesn't deserve an answer. You seem to think you aren't good enough or that there's something wrong with you and you don't deserve to be happy, and I don't understand that."

"It's not that. The guys I like either don't like me or they don't stay around too long." Kevin kept his eyes closed. It was easier talking about this if he couldn't see Angus's face. "I used to have a crush on Harry, Bull's partner in the club. I thought he was interesting, but Harry really liked Tristan, and rather than seeing me, he actually waited Tristan out and helped him when Tristan needed to get rid of the guy who turned out to be a drug dealer. The two of them are happy, and as part of the whole adventure, I met Ken. He was with the police, and he was pretty hot, but he moved away." Kevin pulled his feet back, ready to get up, but Angus held him still.

"You think my life has been a bed of roses? I'm a firefighter. It's what I love to do. But guys aren't particularly interested in someone who works for a solid week, can get called in at just about any time, and who might not come home. It's a dangerous job, and most people can't take it. So for me, it was always easier to just have simple relationships that never went too far."

"Is that the only reason?" Kevin asked, and when Angus turned to him, the darkness in Angus's eyes told him there was a lot more to it. He'd seen that look a few times before, and each time Angus had turned away and hadn't talked about it. "What happened? Is it about your family?"

"I don't have any family. Not anymore," Angus whispered and released Kevin's feet.

Kevin could feel Angus pulling away from him as they approached the same point where Angus had lashed out on their first date. Kevin waited and wondered how Angus was going to react.

"Can you just tell me what happened?" he asked.

"I don't like to talk about it," Angus said.

"Yeah. There are things I hate to talk about too, but I did it anyway, because you asked. So I'm asking. What happened to you?" Kevin sat up and took Angus's hand. "You're so strong all the time, but it's okay to be vulnerable sometimes, especially with people you care about."

Angus shook his head, and Kevin pulled his feet away, slowly standing. He checked the time and yawned once again. "You're supposed to be resting," Angus said as Kevin put the blanket over the back of the sofa. "If I tell you what you want to know, will you sit back down?"

"I keep wondering what could be so bad that you'd hide it like this. Did you kill someone?"

"No."

"Get arrested for something stupid, like streaking at a soccer game?"

Angus smiled. "Where did that come from?"

"I don't know, but it made you smile."

"I don't like to talk about it. That's all. It isn't as though I did anything. I grew up in Scotland, at least until I was sixteen. We lived in Edinburgh in a small house. My dad owned a pub, and he provided pretty well for us. It was good and I was popular with the other kids because… my dad owned a pub."

"What happened?" Kevin asked.

"I was staying with a friend. He'd invited me for a sleepover. When I got up the next morning, his mom was there. She sat me down in the lounge and told me that there had been a fire during the night, and that my mom and dad—" Angus's voice broke. "I can hear her even now trying to tell me through gasps and near sobs that my parents had both been killed. One of the pieces of kitchen equipment had apparently caught fire, and they didn't make it out."

Kevin swallowed. "Is that why you became a firefighter?"

"Yes. Part of it, I think. I always wondered if things would have been different if I'd been there. I might have been able to get them out."

Kevin sat down next to Angus. "You were a kid. Now, I have no doubt that you'd have saved them like you saved me. But then, you could have been killed too."

"So many times I wish I had been," Angus whispered. "After Mom and Dad died, there were no relatives in Scotland. My mom was an only child, but my dad had a brother who lived in Carlisle. So he came over and took me back with him. I was sixteen and ended up moving partway around the world. I'd lost my parents and then everything else I knew.

The kids here picked on me because I talked funny. So I worked hard to lose my accent and try to fit in. I was strong and athletic, so that helped, but it was still hard. Then, of course, I realized I liked guys instead of girls, and that made things even worse."

"What about your uncle? Did he understand?"

Angus sighed. "I don't know. I never told him. Uncle Thad was good to me and treated me well. He was a supervisor in a trucking warehouse, and he worked hard. He never married, and he never talked about anyone he might have loved. As far as I know, he was a bachelor and stayed that way his entire life. Now I wish we'd talked about it, but we didn't."

"Where is he now? Can we visit him?"

Angus shook his head. "He died when I was twenty."

"How?" Kevin breathed and then stopped. The anguish in Angus's eyes told the story. "No way."

"Yeah. I was away at college. Mom and Dad had left some money, but Uncle Thad didn't use any of it. He said it was so I could have a good start in life. Anyway…." Angus shook his head slightly. "I was going to business school. Uncle Thad had said that I should do whatever I wanted and that my mom and dad would be proud of me. I was at school, in class, when I got a call from the police. Uncle Thad had had a massive heart attack. They found him in the basement. He had been dead a few days, and he'd died all alone with no one to help him."

"Jesus," Kevin breathed. "So you quit college…."

"…and became a firefighter. Just like that. There was no question. I had to stop other people from going through that if I could."

"Is that why you rushed back into the building to save me?"

"I guess so. Maybe. Going back in to get you was a gut reaction. I didn't think about it, I just raced back inside."

"So you'd have gone back in for anyone?" Kevin asked. He'd thought that he might have been special and that was why Angus had saved him, but maybe he'd been reading things wrong and Angus had just been doing his job. Of course he'd been doing his job. Kevin knew he was being a ninny and kind of stupid but couldn't stop the disappointment.

"I kept thinking I needed to save you," Angus said. "I couldn't let you die, not if there was a chance. So I raced back inside." Angus leaned closer and slipped his arms around Kevin's waist. "I acted like such an ass when I got mad at you during our date. You were asking about my family, and I don't talk about them because I don't have any. They're all gone, and instead of saying I didn't want to talk about it, I got huffy. Then afterward you didn't call, and I got worried, so I was going to come see you, maybe bring flowers," Angus smiled. "But then I got the call, your building was on fire, and you weren't outside."

"So you rushed in to try to save me."

"Yeah, I did." Angus rested his head on Kevin's shoulder. "Of course I wasn't fast enough and you nearly died from the smoke, and we both could have died when the building collapsed."

"You know it's okay to be scared. Hell, I'm scared of stuff all the time. Every time I meet someone, I keep wondering when they're going to leave."

"And I wonder when they're going to die in a fire," Angus retorted.

"Okay… you win," Kevin quipped, hoping to lighten the mood. "But since I'm the one who would have to die in a fire for you to lose me, I guess we both win… or in this case lose." Kevin's head began to spin. "I'll stop babbling now before you think I'm totally stupid." Kevin leaned back against Angus. "When were the guys going to come over?"

"Zach said about six. They were going to bring food with them."

"Lord. That means enough junk food and chips to feed an army… and nothing else."

"I have stuff here," Angus said.

"So were you a Boy Scout?"

"No. We didn't have that near where I grew up. But I like to be prepared anyway." Angus stood slowly and then guided Kevin until he was lying on the sofa once again. "Rest some more. Give those lungs a chance to heal, and I'll get things ready for your friends."

"I'm not sleepy anymore."

"Then watch television, though how you can find anything on that isn't drivel is beyond me. But you're welcome to try." Angus leaned over the sofa and kissed him. Kevin put his arms around his neck and held on, deepening the kiss until he felt like he was going to cough.

"You said you never got serious with anyone. But I want to know why any of them let you go. You're kind, sweet, gentle, and really easygoing." Kevin breathed as levelly as he could with Angus's lips just inches from his. "You're also super sexy and hot."

"I didn't give them much of a choice, I guess," Angus answered.

"Will you give me a choice when the time comes?" Kevin asked. If that was Angus's pattern, then Kevin figured it was only a matter of time before Angus returned to it. "How long before you decide I'm not worth it and toss me away along with the others?"

Angus straightened up and turned away. "I've never told anyone about my parents and uncle before." That was the only answer Kevin got before Angus left the room, and a few minutes later Kevin heard him working in the kitchen. He took Angus's response as a minimal reassurance. If Angus was willing to open up to him, then maybe there was hope.

Kevin rested and the tightness in his chest eased after a little while. He figured it had been a combination of his lungs and what Angus had told him. Eventually he dozed and was awakened by the doorbell, followed by the guys as they tramped inside.

"Thanks for having us," he heard Tristan say, followed by the rustle of a bag of chips.

"It's really cool of you," Jeremy said. "We've been really worried about him."

He didn't hear Zach, but knew he was there, and soon all three of them had joined him in the living room.

Kevin sat up and got a hug from each of them. Zach hooked up his Nintendo and Jeremy plugged his iPhone into Angus's docking station, and soon the room was filled with dance music. "We thought since you couldn't come to the club, we'd bring the club to you," Tristan said.

Jeremy left the room and returned dragging Angus by the hand. Kevin had never seen him terrified before, but he looked it now.

"I don't dance."

"Come on, you can dance. Everyone can dance." Jeremy tugged him farther into the room, and Angus looked lost. Tristan had moved the coffee table to the side, and he was shaking it in the middle of the floor. Jeremy began dancing as well. Kevin wished he could join them and dance with Angus, but instead he went to his rescue and guided Angus down next to him on the sofa.

"Is it okay?" Kevin asked. "I can tell them to turn it off."

"It's fine. I just look like a dying chicken when I dance."

"I bet you look fine when you dance. Think of it as having sex standing up." Kevin winked, and Angus blushed. The song ended and a slow one came on. Jeremy went to change it.

"Don't," Kevin said and stood up. "Let's dance," he said to Angus and waited for him to stand up. He put his arms around Angus's neck and waited until he pulled him close. "Just move slowly to the music. Okay?"

Angus nodded and swayed back and forth. Kevin rested his head against his shoulder, and it felt like it was just the two of them.

"This is really nice," Angus whispered.

"You know what would be nicer?"

"What?"

"Doing this with you wearing nothing but those fire pants of yours." Kevin grinned. "Or maybe with you wearing a kilt." He knew he was being naughty, but feeling the heat rise in Angus's skin was more than enough indication that he'd hit on something. "You like the thought of that." He kept his voice low enough that only Angus could hear him.

"Yeah," Angus breathed. "If your friends weren't here right now, I'd keep dancing with you, stripping you down until you were naked." Angus slid his hands down Kevin's back and over the curve of his butt, stopping just at the point where Kevin could feel the tips of his fingers touching his tuchus. "I'd press to you and love on you all night long."

Kevin swallowed hard and closed his eyes.

"I'd make you pant and whimper for me… and yes, I'd dance with you in my fire pants or anything else if it would make you happy."

Kevin lifted his head so he could look into Angus's eyes. "What would you like?" The song ended and something more energetic came on. The others began dancing, but Kevin stayed where he was, pretending nothing had changed.

"Just you," Angus whispered and shifted his hips. Kevin felt Angus's erection pressing against his. He closed his eyes as pleasure shot through him. "You weren't kidding when you said dancing was like sex standing up."

"We have to stop or—" Kevin swallowed and pulled away, but not too far. He didn't want to give all his friends a show. Slowly he sat back on the sofa and pulled the blanket over himself and Angus when he joined him. The others continued dancing. He and Angus swayed to the music until the others tired and turned the music down.

"Do you want to play games? I have everything hooked up," Jeremy said.

"Sure," Kevin said.

"I'll go get the food and bring it in," Angus offered.

"He's pretty cool," Tristan whispered once Angus had left the room. "I figured he'd be more straitlaced than he is."

"What's to be straitlaced about? We're playing video games and eating junk food, not plotting to take over the world," Kevin countered. "Angus is really special."

"How special?" Jeremy asked in the way he had that could make any question sound naughty.

"Yeah, how special am I?" Angus asked as he came back in the room, and Kevin snickered at the way Jeremy clammed up.

"I'll explain later. Right now I'm about to kick Jeremy's butt at Mario World." Kevin winked at Angus and then picked up the controller. It had been a while since he'd played, and to his surprise and shame, Jeremy managed to beat him, but just by a little bit. Since he lost, Kevin handed his controller to Tristan. Kevin sat back, watching and hooting as they played, especially when it was Angus's turn. Zach beat him handily, and Kevin begged off playing again, settling on the sofa under the blanket.

"Don't overdo it," Angus said.

Kevin nodded, already fighting to stay awake. At least he'd managed to call the insurance company to get things rolling. Other than that he hadn't done much and felt a little useless.

"I got a message from Janice about an hour ago about a few potential apartments for you. So we'll call her in the morning and look at places."

"Don't you have work?"

"The day after tomorrow. So until then I can help if you want it."

Kevin nodded slowly and leaned against Angus, watching as the guys continued playing. Eventually he curled up on the sofa and fell asleep with Angus next to him.

"Guys, we should go," Kevin heard Zach say after a while. "Kevin is out, and we need to help clean up."

"It's all right," Angus told him, and Kevin stirred, slowly sitting up, rubbing his eyes.

"We can help," Zach said as he gathered snack bags and began closing them. Jeremy gathered trash, and Tristan carried the dishes into the sink. Once everything was put away, Zach unhooked the game console and packed it in the box. Finally, the coffee table was put back into place, and it was like they hadn't been over at all.

"Thanks for having us. When we get together, we can be a bit much, and you're a real sport," Tristan told Angus, who simply nodded. The guys all said their good-byes and then left, with Angus seeing them out and locking up.

"Did you have fun?" Angus said when he came back in the room.

"Yeah. I hate that I was too tired to do much, but it was nice doing something we always do. I know it may look dumb to you, but it's our thing and felt normal."

"They were nice, if a little energetic." Angus extended his hand and gently tugged Kevin to his feet. He led him through the house and up the stairs, turning off the lights as they went. "It's time for bed."

"I'm not sleepy now," Kevin said sheepishly. But from the way Angus looked at him, that wasn't going to be a problem.

CHAPTER SIX

WHAT ARE you doing? Angus sent as a text the following Saturday night. He was just finishing up his shift and was about to go home. He had to be back at the station the following afternoon. Having the evening off had been a surprise, but one he wasn't going to question.

Going to the club with the guys, Kevin responded. *I promise not to dance very hard. I want to go out and have some fun.*

Want company? Angus sent and got a smiley face followed by a sound file that made squee sounds. Angus took that as a yes. He checked his appearance in the bathroom mirror at the station after changing and then left, heading right over to the club.

It was still relatively quiet when he entered and found a table. "You're the guy Kevin is seeing, aren't you?" a huge bald-headed man asked.

"You must be Bull." He extended his hand. "Kevin has told me a lot about you." Bull shook Angus's hand firmly and then released it.

"You were the one who saved him in the fire?" Bull asked as he pulled out one of the chairs and sat down. "Kevin's a nice kid, really nice. He's had some hard luck with guys. I hope you don't plan to add to that."

"No."

"Good. I asked around, and you have a 'love 'em and leave 'em' reputation. Now, I'm all for a man changing his ways. I know I did when I met Zach. But if you're not planning to make some change, I suggest you back away now before Kevin gets hurt. There are plenty of us who would hate to see that happen." Bull glanced to where a small group of men stood at the bar, looking in their direction.

"Is this some kind of joke?"

"No. We're very much for real." Bull smiled. "Just be good to him." He pushed away from the table and joined the others, talking briefly, and then they all separated. Angus actually watched to make sure he wasn't being surrounded. Damn…. He hadn't expected that. Angus wasn't sure if he should be pleased or scared. Bull was intimidating, and his demeanor suggested quite strongly that he could back up any threat he chose to make. That was more than a little frightening, and the guys Bull had been talking with up until a few minutes ago had that same menacing look. But what pleased him was that Kevin had such loyal and caring friends. They thought enough of him to look out for him. Yeah, threatening his boyfriends might be a little much, but they did it because they cared, just the way his friends had cared enough to give up their night out to come to his place and include Kevin in their fun. The evening hadn't been at all what he'd expected, but Zach and the guys could have gone out and left Kevin on his own to recuperate. They hadn't. They'd simply moved their fun to him. That told Angus a lot about the person he'd really come to care about.

"What are you doing here?" Zach asked as he bounded up to the table carrying a drink tray. He pulled Angus out of his thoughts. "Can I get you anything?" Was the kid flirting?

"A beer would be great. But I have to watch what I drink because I'm driving. Kevin asked me to meet him here, but he hasn't shown up yet." Angus watched Zach for a minute. "What the hell are you doing?"

"I'm trying to earn some extra money so I can take Bull on a mini vacation. Harry said they needed a server because one of the guys got sick, so I'm filling in, and if I'm flirty I'll get better tips."

"If you're flirty, Bull is going to flatten anyone you flirt with, and that isn't going to be good for business."

Zach stood up straight. "You're right. I hadn't thought of that." He seemed thoughtful. "Maybe I can use that to my advantage. Tip me good or I'll tell Bull on you."

Angus laughed. "Just be a good server and the tips will come. See, that happens when you actually bring the drinks rather than talking with the patrons." Angus smiled, and Zach rolled his eyes and hurried over to the bar. Angus watched as his order was filled and Zach hurried back. He was something else, but definitely not as cute as Kevin. Angus paid for the beer and gave Zach a good tip.

"A buck?" Zach whined with a smile.

"For a single beer, yeah."

"Shit, this is going to be harder than I thought."

"How much are you hoping to make?"

"I want to take Bull on a cruise. He needs to get away from here for a real vacation. This place wears on him after a while, and after the fire and all, he's getting way too wound up. I guess it's going to take longer than I thought."

"You could just help Bull pay for the cruise, and use the tip money for drinks and spending money while at sea," Angus suggested. He tilted his head toward the next table, where several guys were looking around. "They seem thirsty."

Zach hurried away, and Angus saw Kevin come through the door. He was a sight for sore eyes. They had texted and called a few times, but this was the first he'd been able to see him since he'd returned to work. The tight jeans and gauzy shirt he wore left very little to the imagination. Kevin grinned when he saw him and came right over, plopping his tight little butt on the chair next to him. "Have you been here long?"

"No." Angus kissed Kevin hello, reminding himself that he was in a public place and that stripping Kevin down right at the table was probably not a good idea, even if parts of his anatomy were more than interested. When they broke apart, Kevin was breathing hard, and Angus worried he'd overdone it, but Kevin smiled and didn't cough, so that was good.

Angus signaled to Zach, who hurried over.

"Playing cocktail waitress?" Kevin teased.

Angus smiled. "He's trying to earn some money for Bull, and unless you want to crowd up to the bar all night, be nice to the cocktail waiter."

"For the cruise?" Kevin asked, and Zach nodded. "God, that sounds like fun. Lying on the deck in the sun, a handsome cabana boy to rub lotion on my back and the pool boy to bring me drinks. That would be heaven."

"I don't think it works that way," Zach told him. "You have to bring your own cabana boy, so ask Angus if he'll rub lotion on your back. And as for the pool boys, maybe Angus can do that too. I know I intend to have the biggest pool boy on the whole ship." Zach looked over

119

to where Bull stood near the office door, mouth hanging open a little. Angus wouldn't have been surprised to see him drool.

"Zach," Angus said gently.

"Oh yeah. I'll be right back."

He hurried away and Angus turned his attention to Kevin. "I'd definitely be your cabana boy. I'd rub lotion on your back, and then maybe if no one was looking, slide my hand into your suit, cup your butt, and…."

The sound of a chair scraping on the floor was like nails on a chalkboard through the little seductive dream he'd been trying to weave.

"Hi, guys," Jeremy said as he and Tristan sat down.

"Your timing is amazing," Kevin grumbled as he leaned against him slightly.

"Sorry. We can come back if you're getting busy," Tristan teased.

Kevin smacked him lightly on the shoulder. "Not at a table—that's gross." He giggled, and the others did too. The music had started, and once the others got drinks, courtesy of Zach, they headed out on the floor to dance. Angus and Kevin moved around to the back side of the table so they could watch.

"How was work?" Kevin asked.

"Tiring. Our friend doesn't appear to have struck again."

"That's good," Kevin said.

"I'm not sure if it is or not. I have a feeling that the longer he waits, the more spectacular the next one is going to be. Antonio is doing all he can, but there isn't much of a trail, and the only one who has truly seen him is you. We can't take the pictures we got to the media because they aren't clear enough."

"But they go to the media with descriptions of people all the time."

"Yeah, they do. Mostly when they're looking for witnesses to a specific event. That isn't what we have, and there are a lot of people who match our description."

"I guess." Kevin turned to him. "What I really want to know is who in the club saw him. The guy set a fire right here, and no one knows who he is or got a good look at him. There had to be people sitting or standing right next to him. The place was packed."

"That's the point. He could hide in plain sight because no one was paying any attention to him. It's how he got into your building, and I suspect it's how he tried to get into your office. Only it didn't work, though apparently he was pretty good at evading their cameras. We have a picture of a guy in jeans and a T-shirt, but nothing in detail of his face, just like all the others."

"Damn," Kevin said. It was hard to hear him with the music. "I really wish I could dance. But I'm barely making it through the days on the phone at work. I keep water at my desk all the time, but I have to put people on hold to cough, and I've used the inhaler more than I like."

"You need to give your lungs a chance to rest."

"I need to work or I won't be able to afford the place that your friend helped find for me. Oh, and you never told me that Janice was Mrs. Kranz. I nearly wet myself when I realized who I was talking to. She's, like, the richest lady in town, and you had her help me find a place to live."

"Janice is one of a kind, and as for the money, she put most of it into a foundation to help others. Did you meet her at the church?"

"Yeah."

"She's going to have to move, and she's looking for a place."

"Why doesn't she just buy one? She has lots of money."

"Janice wants the charity to be able to run on its own, and she's been able to do that up until now. She once told me that if she kept putting her own money into it, then no one else would help, and once she was gone everything would die. It makes sense."

"I guess it does. There have to be a lot of places she could use." Kevin paused like he was getting an idea. "Why not ask Bull if we can do a benefit here? She helped me, and I bet she's helped others in the community. She certainly doesn't discriminate, and there are a lot of gay people who end up homeless and in need."

"We can ask her and see what she thinks," Angus said. He leaned closer, kissing Kevin gently. "You are a very special person."

"I'm just me." Kevin grinned. "And who doesn't love a party?" He motioned all around, and Angus had to agree. Everyone was having an amazing time. The music drummed until the building seemed to move along with it. The damage from the fire was gone, and it was as though the incident had never happened. Men jumped and danced shirtless on the floor, sweating and rubbing against each other. It was enough to make Angus want to learn to dance just so he could be in on the fun.

"Do they ever play anything slower?" Angus asked, nearly shouting to be heard.

"I can ask," Kevin said, and before Angus could stop him, he was out of his chair and making his way through the crowd, which had grown considerably in the last hour or so. Angus watched him approach the DJ booth in the corner. He talked to the man, who smiled and leaned close to speak to Kevin. Then Kevin turned and began weaving through the crowd once again. Angus lost sight of him in all the moving bodies. When he reached the table, Kevin pulled Angus to his feet.

"He's here. I saw him. The guy who set the fires. He's in the club right now." Kevin turned and pointed. "He was right over there."

"Did he see you?"

"I don't know. We need to get Bull and tell him. He's wearing a red shirt and really dark jeans. He was carrying a white hoodie or something like it so he could be wearing that too." Kevin scanned the room, and Angus did as well.

"Go tell Bull and the guys. I don't know what this guy has in mind." Angus was already working his way through the crowd toward the front door. As he got there he saw a guy clearly meeting Kevin's description leaving the club. Angus took off and got out as quickly as he could, but there were so many people it was hard to move anywhere fast. By the time he made it to the sidewalk, he saw the guy running away from the club and swore under his breath.

"What happened?" Bull asked as he came through the door.

"Kevin saw the guy who'd posed as the gas man at his building. We think he's the arsonist. The guy took off before I could get very close. We need to check the building to make sure he didn't leave anything. Have your people look in the bathrooms or anywhere out of the way. If they find anything at all, call it in and evacuate the club."

Bull headed right back inside, and Angus followed. Security personnel met him, and Bull gave quick instructions. They all fanned out through the crowd, and Angus returned to where he'd left Kevin. "I didn't get him, but he must have seen us because he took off outside like a scared rabbit. Security is checking to make sure he didn't leave anything, but I doubt he did. This guy wants to see his handiwork in action."

"Should we leave?"

"If they find anything, they're going to need help getting everyone out. So let's be ready just in case."

Kevin took his arm, holding it tight. He stood right next to Angus as they watched the crowd.

"It seems clear," Bull said after he made his way over.

"Good." Angus relaxed and sat down as the other guys made their way back, covered in sweat. Zach showed up to get them drinks and then hurried away once again. Everyone seemed unaware of what had happened, and that was good. There was no need for panic. "I feel as though he couldn't have been here very long."

"After that note he left, I'm surprised he came back at all," Bull said.

"What he says in the notes is less important than him leaving one. It's his signature, and all he wants and needs is the rush he gets from watching a really big fire." An idea occurred to him, and Angus cursed inwardly, wishing he'd thought of it before. He made a mental note to call Antonio as soon as they left the club. He was nervous as he sat back down. He kept looking all around the room. The carefree atmosphere of a few minutes earlier was gone. He turned to Kevin and saw that he was pale and swaying on his feet. Angus guided him down into a seat and asked Jeremy to get some water.

"I need to go," Kevin said. "I don't feel safe here."

Jeremy returned with a bottle of water and set the bottle on the table. Angus opened it and let Kevin drink. "What happened?"

"He was here," Kevin said. "The guy who burned down my building and set fire to the club was here. I saw him. He left, but…." Kevin gulped some more water, and Angus's training kicked in as Kevin began to breathe violently, coughing and trying to catch his breath. Angus stood and lifted Kevin into his arms, carrying him toward the door. All he could think was that he needed to get him out of here.

The crowd parted when they saw him and heard him yell. Angus made it to the door and out into the fresh air in less than a minute. "Breathe slow and steady. You're panicking, but we're outside and okay now." He set him on a small patch of grass near the street and rubbed Kevin's back, and the coughing subsided. Kevin's breathing evened out, and he held on to Angus, making Angus feel like he was the most important person in the world. To hell with other men—he only wanted this one. "Is that better?" he whispered as a car went by, blaring its horn, but the sound barely intruded on the peace he saw in Kevin's eyes.

"Yeah." Kevin breathed slowly. "I want to go home, not to my apartment."

That Kevin meant his house when he said home made Angus's heart do a little flip. Angus helped Kevin up, and they walked away from the club toward where he'd parked his car.

"Kevin," a rough voice called. Kevin stopped and stilled. Angus turned to the source of the call and saw a tall, broad man with short dark hair striding toward them. "Are you all right? I just got here, and Tristan said you weren't feeling well and had been carried out." Before Angus knew what was happening, the man had Kevin in his arms and was holding him tight.

"Excuse me," Angus said and placed his hand on Kevin's shoulder. "Who are you and why are you hugging my boyfriend?"

Kevin pushed away from the man.

"*I'm* his boyfriend," the man said with a growl and turned back to Kevin. "I was a fool for leaving, and I was able to get my job back with the force here. Or they said I could come back if I wanted. So I jumped in the car and drove back. I knew I'd find you here with the guys."

"Ken… you left," Kevin said very softly. "This is Angus."

Ken turned toward him, and Angus gently extricated Kevin from the clingy bastard's arms.

"I don't blame you for taking a guy home for the night. I know I left, but I'm here now, so you can send him home. Then you and I can go to your place and get things back to where they were before I was foolish enough to let you go."

Kevin looked at Angus, and Angus put his arm over Kevin's shoulder. "First thing, bub, I'm his boyfriend, not a pickup, and a lot has changed since you left. Kevin doesn't have an apartment any longer. His building was burned down."

Kevin stood taller. "Angus saved my life when my building was set on fire. But we had started dating before that." Kevin took his hand, and Angus's urge to punch the guy eased a little. "Ken is a police officer in Pittsburgh," he said to Angus. "He used to work here, but he moved about six months ago." He pulled an inhaler from his pocket and used it with a light puff. "I got some smoke in my lungs, and I'm still feeling the effects," he said to Ken.

"I'm sorry I wasn't here."

"Right, you weren't," Kevin said sharply. "You left, and I had to get over you and figure out a way to move on."

"It was too good an opportunity to pass up," Ken said, and Angus wondered just how good it was if he was already back, but he kept quiet. This was Kevin's fight and his decision, no matter how much he wanted to step in.

"And now you're back, so I guess it wasn't all that good." The bite in Kevin's words was unmistakable. "You left me, like most everyone else. Something better came along, and you left, figuring that was more important than me."

"It was my job."

"Yeah, and you made your decision."

Ken looked up at him, fire in his eyes. "And you think Mr. Hot Fireman is going to stick around? I know this guy from when I was on the force. He had his dick stuck in any ass that was willing to roll over and take what he had. And he'll go back to that. Just watch him. I offered to take you with me, remember?"

"My life is here, and my dad is close. He'd be hours away out there, and you know that."

"Hey, let's get you home," Angus said softly to Kevin.

"Mind your own business," Ken said.

Angus stepped forward, thrusting out his chest. "You want to do more than talk? You're off duty, so at the moment, you're just a guy who's accosting him on the sidewalk and I came to his defense, so I'll kick your ass from here to kingdom come."

"That's enough!" Kevin snapped again and then began to cough. That sound knocked the wind out of Angus, and he moved back to Kevin.

"He's right. He needs to rest, but you stay away. Or that job you're hoping to get will evaporate like the fog."

"You threatening me?"

Angus put an arm around Kevin's shoulders. "If I have to. See, I have contacts on the force, and like Kevin said, a lot has happened, including the fact that Kevin saved the club over there during a fire. He's a hero and a lot of people know it. So making trouble for him isn't going to endear you to anyone."

"I'm okay, Angus," Kevin said. "Ken isn't going to hurt me. He just expected that I've been spending the last six months pining away for him, and now he's hurt that I managed to get on with my life. All he did was come here and expect things to be exactly as they were."

"I guess I was wrong," Ken said.

"You could have called or told me what was going on. I haven't heard from you in months." Kevin started to cough again, and Angus did his best to soothe him. Kevin began to shake. "I'm going now." Kevin turned and walked away, still coughing.

"Stay away," Angus grunted and then went after Kevin, helping him to his Mustang. "Leave your car here. I'll bring you back to get it in the morning."

Once Kevin was seated, Angus waited for his coughing to die down. "Are you feeling better now?"

"Yeah," Kevin answered, and Angus stepped back. Kevin pulled the door closed, and Angus walked around to the other side and got in. "I can't believe that he'd just come back and think that everything would be just like it was. That I was some great big loser pining away for him for months."

Angus started the engine. "You know, it's okay to mourn the end of a relationship." He'd done that plenty of times in his life. Of course for him it was death that brought an end to the relationships in his life, but he figured the concept still applied. "And be angry for what he did."

Kevin sat back and didn't say anything. "I really loved him. I thought he was the one. We dated for a while, and when he called and said that he had something big he wanted to tell me, I thought he was going to ask me to move in with him. But he told me he'd taken a job in Pittsburgh." Kevin chuckled. "It was like a scene out of a stupid romantic comedy. I went to his place expecting to be given a key and even some closet space. We were going to be happy. Instead, I nearly tripped over his suitcases, and he told me he was moving for a new job."

"He'd never mentioned it?"

"Not once. He went out there for an interview and everything and never said a word. I was completely floored and figured I must have done something wrong."

"You didn't. He did," Angus told him. "You thought you were building a relationship with him, and yet he didn't tell you that he was looking for another job in a different part of the state."

"We had stopped using protection, so when he left I got tested because… well… who knows what else he'd been keeping from me. Everything was fine, but he scared the hell out of me."

Angus pulled to a stop at a light. "But you still care for him?"

Kevin didn't answer right away. "I'd like to say that he's out of my life, but it's hard. I don't feel the way I did when he left…. It's weird. I don't know what I feel, I guess. Suddenly he's back and everything has been turned around again."

"I see," Angus said, but it was a lie. He didn't understand anything, least of all what Kevin was trying to say.

"If you do, then explain it to me, because I don't get crap. I should be over him and not thinking about him. Yet he shows up for five minutes, and he's all I can think about. But not in a good way." Kevin turned in his seat as the light changed. "I used to think about him all the time, and that was enough to put a goofy smile on my face. Now I want him to go back to Pittsburgh and leave me alone."

Angus heard what Kevin was saying, but there was more behind it, and it settled in a lump in his throat. He understood being upset about seeing an ex, but it was obvious that Kevin still had feelings for Ken that he hadn't worked through.

It was those feelings that scared the hell out of Angus. If Kevin hadn't cared, he wouldn't have been upset and Ken's appearance wouldn't have meant anything.

Angus pulled the car into the garage on autopilot. He turned off the engine and stared at the back wall, seeing nothing. The original plan had been for Kevin to stay with Zach, but through some stroke of luck that had had Angus's heart soaring, Kevin had felt comfortable with him and he'd stayed at his place. Even when Angus had gone back to work and had spent some nights at the station, Kevin had stayed at home, in his bed. That had meant a great deal.

"Come on, let's get you upstairs," Angus whispered, breaking himself out of his own thoughts.

Kevin opened the door and got out. Angus followed him. There was no energy in the way Kevin shuffled up the stairs and then flopped down on the sofa. He yawned and said nothing, sinking into his own world.

Not knowing what else to do, Angus took Kevin's hand and gently helped him to his feet and then up to the bedroom.

"I'm sorry for flaking out," Kevin said.

"It's okay. You'll feel better in the morning. Go get ready for bed. I have a few things to do downstairs, and then I'll be back up." Angus left and went to the kitchen. He puttered for a few minutes and then started a load of laundry. When he went back upstairs, he peeked into his room. Kevin was curled up on his bed, sound asleep. Angus didn't want to disturb him, and for some reason sleeping in the same bed with him didn't seem right. Kevin had decisions to make, whether he knew it or not. His ex was back and very interested in him.

Angus closed the bedroom door and grabbed a blanket and pillow from the linen closet. He used the hall bathroom to clean up and then went into the living room and lay down on the sofa. He was so tired he was asleep in a few minutes, but it wasn't a deep sleep and his dreams were vivid and unsettled.

In the middle of the night, Angus woke, wondering if he'd heard something. But the house was quiet. He got up and checked on Kevin, who hadn't moved an inch, still sound asleep. Angus watched him for a while. The tension he'd seen earlier was gone, his face and mouth at complete rest. He thought of joining Kevin in bed, but ended up back on the sofa, alone.

CHAPTER SEVEN

KEVIN WOKE to an empty bed. He felt better—or at least he had until he woke alone. He couldn't remember Angus coming to bed at all and got up, sleepily wandering through the house. He found Angus asleep on the living room sofa. He watched him for a few minutes and then turned and went back up to the bedroom. He thought he and Angus might have been developing something between them, something special. But maybe he'd been wrong.

Ken had shown up last night, and just like that Angus was pulling away. At least he knew where he stood.

"You're awake. Did you rest?" Angus asked, pushing the blankets away and sitting up.

"Yeah, I slept," Kevin said with a yawn that thankfully didn't end with a coughing fit.

"I didn't want to bother you…." Angus stood in his briefs and began folding up the blanket. "You were comfortable and I didn't want to disturb you, or…."

"What? You didn't want to sleep with me anymore?" Kevin blurted before he could stop his thought. "If that's what you want, that's fine."

Angus took a step back. "I only thought you might need some time to figure out what you want."

"Me?" Kevin blinked a few times in confusion.

"Yeah. You're the one with the hot boyfriend who just breezed into town, and it was all you talked about on the way home, so I thought you needed some space to think. So when you fell asleep, I stayed here. It

129

didn't feel right to sleep with you if you had some other guy on your mind." Angus grabbed the pillow and blanket, stomping out of the room. Kevin heard the closet door open and then slam closed.

"It's over with Ken," Kevin said. He tried to keep his breathing level but felt a coughing fit coming on.

"Are you sure? Because if it was, you wouldn't be so worked up over him."

"He left me, like everyone else," Kevin said. "You should be able to understand that I can be angry about him, but I'm not going to go running back because he showed up. Yes, I loved him, but when he left, he told me what was important… and it wasn't me." He turned away and calmed the cough that threatened. He'd come looking for Angus, hoping they could talk and put this behind them. He cared about Angus, a lot, and Ken was in the past. Ken had left him, and that was something Kevin wasn't willing to let go of.

"Are you sure that's what you want? You were with Ken for a while, and he wants you back."

"Are you pushing me to him because you don't want me anymore?" Kevin had to keep his voice level or he'd break down, and he didn't want to do that. "If that's the way it is, then just say so. I can deal with a breakup. I've been through plenty of those. You don't need to feel sorry for me because of all the stuff that's happened. I'm going to be in my own place once again, and I can go back to making my own life. And you can go back to your roving ways and everything will be just fine." Kevin was nearly yelling, and he didn't know why.

"Kevin, that's not what I want. But is it what you want? Do you want Ken in your life? Or me? Or neither of us? Do you just want to be free and on your own?"

Kevin's head spun. He wasn't sure of anything right now.

"I know what I want," Angus continued, "and I was willing to give you time to figure it out, but now you're angry with me for doing that." They were circling each other, and Kevin glanced at the clock and swore under his breath.

"I have to get ready for work," Angus said.

Kevin wanted to stop him, but he had to do the same.

The two of them moved around each other as they used the bathroom and then dressed. It was like they were strangers and neither wanted to see or touch the other one. After they were dressed, Angus drove him back to the club to pick up his new—well, new to him—car. They didn't talk much on the drive over. Kevin said good-bye, got in the car, and started the engine. As he started to pull away, he saw Angus rush over. He stopped and rolled down the passenger window.

"I don't know what all that was about. I wish I did, but my shift is going to keep me busy for a few days. I don't want you to think I'm angry with you."

Angus reached in the window, and Kevin took his hand. "I guess we have things to think about," Kevin said.

Angus nodded. "I'll be on shift for a few days, and talking is going to be difficult."

Kevin's stomach lurched at the thought of spending a couple of days wondering what Angus was thinking. Kevin hated that kind of relationship drama, but he knew this round of it was most likely his fault. That whole crap with Ken was overwhelming him, and then to wake up this morning and find Angus gone.... Kevin knew Angus was mad at him, no matter what he said.

"Call me when you can. I need to know you're okay." Angus squeezed his hand and then pulled away.

Kevin raised the window and pulled out. He made it to the corner and stopped. He checked his rearview mirror and thought of backing up so he could tell Angus that he cared about him, but he'd already gone back to his car, and Kevin was going to be late for work. He made his turn into traffic and headed toward his office. He tried to put their argument, discussion, whatever it was, out of his mind.

IT DIDN'T work very well. Kevin moped inside his cubicle. He could see around the entire room, so he mostly kept his face turned away from the rest of the room so he wouldn't spread his mopey vibes to everyone else.

His cell dinged and he answered Zach's text, saying he would call him during lunch. Then he answered the next call in the queue. When he finished with his caller, he wrote up notes on the call, hoping he didn't sound as down as he felt.

"What's wrong?" Dort asked from the next cubicle as she hung up her phone. "You look as low as a gopher hole."

"Nothing important, I guess. Man troubles, sort of." He went to pick up another call, but the queue was empty, so he took a breather.

"Tell me about it." Dort had been married at least three times. That much Kevin had gleaned from her stories. To hear her describe them, she picked the three biggest losers in the state. "You know what I keep telling you: just use them for sex and get you a dog for company." Her phone rang and she picked it up. Kevin wondered if she was right and if he wouldn't be better off without a guy in his life. He had good friends and was young enough that he could get sex if he wanted it, and the apartment he'd found would allow him a small dog or a cat, so he could have some company. Kevin knew he was being silly, but he could avoid all this drama.

"Go on to lunch," Tom, his supervisor, said, and Kevin signed himself out of the phone system. He left the area and walked down the long hallway through the development support areas and then continued to the cafeteria. The building had been built over the course of twenty years, so there was very little cohesive design in the place, and in the summer with the air-conditioning on, like now, parts of the building baked while others froze. He made it through the deep freeze portion and into the cafeteria.

He got in line and called Zach. "What's going on?"

"Nothing here. Just working. How about you?"

"Same." He sighed. "Angus and I had a fight. At least I guess it was a fight. It was really weird."

"Why?" Zach asked.

"Because Ken showed up as we were leaving the club. He made a scenelet, I guess, and said he wanted me back."

"I hope you sent the jerk packing."

"I told him he left me and that I wasn't going to take him back. Angus stood up for me when I started to cough, and then we went to his place. He helped me into bed but then he spent the night on the sofa. He thinks I need to think about what I want, but I'm starting to believe that he's getting tired of me and is using this as an excuse to step away."

"So when was the fight?"

"This morning." Kevin paused and placed his order, then paid for his sandwich. "I don't know what to do. I really like him, and he's so good to me—better than Ken ever was. Most of the time he listens to me, and he's been so wonderful since my apartment burned down." He stepped out of the way so he could talk without half the office listening in.

"So why did you fight? Just tell him that things are over between you and Ken and that you want to be with him."

"But what if he's just using this as an excuse to get away?"

"What if he isn't?" Zach countered. "Ken shows up out of the blue. He's your ex, and Angus knows you had feelings for him. Angus isn't a mind reader. And most people can't just turn off their feelings. So maybe he's scared you'll go back to Ken."

"Hold on," Kevin said as he took the tray with his food and carried it to a table. He sat down and picked up his phone again. "Sorry."

"Think about it. If one of his exes suddenly showed up, you'd be on the phone to me, crying because you were afraid that Angus was going to go back to… Liam, or whatever his name was. Give the guy a little reassurance and show him that you care. Sometimes you boys are so obtuse."

"You're six months older than me," Kevin groused.

"Fine. But if you care about him, then show it. Things aren't that hard if you're willing to put yourself out there a little and take a chance."

"But what if he's just using this as an excuse?"

"Then you'll know and can move on. What part of take a chance don't you understand?" Zach paused, and Kevin wondered what he was doing. "Do something. Take action. You'll feel better, and then you'll have answers to all the questions you're stewing over." Kevin heard more rustling. "I have to get back to work, but I'll talk to you later."

"Thanks," Kevin said and hung up, put his phone in his pocket, and then began eating his lunch.

When he was done, he returned to his work area and signed back into the phone system. He felt a little better, even if he still didn't know what he was going to do.

ONCE HE was done with work, Kevin got into his car and wondered where he should go. Since the fire, he'd gone to Angus's. But now he didn't know what to do and called Zach, who told him to come to his place. Kevin hurried to Angus's and used the key he'd given him to go inside. He tried not to think too much about where he was or the things he and Angus had done there. He grabbed a change of clothes and then locked up and left again.

As he headed for his car, a man ran across the street about two houses away. Kevin tensed and ran the rest of the way, started his car, and pulled away as fast as he could. He turned on the Bluetooth phone system in the car and told it to call Angus. "Please answer."

"Kevin, I'm on my way back from a call," Angus said when he answered. It was noisy in the background.

"I saw him. He was on the street where your house is. I just saw him." Kevin pulled to a stop at the first light and then made the turn so he could get over to the freeway. "I don't know if he's following me or not, but I saw him and he knows where I was staying and where your house is."

"I'll call Antonio."

"I'm going to Zach's. I didn't want to be at the house alone…." He left off the rest of his thought. It wasn't any use going into it now. "It was a good thing, because I don't know what he's planning, and…." The truth was he was terrified that Angus's house was going to be next.

"Okay. When you get there, call Bull. Tell him what's happening. He can help keep you safe. I'll call the police and see if they can get someone over to the house. I have to go because we just got back and there's another call. So we're doing a fast turnaround." Angus already sounded tired.

"When can I see you?"

"I should be off duty on Wednesday."

"Okay," Kevin said and turned onto the freeway on-ramp, going as fast as he dared. "But call me with what you find out." Kevin hung up and continued driving. He called Zach back and told him what had happened.

"Bull is on his way to the club. Let me call him so he can swing by Angus's just in case." Zach hung up, and Kevin did nothing but worry until he pulled into Zach's driveway and his friend came out to meet him.

"Bull says everything is fine at Angus's house. There was no sign of anyone, and he wandered around to make sure it looked okay from the outside. He said that as he was leaving the police showed up, so it's getting plenty of attention."

"That's good. I spoke to Angus, and he said that he was going to call them. He also said that he won't be off shift until Wednesday."

"Then you can stay here if you want."

"Hopefully I can get into my new apartment soon." He wanted to have his own place and start building his own life once more. He needed some independence again. Maybe then he wouldn't be so scared and feel so needy all the time. "They said it needed to be cleaned and that they would call me when it was ready. I have the money from the insurance company for what I lost in the fire, so I can get furniture and stuff, but I didn't want to buy anything until I was settled."

Zach led Kevin inside the house. "I cleaned up the guest room for you, and Bull will be gone until after the club closes."

"Are you going to go in?"

"No. Bull says I'm going too much and that he can't get his work done when I'm there because I'm too distracting." Zach rolled his eyes. "It seems I've still got the power to make him forget himself." He grinned evilly. "But I try to use it only for good."

"Yeah. I've seen how you wrap that man around your little finger. And he loves you more than life itself." Kevin sat on the sofa. "Do you know how hard it is to watch that all the time? I thought I'd found my prince, and then Ken goes off and leaves me for some job that was so important that he jumps at the chance to come back and expects everything to be exactly as he left it. Like I'm some toy he can play with and put away until he wants it again."

"You don't sound like someone who's over the guy," Zach said as he left for the kitchen.

Kevin turned to face that general direction. "I'm so over him I could scream. It just pisses me off, is all."

"Why?" Zach asked, the refrigerator closing with a rattle and bang. Then Zach came back in with two Cokes and handed one to him. "Why do you care? If Ken is history and you have someone else who is interested and, quite frankly, seems like a much better man than Ken ever was? Even if I give him grief sometimes. He's a stand-up guy."

"You thought Ken was too," Kevin countered. He remembered when all the guys had loved Ken and thought he was the cat's meow, especially the way he'd helped when Tristan was kidnapped.

"What Ken was or wasn't isn't the issue." Zach sipped from his can. "You need to figure things out. Stop trying to determine what everyone else wants or what their opinion is. It doesn't matter what I think of Ken or Angus. The four of us will always be friends, and even if you were to date Bozo the Clown, you know it wouldn't matter. So as far as boyfriends go, choose Ken, Angus, or no one at all. We just want you to be happy."

"Thanks," Kevin said, batting his eyelashes. "You make me sound like a distressed princess."

"Maybe. But think about it. Are you really still in love with Ken? Or is your pride still smarting because he left?"

Kevin swallowed and then opened his soda. He needed something to give him a chance to think. "I'm over him. Even if I wasn't—and I am—I'm not going to go back to a guy who thinks so little of me and my feelings." It made Kevin angry just thinking about it. "I'm not interested in him other than to smack him upside the head and tell him to get lost."

"Then why didn't you tell Ken that last night? That's all you would have had to do, and then Angus would have known that Ken isn't a threat and he wouldn't be distancing himself. I mean, Angus is hot—not as hot as Bull, but he's hot—and I might have made a play for him if I didn't have the best guy on earth."

"One who scares everyone he sees," Kevin teased. Bull was the most intimidating guy he knew. He still intimidated Kevin sometimes, especially when he crossed his arms over his chest and gave him that stare that Kevin swore could turn people to stone if Bull wanted.

"Maybe he does, but it's part of who he is. Doesn't work on me." Zach grinned. "Anyway, let's get back to you. Do you really care about Angus?"

Kevin sighed. "Yes."

"Then like I told you before: tell him or show him. And don't be a wiener about it." Zach jumped up off the sofa and raced back into the kitchen.

"What are you doing?"

"Getting something to eat," Zach called. "We're going to need food if we're going to plan just how you're going to win Angus back."

"I never lost him."

"Maybe. But this was your first real fight, and let me tell you, make-up sex is the best kind, so you have to get his attention. Show him that you care. Words only go so far. Lord knows Bull uses very few of them. Men like him and Angus are guys of action. It's what they understand. Sometimes they're a little dense, but they always understand that. And the way to a man's heart is through his stomach."

Kevin nodded and then lowered his head. "Mrs. V used to handle that part for me. She baked stuff for me to take to the firehouse after the first fire in the building." Kevin sighed. "I miss her."

Zach nodded. "Do you know what happened to her? I mean, after…."

"I understand. She didn't have any family, so they cremated her. I requested the ashes, and I thought I'd spread them on the river or something to say good-bye. They haven't released them yet because they have to wait so long after the death announcement for some long-lost relative who might show up." Kevin wiped his eyes with the back of his hand. "I hate that she's gone. Mrs. V was so much fun to talk with, and she'd seen so much. She met Ken once and hated him on sight, said he was too full of himself, and I guess she was right."

Zach sat still and sipped from his can, listening. It was what Kevin needed so badly right now.

"If she were here, she'd be down in her apartment, whipping up a batch of baklava that she'd say was guaranteed to wrap any man around my finger. But she's not and it's my fault." Kevin managed to set the can on the coffee table before falling to pieces. "Everything is my fault— losing Mrs. V and pushing Angus away. I should have told Ken to fuck off right there, but I was in shock and I think part of me loved that he wanted me back. I mean, he left me, but he was crawling back to me, Kevin Foster, the guy everyone leaves."

"Sweetheart," Zach said softly and then hugged him as Kevin began to cough his brains out. "It wasn't your fault that Mrs. V died. It was a psychotic arsonist."

"But he's after me and he got her," Kevin breathed once the coughing subsided.

"It's all in his head, and this guilt is all in yours. No one else thinks that but you." Zach raised his chin so they could see each other. "Have I ever lied to you about anything?"

Kevin shook his head.

"Then why would I lie now?" Zach pulled him into a hug once again. "Part of this whole fight with Angus is that you've been through so much already."

"What do you mean?"

"The fires, the guy hanging around. It's too much. You need some time to rest and think. Decide what you want," Zach said.

"Now you sound like Angus. I know what I want, but no one seems to believe me." Kevin wiped his eyes.

"Okay. Then rest for a while, and after that we'll do something in Mrs. V's honor. We'll make something and take it over to the station. The way to a man's heart is through his stomach, and the way to get a man's attention and keep it is to feed everyone he knows. Then not only do you get his attention, but all his friends like you too."

"Okay." Kevin sat back on the sofa, and Zach turned on the television. They watched *Storage Wars* for a while, and Kevin finished his soda. "I hate being this tired all the time," he whispered.

Zach moved to the chair. "Lie down if you want, and I'll get you a blanket and pillow." He was back up and out of the room like a shot. When he came back, he got Kevin settled on the sofa, and Kevin had to admit he was comfortable. Soon he was having dreams about buying jet skis inside storage lockers. It was weird and his mind didn't seem to settle.

When he woke, Zach had left the room and the most heavenly smell drifted in from the kitchen. Kevin pushed back the blanket and followed his nose to where Zach was pulling cake layers out of the oven. "This is Bull's favorite. His mother gave me the recipe, and it's amazing. I thought we could let them cool and then tomorrow you could take Angus a cake. Feed the man and he'll never forget you."

"I hope you're right," Kevin said, pulling out one of the stools. "Do you want my help frosting it?"

"The layers have to cool first, so we'll frost it tomorrow and then you can take it to him." Zach set the layers on racks. "Are you feeling better?"

"A little. Every day the urge to cough my lungs out on a constant basis is a little less, and I'm not using the inhaler much." He leaned on the counter.

"Don't worry yourself over Angus. He's working, and he did take your call, right?"

"Yeah. He sounded concerned."

"See? He does care. So don't mope about it, just talk to him when you can." Zach's phone rang and so did Kevin's. "Tristan."

"Jeremy," Kevin said before answering it.

"We're going out tomorrow night," Jeremy said. "I just got really good news. I'm getting a better position and a raise. So we need to celebrate. We don't have to stay out late because we all have to work, but I feel like dancing."

"What about Spook? Don't you want to celebrate with him?" Kevin snickered.

"I plan to do a lot of celebrating with him just as soon as he gets home."

"Then are you sure you're going to want to dance?" Kevin teased. More than once after his and Spook's "celebrations," Jeremy had difficulty walking straight. Come to think of it, each of his friends had had that problem at one time or another. Everyone except him. "And we're all going. Tristan is telling Zach right now."

"I know. I'm with him." He looked over at Zach, who met his gaze and nodded. Kevin nodded back. He had to take it easy, but he really wanted to go dancing, so he agreed, and Jeremy whooped a little.

"We're meeting at seven. We'll have a little dinner and then go dancing. It's a Tuesday, so the place won't be super busy, but that's good. It'll still be fun. It isn't like any of us are there to pick up guys or anything."

"Sure," Kevin agreed. "Hey, there's this charity that Angus works with and they were really helpful, so maybe we can plan a benefit at the club or something for them."

"Fabulous. I'm always up for planning a party."

The cake was a good idea, but helping an organization that Angus thought highly of was an even better way to show how much he cared.

"Then bring your ideas and I'll see you tomorrow," Kevin said. Jeremy's excitement was catching, and by the time Kevin hung up, the last of his doldrums seemed to have passed. When Zach hung up too, Kevin told him about his idea.

"Awesome," Zach said. "I'll talk to Bull as soon as he gets home, and we'll see about a date." He grinned, and they went back into the living room. Zach got a notepad, and they began tossing around ideas to both attract attention and get people willing to fork over a high cover charge and pack the club for a good cause.

"I heard about a fire company in Carlisle that had a dinner where the firemen served in nothing but their fire pants. Apparently it was a huge success," Zach said. "We could see if Angus has friends who are willing to do that."

"I remember. Chicken and Beefcake," Kevin grinned. "But I don't think so. It's been done, and we need something original. I'd ask Angus, but…." Kevin sighed. "I thought all this angsty crap would be over once I left high school. This is ridiculous. He and I are adults, and we should be able to just talk about things."

"You will once he's no longer on shift. I bet he wants the same things you do. Just listen to what he has to say this time rather than getting all wound up in all those old feelings that seeing Ken stirred up." Zach lightly punched him in the arm. "Now, let's focus on this. Remember this is part of that plan. You're showing support for something he cares out."

"I know…." Kevin put his mind back on the task at hand. "I've got nothing at all. We could do strippers, but that's a regular thing and not everyone goes in for that. It has to be special to grab attention."

"Hmmm." Zach's thoughtfulness turned to a slight smile and then morphed into a huge grin. "I got it: a kilt party. I bet Angus has one, and…." Zach put his hand over his face. "We could have a 'man in kilts' auction to help raise money. The winners get to see exactly what the guys wear under their kilts." Zach began to blush. "Privately, of course."

"You are so bad, and that's a great idea." Kevin leaned back. "God, I hate being tired all the damn time." Not even something as exciting as the image of Angus in a kilt was enough to raise his energy level. His heart beat faster at the idea, most definitely, but that led to quicker breathing and the fear that he was going to start coughing again. How fucking sexy was that? Not.

"Let me heat us up some dinner. I made some ravioli the other day that I can reheat." Zach bounded up off the sofa as the door from the garage opened and Bull came inside. He greeted Zach as though he hadn't seen him in days, and Kevin smiled and turned away to give them some privacy. "I'm just heating up dinner," Zach said to Bull, and then Kevin heard him whisper that he and Angus had had a disagreement.

"I'm sure it will be okay," Bull said as he came in the room. "The last time I saw you together, Angus couldn't keep his eyes off you. That says a lot."

"Thanks, Bull," Kevin said softly. "Ken showed up last night, and I didn't handle things very well."

"People have disagreements. It happens. Zach and I do. But we talk them through and don't let them fester."

"I know. But he was angry and hurt. I'm over Ken, but I let him get me all flustered, and Angus thinks I have all this thinking to do, but I don't."

"Hey. You've been through a lot lately, more than you should have, and it's a lot to deal with. So give yourself a break, and I'm sure Angus will too."

"I thought you had to work," Zach said once he got the microwave going with its soft hum.

"Harry told me to go home while it was slow." Bull put the footrest up on his recliner and turned on the television. "God, I'm beat. Between making repairs and getting the club open again, the investigation into the guy that got trampled, and now the extra security to try to keep it from happening again, I'm exhausted."

Kevin had never seen Bull seem defeated or look this tired. The guy was as stalwart as they came, a tower of strength.

Zach brought Bull a plate and handed Kevin one too. He ate a little, but he wasn't very hungry, even with the lingering scent of chocolate cake in the air. Still, he ate what Zach gave him and felt better once he was done. He was still fatigued, though, and excused himself. Zach got him settled in the guest room, and Kevin cleaned up and turned in early, not only because he was tired, but to give Zach and Bull some time alone.

From the muffled sounds he heard coming from the other room a little while later, he knew they'd taken advantage. But the happiness that seemed to spread through the house just because they were making love only made Kevin a little jealous and regretful. He rolled over and did his best to put it out of his mind, but Angus kept returning to his thoughts and his dreams.

CHAPTER EIGHT

"Why have you been acting like a bear with a thorn in its paw?" Clark asked Angus on Tuesday morning. "Did the guy you've been seeing dump you or something?" He held up his hands. "I'm being nice here, so I don't want no details."

"I don't know. His ex showed up, and it was pretty much a mess."

"What? Did he dump you to go off with him or something?"

"No. But I could tell he still had feelings for the guy."

Clark rolled his eyes. "So you did the gentlemanly thing and backed off to give him time to think about what he wanted."

"Yeah. He had to decide," Angus said, and Clark looked like he was about to smack him hard.

"I'm not an expert, but if I had a cute girl that had me as starry-eyed as you've been for the last few weeks, and her ex showed up, I'd have stood between them and fought for her so she'd know I was serious. I wouldn't have backed away. You care about this guy, right?"

"Yeah. Of course I do," Angus growled with more force than he intended.

"Then instead of giving him time to think about things and let the other guy get his foot in the door, you sweep him off his feet so he's only thinking about you and can't remember this ex's name." Clark looked at him as though he were completely stupid.

"I'm not a Neanderthal," Angus said. Clark shook his head and went back to directing the guys to clean the engine from last night's run. Angus figured he should check his own equipment and make sure it was ready when called upon. He'd cleaned his jacket, pants, and helmet when they'd returned, so he checked air tanks and made sure all were filled and ready for use. It was a solitary job, one he needed at the moment.

Clark poked his head in just as Angus settled down to get started. "It looks like you are the luckiest son of a bitch to walk this earth."

"How so?" Angus asked, but all Clark did was tilt his head toward the front of the station. Angus got up and walked to the doorway, peering out. Kevin stood in front of the large overhead doors talking to Mark, one of the intern/volunteers with firefighter dreams.

Angus knew the second Kevin saw him. He broke into a smile, and Angus walked toward him. "What are you doing here?" Angus said, and Kevin's smile faded to nervous worry.

"Zach and I baked this," he said as Mark stepped away and Angus got closer. "I felt bad and didn't want you to be angry, so…."

Angus sighed and motioned toward the stairs. He followed Kevin up, and Kevin put the cake on the counter. "Make sure you get a piece," he blurted, already heading for the stairs. "I'm sorry I bothered you."

"Kevin," Angus called, but he was already halfway running down the stairs like a frightened rabbit. Angus swore under his breath, hurrying after him. "Kevin, stop."

Kevin stilled at the bottom of the stairs, looking up at Angus, hurt and shame clear in his expression. "I won't bother you anymore."

"Shit," Angus whispered and hurried down the stairs. He grabbed Kevin's hand and tugged him back up the stairs. There was very little privacy in a firehouse. If you were scheduled to stay there, you slept in the dorm, one room for everyone. Thankfully it was empty at the moment. "I'm not mad at you, just surprised, and that you brought me a cake was so sweet."

"I'm sorry about Sunday."

"Hey. That wasn't your fault. It was mine letting my stupid insecurities run away with me. I'm the one who doesn't do relationships, and I was getting scared. I wanted you to be sure about what you wanted."

"I don't want Ken. He showed me how little I meant to him when he left me."

"But can you forgive him?" In the back of his mind, Angus knew he was testing Kevin. This was something he had to know.

"Yeah, I guess I forgive him, but that doesn't mean I want to get back with him." Kevin paced the small open area at the one end of the room. "And next time you need to, ask shit, okay? We both can do better. Talking and listening are skills Ken and I never particularly mastered. I guess if we had, I'd be with him, and you'd be out in the cold and not getting any of this." Kevin flashed him a quick view of his backside, and Angus laughed.

"Yeah." Angus smiled and tugged Kevin to him. "We need to talk to each other more."

"What we need to do is listen to each other. Ken and I never did. He wasn't happy here. I realized that after he left, but I didn't want to see it at the time because I thought he was the living end. He wasn't, of course, and if I'd listened to what he was saying, maybe things wouldn't have come as such a surprise. But you have to listen too. I told you I didn't want Ken, but you just went on and assumed that I had some grand decision to make and cut me out."

"I suppose."

Kevin smacked him on the chest and then shook his hand. "What are you made of, rocks?" Then he giggled. "I like that you're all hard everywhere, and I like how you feel when we're together." Kevin stood on his tiptoes. "I wish we could be together right now. I could pull your big cock out of your pants and you could fuck me right now."

Angus groaned as his cock swelled down his leg. "I can't."

"I know. And I have to go to work. But that will give you something to think about." Kevin backed away with a grin. "And something to look forward to."

"You're a tease."

"I know. That was the point. Now you have things to do, I'm sure, and I have to get to work."

Angus grabbed Kevin and pulled him right up to his chest. "Just wait till I get you alone and strip you naked. I'll suck you and then eat that pretty little ass of yours until you can't see straight. Then, when you beg me for it loud enough, I'll slide inside you." Angus sucked on Kevin's ear. "And ride your tight ass until you scream at the top of your lungs." Kevin quivered like a leaf in his arms. "See, two can play that game."

"Bastard."

"I'll see you tomorrow." Angus reluctantly released him. "I have to get back to work, and I suspect your boss isn't going to be happy if you're late."

"He isn't going to happy if I show up with an obscene boner on display, either." Kevin backed away, and Angus led him out through the station. "I'll see you tomorrow."

"I'll call you when I know I'm through for the day," Angus said, trying to keep his anticipation to a minimum and failing. "What are you doing tonight?"

"I'm feeling better, so the guys are taking me out to the club. We're going to plan the benefit for Janice's Homeless Aid." Kevin looked around. "We're thinking of having a kilt party, and I was hoping you'd come.... That is, if you have one. Not that I'm saying that because you're Scottish you have to have one.... Am I being insensitive?" Kevin colored instantly.

"Of course I have one, and I'll come."

"But no one sees what's under it but me," Kevin said seriously. "And you will not be part of the auction."

Angus's curiosity was piqued, but he needed to get back to work. "You'll have to fill me in on that." As much as he wanted to know, he couldn't spend any more time talking to Kevin. The equipment had to be ready in case they got a call. "I'll call when I can." He wanted to lean in and kiss Kevin within an inch of his life, but not with every guy in the station watching them. So instead he smiled and walked inside, turning to make sure Kevin got in his car and drove away. Then he hurried back to the equipment room and began checking all the breathing equipment.

Thankfully the station was quiet and he was able to clean and prep everything, including all the secondary equipment.

"So I take it by your smile that things are better," Clark said when Angus stepped out, wringing with sweat. On days like this with the doors open and the guys washing and cleaning, the humidity went through the roof.

"Yeah. We're talking again."

"You don't sound convinced."

Angus sighed. "How did you know your wife was the one? That you really wanted to spend the rest of your life with her?"

Clark shook his head in that way he had. "Look, I was raised Catholic—no sex before marriage or my mother would have cut it off. She said it so many times that damn if I didn't believe her. That woman is a menace. I love her… but she's scary. So when I met Michelle, I fell for her and figured my balls were going to fall off, either that or my hand, so when we got serious, I asked, she said yes, and I instantly won the lottery because she's amazing. And I dodged a bullet the size of Pittsburgh. She understands about my work and schedule, never complains, is always there, and I love her more now than I did the day I married her."

"So blind luck," Angus supplied.

"Pretty much. There wasn't some grand plan. We were in love, and I was in major lust and I let my dick do the thinking, and for once it was the smart head. Go figure."

"You're no help," Angus said.

"Kid, I've been around the block, and after a decade together and three kids, I know more than I did then. I got lucky. She really loves me." He walked in the direction of the truck they were cleaning, and Angus followed, absently picking up a cloth to help. "If you want my opinion, you've known this guy, what, for two weeks or so and you're wondering if he's the one?" Clark scowled at him. "At least date, get to know the guy. You kids just jump into bed and want to fuck first and then see what happens. I got to know Michelle before we jumped into bed."

"I guess, but…." Angus smiled. "I get to jump into bed and have great sex. What's wrong with that?"

"Do you know what food he likes? What his favorite movie is? Maybe you could go to the department store and actually pick out a shirt or a pair of pants he likes?" Clark raised his eyebrows, and Angus had to admit he didn't know any of that stuff. "Everything is instant, and you want an instant relationship with instant compatibility, no fights, and love that goes on forever."

Angus realized the entire station was listening in on their conversation, but Clark had a good point. "Don't worry so much."

"Or bed-hop so much." Clark had gotten on his soapbox and had warmed up to his theme. "There are dating sites, speed dating, clubs, bars, and God knows what else, and all of it to find Mr. or Ms. One-Night Stand. Then you wonder why you're all miserable and alone." Clark shook his head once again and then looked around. "Get back to work," he bellowed. "This truck isn't going to clean itself."

They all scurried to get back on task, and Angus chuckled. "I see your point."

"It's like a damn buffet, and you eat your fill but wonder why the food doesn't taste very good." He turned and went back to work.

Angus took a few seconds to pull out his phone and ask Kevin on a date for Thursday night after work. They'd been out once, but it should be something they did regularly. He told Kevin to pick a movie he'd like to see. At least then he'd know the kind of movies he liked—two birds with one stone. *I'll pick you up on the bike, and we can ride if you like.* He shoved his phone back in his pocket and went back to work.

By the time he was ready for a break, Angus went upstairs to find the cake nearly gone. That served him right for not putting his name on it. Not that he'd have been selfish, but it would have been nice to have had a piece before everyone else in the station. "Did you get some?" Angus asked Clark when he came up. Angus ended up cutting two small pieces from what was left and handed the other slice over.

"They're worse than vultures around here," Clark said with his mouth full.

Angus laughed and took his first bite, moaning softly. If food were sex, then this was wild monkey love. He grinned and took another bite as the station alarm sounded. Angus took one more bite and set his plate aside, then slid down the pole and jumped into his gear. Most people thought the pole was quicker to get down, but many times it was because the stairs would become dangerous if everyone tried to take them all at once. Angus jumped into the engine, and as soon as everyone was onboard, he pulled out of the station and headed to the call.

HE BACKED the engine into the station a couple hours later, grateful that the call turned out to be a false alarm for the most part. The fire department was called for nearly every reason, including ambulance and other emergency calls, so some calls had little directly to do with them. But they were the central dispatch, so they always went and sometimes stood around waiting to be told they weren't needed.

"At least our fire starter has been quiet. I hope to hell he's moved on," Mark said.

Clark lightly smacked him on the top of the head. "What you hope is that he's been caught and is in jail. Never wish our problems off on someone else, because the reverse can always happen."

Mark rubbed his head and glowered at Clark. "You can't do that," Mark said.

"Yeah, I know. But you'll remember the lesson."

Angus stepped away and let the two of them hash things out. He had to agree with Mark that he hoped 'quiet' meant 'gone,' but he wasn't counting on it. Whatever happened, when it did, was sure to be big and destructive. The arsonist was building up his need like a junkie, and the fix required got higher and higher as the days passed.

Angus used the few minutes he had to respond to Kevin's texts that he was looking forward to seeing him too, and *Woman in Gold* was a fine movie choice. He'd expected an action flick, but something cerebral was fine with Angus too.

"Angus," the captain called down the stairs. "I'm supposed to remind you it's your turn to cook."

He groaned and began climbing the stairs. He usually tried to prep something in advance so all he had to do was heat it up, but he'd forgotten. When he got to the kitchen, he found Randy Trump, one of the other firefighters, who'd been there about a decade longer than Angus, getting things ready. "You're a lifesaver."

"Since you were out on a call, I started sloppy joes. They can eat those as they're hungry and when they aren't busy with other things." Randy loved to cook and did a great job.

"That's awesome." Angus got to work, and soon they had food hot and ready. It wasn't gourmet, but it was filling, and the scent called the other guys to dinner.

One by one they came in, filled plates, and wandered away. Some sat in the television area to watch the news as they ate, while others took the time to be by themselves. On television, fire stations always ate together like some huge family of brothers, but Angus had found that varied depending on the guys. Mark got his plate and watched Clark, then headed in the opposite direction. They'd work it out eventually, but in Angus's opinion, Clark was in the wrong on this one, and if Mark chose to make an issue of it, Angus would have to tell the captain what he'd seen.

"I hope it stays quiet. We've been run ragged for days," Randy said as he sat down across from Angus. "Tell your… friend that the cake was delicious and thank him for bringing it." The hesitation was a reminder that while Angus was pretty open about who he was, not all of the men were comfortable with it. The central part of Pennsylvania was conservative, but Angus never thought them unaccepting, just not quite sure how to take gay people in their midst. It continued to surprise him how men like Randy lived their lives, having never traveled more than a hundred or so miles from where they were born, even in this day. Randy knew that Kevin was more than Angus's friend, but he'd made the effort and that was enough.

"I will. He'll be thrilled to know that everyone liked it."

Mark strolled in for seconds and helped himself to sloppy joes. "If you keep seeing Kevin, will he keep bringing in food? 'Cause if he does, you should marry him. Heck, I'd consider marrying him."

"I think Laura would have something to say about that." Mark was marrying his high school girlfriend in a year. Apparently they had been dating for nearly five years, and he had finally asked her to marry him a few months ago.

"Yeah, I suppose she'd never understand that." Mark laughed nervously, and Angus wondered if there was more to his comment.

"Actually, Laura is the smart one of us," Mark said. Angus motioned for him to sit, and Randy got up, leaving the two of them. "I was really shy. I still am, I guess. But not as bad as I used to be. See, in high school I couldn't read very well. The words got all messed up. They still do, but I understand it now."

"You're dyslexic. Wow, I've never seen any sign of it."

"I can handle it now. Anyway, Laura asked me out when we were in the eleventh grade. She said she thought I was cute and that she'd grow old waiting for me to make the move." Mark chuckled, and Angus smiled. "After a while I think she figured out I couldn't read well, but she never said nothing. She waited until I told her. I'd been faking it a long time with everyone, even my mom. I figured she'd leave me when she found out I was a dummy, but she got me help."

"Why are you telling me this? Not that it isn't a great story, and Laura has to be an amazing person, but I thought that already."

"I heard you talking to Clark." He made a face, and Angus knew the feud wasn't over. "He talks like he knows everything, but you wanted to know how he knew if his wife was the one." Mark looked down at the table, and Angus waited for him to continue. "I think what Clark said was so full of crap. I think you know you've met the right person when you can tell them your greatest fear, the one you'd never tell anyone, and they love you more not in spite of it, but because of it. Then that's the person you should be with." Mark smiled quickly, nodded, then stood up and left the table.

Angus watched him go and then turned back to his meal, finishing the last of his sloppy joe. The name was appropriate—he had to be careful not to end up with it all over his shirt. He could remember his mother telling him he wore more of his food than he ate. "I'm sorry," he whispered to the memory, keeping still for a few seconds. He didn't realize he was still holding the bun for a minute. Angus ate his last bite and took care of his dishes. Then he thanked Randy for all his help and went in search of something to do.

He hadn't expected the discussion of relationships he'd started to circle around and then knock at a door deep inside that he'd kept locked and thought hidden, even from himself, for a very long time. But now he stood right in front of it, black and ominous. He was afraid to even touch the knob for fear it would burn him.

"Angus," Mark called as he approached. "I was hoping you'd show me how to maintain the breathing equipment. That is, if you have a few minutes."

"Sure," Angus said, relieved that he had something to do to keep his mind off his immediate problems. "Let's go down and I can run you through the process." Angus checked the clock on the wall—just after eight—and wondered what Kevin was doing right now. Then he blinked to bring himself out of his daydream and led Mark down the stairs.

"Everyone relies on this equipment during a fire to breathe, so it has to be kept in top condition. Valves are checked and all the hoses must be free of wear of any sort. If not, then they're changed. We use compressed air, not oxygen, in the tanks. Otherwise they could become an accelerant in a fire." Angus walked Mark through the equipment and its maintenance and care. He was just about to call it done for the day when the alarm went off. As soon as he heard the address, Angus went completely cold for a few seconds, then his professionalism kicked in and he jumped into his gear, raced to the engine, and drove to the destination he knew all too well.

CHAPTER NINE

KEVIN WAS having a ball. The club was rocking even if it wasn't super busy. The guys who were there were all having an incredible time. "I can get into my new apartment on Friday," he told Zach when he saw the e-mail from his new landlord saying that everything was good to go. Not that he had anything to move into the place, but at least he'd have a home to call his own once again, and he could furnish it as he went.

"When you buy furniture, we'll help you move it all in," Jeremy said, looking around the table. "So I take it that the benefit-planning portion of the evening is over."

"Yeah." Kevin closed the notebook he'd brought along. "I have lots of ideas that Angus and I can run past Janice and see what she thinks."

"The kilt-party idea is awesome," Tristan said as his gaze traveled over to the office door, where Harry was just coming out onto the club floor. "I bet Harry would look good in a kilt. He has great legs."

"So does Bull," Zach said.

"Lowell would never wear a kilt—too conspicuous—but if we're talking about our boyfriends' legs, then Lowell's are pretty awesome." Of course he looked over to where Spook stood off to the side watching the crowd. Kevin sighed and refrained from saying anything out loud. Angus's legs had them all beat; that he was pretty sure of. He was also the only one whose boyfriend wasn't there.

"I have a few questions for Bull about the benefit," Kevin said, slipping out of his seat and walking carefully around the dance floor to where Bull stood talking with Harry.

"Hey, Kevin," Bull said without pulling his attention off the floor.

"I was wondering if I could talk to you about a benefit I want to hold here at the club." He followed Bull's gaze and waited.

"Sure. Go on into the office. I'll be there as soon as I can," Bull explained, and Kevin used the access code to unlock the door and head inside. The door closed behind him, and he went down the short hallway toward the office. As he approached the door, it opened and a man came out. Kevin didn't recognize him until he turned at just the right angle.

"What are you doing here?" Kevin asked as the arsonist turned toward the back door to get away. The scent of petroleum reached Kevin's nose.

"I wouldn't suggest that," the arsonist said as he grinned and pointed inside the office. "I've already laced the room with gasoline. All I have to do is light a match and it goes up in a whirl of dancing flame."

Jesus, the guy thinks he's a poet or something. "What do you want?"

"You, Hero Boy. My nemesis. I want you to see that I'm better than you, and that I get what I want. Your apartment was gorgeous: flames reaching for the sky, shooting out of windows, and the building collapse was spectacular." The guy was practically salivating, and Kevin couldn't miss the prominent bulge in his pants. God, he was sick.

"You hurt people," Kevin said quietly.

"I never meant to. All I wanted was to build a spectacular fire, bigger and higher than before." He shook and trembled with excitement. Kevin could almost feel it. The guy was getting off on what he'd done and what he thought he was going to do. "I just wanted to see my work on the news, to be able to watch it over and over again."

Chills went up Kevin's spine, and he wondered how in the hell he was going to get out of this. "What do you want with me? I never did anything to you," Kevin said as gently as he could, wishing he had a baseball bat to knock the guy's head in. "People are going to be coming back here soon." The gasoline aroma was getting stronger, starting to burn his nose.

He shrugged and smiled. "Let them. As soon as that door opens again, I'll light the office and the air flow will carry the flames out to the club like a flamethrower. It'll be glorious, a pyre worthy of a master of fire."

"Okay," Kevin said, worried Bull was going to come in at any time. "What do you want?"

"I want you to see my work up close and personal. You stopped me here once, but not a second time." He smiled and pulled a lighter out of his pocket, his eyes wild and his gaze darting around. "If the door stays closed, there will be time for everyone in the club to get out. But if it opens, whoosh!" He waved his arms over his head, and when he did, the lighter dropped to the floor. Kevin knew it was now or never so he rushed him, knocking the man to the ground. He didn't get up right away, and Kevin grabbed the lighter and ran for the door, burst through it, and slammed it behind him. He knew he might have just seconds.

"Bull, get everyone out," Kevin said as he yanked on his arm. "He's in the back and it's doused with gasoline." He was surprised he didn't cough. "The arsonist—he's going to set the club on fire." Bull raced over and pulled the newly installed fire alarm behind the bar. Lights flashed and an alarm sounded. The music in the club died instantly, and people hurried toward the doors. Additional alarms sounded as secondary door alarms went off, but no one paid attention. The overlapping sound was nearly deafening.

"Everyone out! Go to the nearest exit. That includes the front doors as well as all emergency exits. Don't run, but move quickly," Bull boomed over the din.

The club emptied of people quickly, and Kevin was about to follow when he saw the office door open. He tried to slam it closed but was too late. For a second the air seemed to get sucked away, and then flame burst through the door. Kevin got knocked to the ground, but he remained conscious. He stooped and hurried to the front door. He made it and looked back to see Bull lying still on the club floor. He hurried back inside and grabbed him by the arms, then started dragging him toward the door.

Flames seemed to be everywhere above him, and the heat intensified by the second. Glass shattered and exploded, then the bar off to the side became a blaze of fire as bottles broke or fell to the floor, adding fuel to the already manic flames.

Slowly he pulled Bull closer to the door. "You gotta wake up, Bull." He kept moving as the smoke built, making him cough and then want to throw up. But he kept going as best he could. He turned and saw light for a few seconds, but then it was gone. Kevin hoped he was going in the right direction. The fire was less intense over there, so he hoped like hell it was the way out.

Someone in a firefighter suit and mask pulled him away. Kevin pointed, and the figure grabbed Bull and together they got him moving. The firefighter pointed toward the front, and Kevin understood that he needed to get out. Bull was in good hands, and they were near the door. He got to the opening and stepped out as a crash sounded behind him.

He turned in time to see part of the ceiling fall. Kevin was about to rush inside when he was grabbed around the waist and moved farther away. Kevin saw two other firefighters race into the inferno. He couldn't help wondering if one of them was Angus.

"Can you breathe? Are you okay?" the firefighter asked when he pulled off his mask.

"Yes. I'm okay," Kevin said and then coughed a few times. His lungs settled down, and he took a deep breath of fresh air. "Go do what you need to. I'll be fine."

Tristan, Jeremy, and Zach rushed over, and the four of them shared a group hug.

"Have you seen Bull?" Zach asked.

Kevin looked toward the door as two firefighters came out with Bull between them. Zach broke away and hurried to where they were laying Bull on the ground. By Kevin's count there was still one firefighter unaccounted for, and the thought had him coughing again.

"It's too dangerous," he heard the fire captain say, holding his men back.

Flames leaped high into the air as parts of the club collapsed. Kevin found it hard to breathe as he watched the door. In his heart he knew the man who'd first helped him was Angus. He hadn't been able to see his face, but he just knew it was him. And he knew where he was now.

A figure appeared in the doorway, lumbering out of the wrecked club. He took a few steps and went down onto his knees. Men scrambled to help him as water was poured onto the dying nightclub, steam and smoke rising high into the air.

Zach hurried over to where Kevin waited with Jeremy and Tristan. He threw his arms around Kevin. "You saved Bull. He's going to be okay," Zach sobbed. Kevin wasn't going to argue. He hugged Zach back and let him release the fear and panic that had obviously gripped him.

After a minute Zach calmed slightly and went back to where Bull was being loaded onto a stretcher. Zach got into the ambulance with him. Kevin stayed with the other guys as the outside walls of Bronco's, their home away from home for years, collapsed in on themselves. Kevin held the other two and did his best to keep the tears from falling.

"It's gone," Jeremy said softly.

Harry and Spook joined their group. Soon the only one not being comforted was Kevin. But finally he saw Angus looking around, searching for someone. Kevin realized it was him as soon as Angus looked his way.

"Don't you ever do that again," Angus yelled, but Kevin didn't get to find out what he'd done because his arms were filled with firefighter and then Angus was kissing him, hard, right there in front of everyone. "You scared the shit out of me when I saw you in that building," Angus said when he broke away.

"You should have gotten out earlier." Kevin whacked him on the shoulder. "I knew it was you inside the building. I saw the roof collapse and thought you were gone. Then they got Bull out, but…." Kevin closed his eyes. "Fuck, I'm not going to cry like a baby."

"I'm fine," Angus said.

"I know that. But I'm angry with you." Kevin shook and he wasn't sure why. He only knew he was angry and totally overwhelmed.

"Come with me. They need to check you out and make sure you're okay." Angus gently guided him toward an ambulance.

"I don't need to be checked out. All I need is to know that this is over and that I'm not going to have anything else burned out from under me—the club, my home, my work, now the club again." The trembling got worse. "He was here. I talked to him."

Angus stopped. "You what?" he asked in disbelief.

"He was in the office. He doused it with gasoline and set the place on fire. I hit him and got out. Bull was getting people out of the club when the arsonist opened the door. I think everyone got out but Bull and me. The flames roared through the place, and Bull got knocked to the floor, so I was trying to pull him out." Kevin coughed and reached into his pocket. Fuck… no inhaler.

"I saw. I would have told you it was me, but all I could think about was getting you out of the fire. When I got in there and saw it was you, it was all I could do to stick to my job and not carry you out of there right away."

"I think the arsonist probably died in his own fire, unless he went out through the back exit, but I doubt it. That's past Harry and Bull's office, and that's where he started the fire," Kevin explained and began coughing once again. "That's from last time. I wasn't in there long enough to hurt."

Angus was having none of it. He got Kevin over to an ambulance.

"What happened?" one of the EMTs asked. "Oh, it's you… again. What is it with you and fires?"

Kevin looked into a familiar face. He didn't know his name, but he was the man who helped him at the fire Mrs. V had started. As soon as that thought entered his mind, Kevin put his hands over his face and did his best not to cry. He failed, and the tears came quickly.

"Not a good question," Angus said. "Our fire starter fixated on him after the last incident at the club. So he lost his apartment building as well as a friend, and now another friend's club, so he's been through a lot." Angus gently stroked the back of his neck, and Kevin leaned in, needing the touch. "Captain," Angus called.

Kevin didn't lift his gaze. He just soaked in the comfort as the EMT put an oxygen mask over his mouth. Then he leaned against Angus and breathed.

"Did you find a note?" Angus asked.

"Not this time."

"Kevin here said the arsonist confronted him in the office area and he doesn't think he made it out. We'll need to look for a body when the heat dies." Angus turned to him. "Just nod. Were you and Bull the last people in the club?"

Kevin nodded. "I think so. We were trying to get people out."

"Dang it, kid," the captain said to him. "Have you ever thought of being a firefighter? You sure have the guts for it."

Kevin smiled and shook his head. He was all through with fires for the rest of his life.

"I got a call from the unit at your house. There was no real damage," the captain said.

Kevin pulled off the mask. "Your house?"

"Put the mask back on. Yeah, he set a fire at my house, probably as a diversion. We were there fast and put it right out. Basically my garden shed in the back is a total loss. This was obviously his main target." Angus turned to the captain, and Kevin put his mask back on. "I wonder how he got into the office."

"According to the owners, it uses a numeric code to get in, and he probably watched until he had the code, maybe over the last few days."

Kevin nodded his agreement. "What I really want to know is how he got gasoline inside and past security."

"Gasoline?" Angus said.

"Yeah. I could smell it, and he said he'd coated the office with it." Kevin handed the mask back to the EMT. "I'm okay now. Thank you."

"Are you sure?"

"Yeah. I wish I had my inhaler, but other than that I'll be fine." *As long as people quit burning things down around me.* "Maybe someone helped him," Kevin offered.

"These guys generally work alone. We'll sift through everything and see what we can find once the fire is out. It's too early for speculation. But thank you for all your help." Angus's captain came closer. "I know you've been through a lot lately, but you really were brave and cool under fire. Most people would have run screaming from the building, but you stayed and tried to help."

"I brought Bull partway," Kevin said.

"And that could very well have saved his life. I'm told the roof at the back of the club went first. So you have something to be proud of. I know you lost a lot, especially in the fire that took your apartment."

"And cost my friend her life," Kevin said, sniffling and wishing he had a tissue.

"Yes. I hope all this is over now." The captain turned toward where his team was still pouring water on the pile of rubble and partial walls that had once been Bronco's.

"Is Bull okay?" Kevin asked Angus.

"Yes. They transported him because he was knocked out and we aren't sure if he has a concussion or not, but he was awake and talking when I saw him last. Everyone else seems to have made it out. The police are double-checking, but it looks like the only possible loss of life is the one who started it all."

"He was sick," Kevin whispered.

"How do you mean?"

"He got off on setting fires. Like, it turned him on." Kevin sighed.

"That happens. Sometimes it's hard to understand why they do what they do, but sexual gratification is a powerful motivator." Angus gently stroked his hair. "I hate to say this, but I have to go back to work. I don't really want to leave you alone." Angus strode away, and Kevin saw him talking to his captain, then he returned.

"What's going on?" Kevin asked when Angus began herding him away.

"I'm taking you home. He said we've had enough excitement."

"You don't have to do that for me. I can stay with Jeremy or Tristan."

"You're coming home with me. My shift was over this morning, and the captain said he can get someone to cover for me tonight. We have each other's backs, and I've helped out the other guys plenty. I just have to get back to the station to get my gear."

"I can take you," Kevin said hopefully.

"Meet me there in an hour. I have to help get this wrapped up and make sure the fire marshal and the police have my statement."

"They're going to want mine too," Kevin said and yawned. It had been a long day, so he sat on a tiny patch of grass and waited. He stifled a groan when Antonio came over to him. "Are you going to be civil?"

"I'm always civil," Antonio said. He stood as though he expected Kevin to get up. That wasn't going to happen. Antonio could either sit or stand; Kevin was beyond caring. "I understand you saw him."

"He was in the office area when I went back there. I was planning a benefit, and I wanted to ask Bull some questions, so he said to wait for him there. The same guy who had posed as the gas man before my building burned down was back there, and he was pretty crazy." Kevin told him everything as close to word for word as he could. "I think he may still be in the building, but I'm not sure. The fire captain said they'd check once the fire was out."

"Okay. Is there anything else?"

"This whole thing has ripped my life apart, and I want a chance to put it back together." A new apartment, an opportunity to lay Mrs. V to rest, time to take a chance on Angus and see what happened, maybe get a chance to see him in a kilt and find out just how little was under it. "I'm tired and I've been through a lot." Kevin had cried enough, and he wasn't going to do it again. "Angus said a fire was set at his house as a decoy or something. Apparently his shed is gone, but the house is okay. I just hope it's over."

"We'll check once we can get in what's left of the building."

"I hope he's in there, and I hope he's fried completely," Kevin said acidly. "And I hope if he is, that it was miserable and that he died painfully, writhing and choking. And I hope now that he is dead that he's in hell and it's even hotter and more miserable than I could ever imagine."

"Not in a forgiving mood?"

"He tried to kill me, and all my friends. He did kill Mrs. V, and that guy who got trampled the first time he set a fire in the club. I think forgiveness is something that's long beyond him. None of us deserved the hell he heaped at all our doorsteps. Bull and Harry didn't deserve to lose their club, and I didn't deserve to lose my home and my friend, so don't try to mention the word forgiveness in the same breath with that asshole. If he's dead, the world is better off," Kevin spat and then coughed. Another reminder of the piece of shit.

"He's not likely to get any sympathy from me," Antonio said, and Kevin nodded. "I understand you were venting and you can do that all you want. But are there any facts you haven't shared with me?"

"I don't think so," Kevin said.

"Okay. Will you call me if you remember anything else?"

Kevin nodded. "You know sometimes you sound like one of those guys on television. Maybe you should try to come up with a different shtick." Antonio grunted at him, and Kevin got to his feet. "Thanks for everything. I know I give you a hard time because of what happened that first time we met, but I appreciate everything you did."

"I honestly didn't do much. I like to think that in the end, we might have put enough pressure on him that he finally made a mistake."

Kevin turned toward what was left of the club. "I hope so." The cost had been so high, though. He yawned and stumbled when he took his first step, but righted himself.

"Have you been drinking?" Antonio asked.

"I had one hours ago. I'm just tired. Thank you, though." Kevin pushed the fatigue from his mind and went to find the others. Jeremy and Tristan were standing with Harry and Spook. "Is there anything I can do?"

"No," Harry answered. "There's a lot to go through, and then Bull and I can decide what we want to do. But for now, you might as well go home. They're going to be here for a while because they need to see if there are any bodies." He sounded as tired and drawn as Kevin felt.

"I'll be at Angus's if anyone needs me." Kevin shared hugs with each of them, clinging to Harry the longest because he needed it the most right now. "It will be okay. You can rebuild."

"I know. Not sure I want to," Harry said, and Kevin realized in that instant that a part of Harry's gayhood, his coming of age and realizing the person he truly was, had been taken away forever. Even if it was rebuilt, Bronco's would never be the same. Kevin held Harry a minute longer, keeping his eyes closed so he could remember the club the way it was.

"Is he okay?" Angus asked from behind him.

Kevin released Harry, and Tristan took his place, comforting his partner while Kevin stepped away.

"He'll be okay. We all will," Kevin said and took Angus's hand. "Can you go?"

"Yeah. I'm done here." Angus walked with Kevin to his car. "I'll meet you at the house."

"What about the station?"

"I'll pick up my stuff and go home. Just meet me there." Angus patted the car lightly and then stepped back. Kevin pulled out and drove slowly through town to Angus's house.

When he parked and got out, the scent of wet and charred wood hung in the air. He walked around the side of the house and peered into the backyard. The scent was stronger, coming from the small pile of burned wreckage that filled the back corner of the yard. This all had to be over. That was all there was to it.

Kevin heard the garage doors open and walked back around to see Angus getting out of his car. Kevin helped him with his gear, which Angus left in the garage because of the smell. Then they went up into the house. Kevin honestly expected to be led right up to the bedroom, but Angus motioned to the living room. "I'm going to take a shower, and then I'll be right back."

He wasn't sure what was on Angus's mind, so Kevin settled on the sofa to wait. The cushions were comfortable, and he yawned and rested his head back. He was half asleep when Angus returned and sat next to him. "What is it?" Kevin asked when he saw the serious expression on Angus's face.

"I have something I need to tell you. Something I never told anyone... ever. See, I'm not a good person." Angus fidgeted on the sofa. "We were talking at the station, and one of the guys said something that stuck with me. I won't go into all that, but I think it's important that you know something. See, I became a firefighter—"

"Because of your parents and uncle," Kevin said.

"Yeah. But that isn't all. Back in Edinburgh, when our house burned down and my parents died...." Anguish filled his voice and tears ran down his cheeks. "It was all my fault. The fire.... It was because of me. I used to like candles, and I had lit some in the house... and.... They said the fire started in the living room, where I had lit candles while my parents were out, and I must have forgotten one...."

"So you weren't staying with a friend?"

"I was. Mom and Dad had gone out, and when they got back, I left. But I had filled the house with candles, and I must have forgotten one. If Mom and Dad didn't know, then...."

"Wait. You think you started the fire that killed your mom and dad?" Kevin asked. Angus nodded. "And you've carried this around all those years."

"Yeah." Angus covered his face. "I became a firefighter to try to make up for what I did, I guess. I don't know. I can never bring my parents back."

"But you don't know exactly how the fire started."

"No. I was away." But in his mind Angus did know. It was written in the misery on his face.

"But you've held on to this all this time?" Kevin asked. "You need to let it go. The candles may have had nothing to do with it."

"I kept telling myself that for a long time, and I kept hoping for some kind of answer."

Kevin knew that doubt mixed with guilt and then left to fester and build for years couldn't be erased with a single conversation. "You know that what happened has nothing to do with how I feel about you." Kevin cupped Angus's cheeks in his hands.

"But I could have been responsible for killing my parents. How could you care for someone like that?" Angus asked, and Kevin brought his face closer and kissed him, softly, on the lips.

"Because it doesn't matter. Not to me. And for the record, I doubt you had anything to do with that fire, and I can be just as stubborn as you." Kevin folded his arms over his chest and set his jaw. Angus smiled and shook his head slowly. "You don't know what happened, but you've assumed and let guilt take over the rest. I know your parents died in a fire, and that's all you know as well. The rest is supposition, and you need to let that go."

"But...." Angus seemed confused. "I just told you the one thing I'm...."

"Most ashamed of?" Kevin supplied.

"Yeah, and you don't seem to care."

"I care that you're hurting because of it. But it doesn't change the way I feel about you." Kevin leaned closer, placing his forehead against Angus's. "Think of it this way. Things happen for a reason. You became a firefighter because of that, didn't you?"

"Yeah," Angus answered.

"And you never told anyone else?" Kevin asked. Angus only shook his head. "Not even your uncle?"

"No."

Kevin stood and held out his hand. "I'm not making light of this, but it doesn't affect how I feel about you. Well, it does in a way...." Kevin saw worry flash across Angus's face. "Because it means you trust me, and I trust you. You've saved my life twice, and you'll always be my hero." Angus put his hand on Kevin's, and he tugged Angus to his feet.

"That's it?"

"What were you expecting?"

"I've held that inside all these years, and you act like it's not a big deal. Like the fact that I might have been responsible for my parent's death doesn't...."

"Make you a monster? Is that what you were going to say? Because it doesn't. You were a kid, and like I said, you don't know what happened. But let's just say you did leave a candle burning, and it did start the fire…. It still doesn't change how I feel. Why should it? It was a mistake." Kevin didn't say that he thought it strange that if a candle had been left burning that Angus's parents wouldn't have checked the house before they went to bed. "But I'm not willing to concede that you had anything to do with it at all."

"Damn, you're as stubborn as a mule." There was no heat in Angus's voice as he pulled Kevin to him, their warmth mingling.

"You love it," Kevin said.

"Yes… I do." He leaned closer and kissed him, hard. Kevin wasn't totally sure what had gotten into him. But when Angus lifted him off his feet, Kevin giggled.

"Put me down, I can walk," Kevin said as he laughed.

Angus didn't argue and instead kissed his words away as he carried him toward the bedroom. When Angus set him on the bed, Kevin held him around the neck, deepening the kiss as Angus quickly divested him of his clothes.

"I don't understand what's gotten into you," Kevin said as Angus pulled away his briefs, leaving him naked and most definitely confused. "Whatever I did, tell me so I can be sure to do it again."

Angus pressed him back on the bed, stroking his chest and down his belly. "You didn't reject me," he said and kissed just above his navel.

Kevin cupped Angus's cheeks in his hands. "Why would I?" He brought Angus up to him, eye to eye. "We all have things we're afraid of or ashamed of. It doesn't mean we should spend the rest of our lives alone or hating ourselves because of them. I'm honored that you told me, but it doesn't change anything. I still think you're the hottest, sexiest man I've ever met."

"Is that all?"

"No. You're my hero." Kevin felt his eyes well with tears, and he didn't know or care why. Angus's might have done the same. All he knew was that his heart was bursting. "You'll always be my own personal hero." He tugged him down and held him, kissing, pulling at Angus's shirt.

Angus pulled back and got off the bed. Kevin watched as he frantically yanked off his clothes, and then he was back, heat on heat.

"I need you," Angus whispered. Kevin hugged Angus around the shoulders, holding him tight, pressing their bodies together, soaking in Angus's heat and strength and giving Angus what he seemed to need. After a few seconds Angus trembled against him. Kevin thrust his hips upward, sliding his cock alongside Angus's, earning a soft moan. Kevin didn't fully understand what had happened, or why Angus seemed so passionate, but he drank it in.

"I love you," Angus whispered, and Kevin stopped, all his wondering ceasing in an instant. "I know it's too soon, and you don't have to say it back, but I love you." Angus's eyes shone.

"You do? How? I...." Kevin wasn't sure what he should say. "I love you too. But I didn't expect...." He'd waited so long for someone to say that to him, and now he'd messed it up.

"Hey," Angus said, locking his gaze onto Kevin's. "I do love you. I knew it the minute I raced into that club and saw you trying to help Bull. You're the most unselfish person I've ever met."

"Then what was all that about your parents and the fire? I don't understand."

"One of the guys said that if you tell someone your biggest secret, the thing you're most afraid of, and if they love you anyway, then they're the person you should be with. The person who loves you more than anyone else. I don't know if Mark was right, but as scared as I was when I saw you in that fire, I had to tell you my secret, the one thing I feared most."

"So that was a test?" Kevin asked.

"No. More like a leap of faith." Angus swallowed, and Kevin kissed him once again, making sure that Angus knew his faith hadn't been misplaced. Being trusted with something held so deep and close all that time was heady. And when Angus pulled back, gazing down over him, he heated even more under the fire that burned in Angus's eyes.

"I used to dream of someone looking at me like that," Kevin whispered, arching his back as Angus trailed his fingers over his belly. The touch was barely there, and yet it burned straight to his heart. "I watched all my friends find these grand passions that took them away from me... in a way. They all found love, and I thought I had too, but... he... never looked at me like that."

Angus lifted his gaze. "How exactly is that?"

"Like you're dying of thirst, and I'm the oasis on the horizon."

Angus grinned, wide, his smile lines going all the way to his eyes, and damn if that wasn't bright enough to light the night for miles. "You are my oasis." Angus claimed his mouth in a ravenous kiss that damn near blew the top off Kevin's head. Heat coursed through him, pulsing through his veins. He clung to Angus, body thrumming, cock so hard it ached and jumped between their bodies with each beat of his racing heart.

When Angus broke the kiss and slid down him, licking a blazing trail across his skin, Kevin had to remember to breathe so he wouldn't break into a coughing fit. Not that it mattered, because when Angus opened his mouth and sucked him between his lips, Kevin gasped deeply as the sensation of heat and pressure washed over him. "Angus!"

He stopped. "Do that again. Call my name with such need…." He sucked him once more, and Kevin did just what Angus wanted, crying out his name over and over until all his senses centered only on him. "I do love you, Angus."

"Aye, and I love you," Angus said, letting the accent that hardly ever showed come through loud and clear. He smiled and went back to sucking Kevin's cock as though it were candy, gripping him with his lips, pulling like he was trying to yank his release from him. When Kevin came in a rush, screaming, "Angus," at the top of his lungs, Angus swallowed, taking it all.

Kevin slipped from between Angus's lips, and he lifted his head. What he saw stole his breath once again. Angus leaned over him, a smile on his full lips, the light from the hall shining in his beautiful blue eyes. Kevin knew this was what it felt like to be loved. Warmth spread through him, filling him from head to toe as he basked in the heat of a single smile.

"Kevin," Angus whispered, almost as though he were praying.

"Yeah?" he whispered.

"Why couldn't I have met you a long time ago?"

"Because you weren't ready for me. Like I said, things happen for a reason. Maybe those fires and all that's happened in the last few weeks had to happen so I could meet you." Kevin shrugged and wound his fingers through Angus's soft, curly hair. "I know it sounds dumb and extreme, but having something good come from all this helps me get through it."

"I'll help you get through everything you need," Angus whispered, and Kevin nodded. "So I guess the big question was, was it worth it?"

Kevin smiled. "Only time will tell. I know that's a cop-out, but it's too early to give you an answer. That's a question that can only be answered with distance." Kevin pressed to Angus and rolled him on the bed until he lay on top of him. Angus wound his legs around Kevin's, stroking down his back. Kevin gasped when Angus slid his hands over his butt, rubbing and teasing.

"I want you so bad. I have for days, but I didn't want to hurt you," Angus whispered as he sucked lightly on Kevin's ear. "And I won't now."

"I know you never would."

"How?" Angus asked. "You haven't known me that long."

"It's the way you look at me. Like I hung the moon."

"In my eyes you did." Angus tugged him into another kiss.

Kevin straddled Angus's hips, rolling his pelvis so his cock slid back and forth on his belly. Damn, that was hot and slick. Angus cradled his ass in his strong hands, kneading and pressing him back.

"I need…." Angus's voice broke and the last words came out only as the movement of his lips. Kevin ceased his hip rolls and reached to the bedside table. He found a condom and some lube and slicked his fingers.

"Jesus God, I want to see," Angus said with a shaky voice as Kevin slicked himself.

"You'll do more than see," Kevin said huskily, pulling his fingers from his own opening and grabbing the condom from where he'd dropped it on the bedding. He opened it and slid back, running his fingers along Angus's thick shaft, listening as his groans filled the room. Then he rolled down the condom, slicked it good, and positioned himself before slowly taking him in.

"Holy hell," Angus swore as Kevin rolled his eyes and gasped, stretching to take all of Angus inside him.

"I forgot how big you are. Not something I'm going to do again." Kevin's mouth dropped open, and he whimpered. The burn and stretch felt amazing, the flash of pain morphing into mind-numbing pleasure. He heaved for breath, thankful he didn't cough, as his butt rested against Angus's hips. He stilled, breathing deeply, and then Angus thrust upward.

Light exploded behind his eyes, and Kevin shook as Angus dragged his cock over that spot inside, sending lightning up his spine to his brain.

"You are so beautiful like that," Angus whispered. "Stretched out, covered in sweat, eyes sparkling, hair a little wild."

Kevin tried to smooth it down, but Angus stroked down his arms and then threaded their fingers together as he thrust up into him. "Angus, I…." Kevin clamped down on him, using his thighs like he was riding a horse. Hell, Angus felt like a damn horse. "What are you doing?" Kevin asked as Angus slid both of them toward the edge of the bed. He released Kevin's hands and wrapped one arm around his back and the other under Kevin's ass. Then he stood and Kevin circled his legs around Angus's waist. "Were you in a circus?"

Angus turned Kevin around and laid him on the side of the bed. "I want you, Kev. I want to be in control." He leaned over him, his lips inches from Kevin's, close enough to feel his hot breath on his lips. "I made you a promise, and I intend to deliver." Angus snapped his hips and Kevin gasped. "I want you to promise that you'll give us a chance. I want you in my life."

"I want that too," Kevin groaned. "But this isn't fair. Fucking me to get the answer you want."

"I want to be in your life too. Will you do that?"

"God yes," Kevin agreed. He stretched on the bed while Angus drove into him, taking him to passionate heights he'd only dreamed of. When Angus leaned over him once again, Kevin pulled him down. The kiss was sloppy and inelegant, but hot as sin. He held on and let Angus drive him higher and further until he could take no more. He came in a rush, shaking, cursing, and gasping, with Angus following right behind him and falling on top of him.

"Am I hurting you?" Angus asked without moving to get up.

"No. I like it." Kevin stroked the back of Angus's head and closed his eyes. Being held and loved felt amazing, and he didn't want it to end for anything.

"You've been staying here for the better part of two weeks. Are you sure you want to get an apartment?" Angus whispered in his ear. "You could stay here with me."

"I can't. We need to take things a little slow for a little while." Kevin stroked Angus's cheeks. "My new apartment is just a few blocks away, and we'll see each other whenever you're off shift. But I need the chance to put my life back together after all that's happened, and I need to be independent to do it. So much has happened and there is so much I want to do." Kevin sighed when Angus backed away. "It isn't that I don't love you. I do. But I need a chance to get my feet under me again."

"I see."

"No, you don't. I'm not pushing you away, not for a second, and don't think I am. I need to be myself again so I can be a proper part of us." Kevin sat up and kissed him. "I'm asking for a little time."

"I can do that," Angus said, his expression unreadable. "I suppose it's too early. But I'm selfish and I want you here. I love having you in my bed." Angus took care of the condom and then lay down on the bed. Kevin curled around him, a sticky mess and not caring in the least. "You know, you're the first guy I've slept with all night where fucking wasn't involved," Angus said.

"You've never slept with someone before just because it was nice?"

"Only you, and you're the only one I want to," Angus told him, which pleased Kevin no end. "But I'll give you all the time you need." Angus put his arms around Kevin, gently stroking up and down his side. It was nice, soothing, the rhythmic caresses relaxing Kevin half to sleep. "I know what's important. I didn't before I met you, but I do now."

"I think I do too," Kevin breathed. He'd been so broken up about Ken, but Ken had left as soon as something better came along.

"I won't leave unless you tell me to go," Angus said softly. "That I can promise you."

"I know," Kevin whispered as his eyelids got heavier and heavier. "And I'm the same."

"Good," Angus said and held him a little tighter as Kevin drifted off to sleep.

EPILOGUE

February

"COME ON, we're going to be late. We spent too much time at the firehouse," Kevin said nervously. He knew he shouldn't have scheduled the initial run-through of the fire-simulator program today. There was too much going on. "Sorry to rush."

"I know. But they loved the program at the station and wanted to spend more time with it. That's good, right?"

"Of course it is, but I'm nervous enough tonight." He had spent a lot of his extra time working with Angus and Zach on the program, and he was thrilled the firefighters liked it. They also offered great suggestions, which he wanted to incorporate before the next run-through. Still, it was lot in one day. "I have your long coat. It's really cold outside, and I don't want any of the special parts to freeze off." He waited in the living room—their living room as of a month ago—for Angus to join him.

"Do I look okay?" Angus said as he came in the room, and Kevin forgot his own name.

He dropped Angus's coat over the back of the sofa. "We're not going," he pronounced. "No way, no how."

"Why? What's wrong?" Angus walked over to the nearest mirror.

"Nothing. I'm going to have to stand guard over you with every guy in the place." Kevin wanted to pull off his tuxedo and lead Angus back to what was now their bedroom to slowly take off everything Angus was wearing—

except the kilt, of course. That was staying right where it was. Kevin figured he could use it like reins while he rode Angus to bliss.

Angus chuckled. "No one is going to see me once they get a look at your handsomeness." He strode over to him and tugged Kevin into a kiss. "Janice is counting on both of us. And you're the master of ceremonies for this evening, so if you don't show…."

"I know, but damn, you're edible."

"So are you," Angus told him, which made Kevin smile. He knew he wasn't as good-looking as Angus, but hearing and seeing that Angus only had eyes for him always had him walking on cloud nine. "Now let's go, sweetheart." Angus retrieved his coat and put it on while Kevin did the same. Then they left the house and walked down the stairs to the car.

As they rode, Kevin couldn't help running his hand up Angus's bare leg. When Angus growled for the third time, he pulled his hand away and let the man drive in peace… for now.

To say Angus was stunning was putting it mildly. The red and blue tartan plaid looked amazing, as did his white shirt and the socks that hugged Angus's meaty calves. Of course the best parts were underneath all that, and God help anyone who tried to grab a peek. Kevin was definitely prepared to claw eyes out if necessary.

"Calm down, sweetheart. No one is going to touch what's yours." Angus patted his leg. "Just remember that tonight you're doing something pretty special and helping people who need it. That's why we're there." Angus parked and they got out of the car. As soon as it was locked, Angus joined him on the sidewalk and took his hand.

Searchlights filled the sky outside the brand-new Bronco's, with its huge neon sign and laser projectors that made patterns on the building and sidewalk outside the door. The body of the arsonist had been found in the ruins of the club, outside the office area. Bull and Harry had decided to rebuild after the fire and to make the club better than ever. Lighting, sound— everything was state of the art. Angus had been brought in to help design the fire-suppression systems, and Zach and Kevin had designed a custom video and camera system that could project not only images, but could turn the crowd into cartoons and even create a custom comic book of the evening.

Janice met them at the door, looking stunning in a cashmere coat. "This looks amazing."

"The official opening is tomorrow night," Kevin said as they approached. He reached out to shake her hand but was tugged into a hug instead. Then Angus gallantly kissed her cheek. "But they agreed to let us have the club for the benefit tonight. Would you like a tour?" Kevin asked as they passed inside. Angus took their coats, and Janice took Kevin's arm as he led her through.

"What is all that?"

"Lasers. They can project images onto smoke or the ceiling of the club. The video screens can also play videos, or they can be linked together so images seem to move around the club. There are cameras in the two corners of the room that take special images that are turned into computer caricatures. They can be inserted into a comic-book sequence that people can buy if they want."

Janice looked around the space, which was a full story higher than the old club had been. "What's the catwalk for?"

"It can be raised to the ceiling or lowered to become like a stage for dancers and things." It was where the strippers would perform and go-go boys would dance, but he figured he didn't need to go into that much detail. "Also, when it's raised, security can watch the crowd from there to keep everyone safe."

"We're not having the auction from up there, are we?" Janice asked.

"No," Kevin giggled. "We don't want to give away the goods for free. The stage area over there is where we'll hold the auction, but I do have dancers who will be using the catwalk. Advance tickets sold out a week ago, and we'll be selling tickets at the door tonight." At almost twice the price, and given that the website had been pegged, he expected people to start lining up soon. "It's a cash bar."

Angus tapped him on the shoulder. "I'm going to check on the waitstaff. Let me take your coats into the back," he said, and he leaned in to kiss Kevin. "I'll be back."

Kevin watched him go and swallowed hard.

"I know just how you feel," Janice said from next to him. "That's one stunning man, with a heart of gold."

"Yeah, he is." Kevin pulled his attention back to Janice. "As Angus said, we'll have waiters passing hors d'oeuvres for most of the evening.

They aren't going to be shirtless, but they'll be sleeveless, to show a hint of muscle."

"Sounds lovely."

"We got all the food donated, and bar proceeds will go to the charity as well."

"Hi, Janice," Zach said as he hurried up with Tristan and Jeremy. "You've all done an amazing job. How can I thank you?"

"You helped Kevin when he needed it. That's thanks enough," Zach said. "There are local news trucks outside. You two should go out there and talk to them. Bull will be right out to join you."

Kevin wasn't so sure how he felt about being on the news, but Janice took his arm. "Come on, young man, let's make your television debut." She led him toward the door, and Bull joined them. Once outside, Kevin was thankful that they wanted to talk to Janice and Bull primarily. He said a few words and let the others do most of the talking. When it was over, he was shocked at the size of the crowd waiting to get in. The word was obviously out, with a lot of the men in line wearing kilts.

"What will we do with all these people?" Janice whispered as they went back inside.

"Bull and his team will manage the front door. They're really good at that. As people leave for the evening, others will be let in once we reach capacity." Kevin was so excited he could hardly stay still. Angus returned, and Kevin excused himself. Janice smiled and nodded, continuing to look around.

"We're going to open the doors soon and start letting people with tickets in. Is there anything else you need?" Bull asked.

"If you're ready, then we are too," Kevin said. Angus joined them and handed Kevin a drink. He downed it, the warmth spreading through him.

"Feeling better?" Angus asked, and Kevin nodded and handed the glass to one of the bartenders. Angus immediately took him into his arms and held him close. "Everything is going to be great. You've done an amazing job with this." Angus kissed him as the music started and lights began to flash. "I'm so proud of you."

Kevin moved closer, and Angus looked up. Suddenly the music shifted, slowing, and Angus began to move, propelling him slowly around the floor. As they moved, Kevin saw Zach drag Bull out onto the floor. Soon Jeremy brought Lowell, and Harry joined them with Tristan, the eight of them dancing together. Kevin kept glancing around, enjoying the fact that each of his friends had found love.

Angus touched his chin, and Kevin centered his attention on the man who filled his heart. For a few minutes there was just the two of them, moving and dancing on the nearly empty floor. "God, I love you," Angus whispered. "You make each day special and never stop amazing me with your talent." Kevin blushed and then blinked at the intensity in Angus's deep cobalt eyes. They stopped moving, and Angus leaned in to kiss him. They got lost in the kiss until the music stopped and silence settled around them.

"I love you too," Kevin said as he heard similar whispers around him. The club remained silent for a few seconds as they all basked in the glow of their happiness. Kevin could feel it like a warm hand on his shoulder.

Then he heard a door open and close and saw the waiters fan out through the room. It was time to open the club and start the next chapter in their lives, and as long as he had Angus, Kevin knew he'd be ready for whatever came next.

Bronco's Boys: Book One

Former mercenary Bull Krebbs now heads up security at his nightclub in Harrisburg, PA. Working the door night after night, he's seen it all. Though tough on the outside, he's a little hurt that people find him unapproachable. Then he pulls a cute twink out of line to perform a random search, and he's surprised when the guy giggles and squirms.

Zach Spencer, graphic artist, twink, and seriously ticklish, isn't intimidated by Bull. He's in awe, and when Bull saves Zach from being trampled on the dance floor, Zach finds his inspiration for the superhero in his graphic novel.

Soon Zach wants more and makes his move by asking Bull on a date. Though small, he has a backbone of steel. He'll need it— their happily ever after is thwarted at every turn, including by Bull's interloping mother showing up unannounced and enemies from Bull's past threatening to pull him to the other side of the world.

www.dreamspinnerpress.com

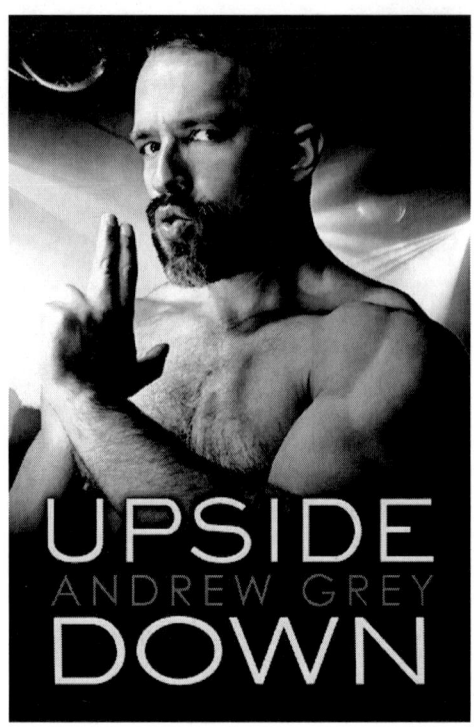

Sequel to *Inside Out*
Bronco's Boys: Book Two

Lowell Cartwright's life as a mercenary problem solver has taken its toll, and after one more difficult job, he wants out. For help, he turns to Bull, a soldier of fortune turned club owner—not exactly a friend, but the best chance Lowell has. He visits Bull's club to scope it out and meets Jeremy Hodgson. The twink captures his attention in a big way. Bull tells Lowell to stay away from the club until he decides whether he can help, so Lowell stays in town. When he spots Jeremy passed out on the floor of a convenience store, he goes to Jeremy's aid.

Lowell piques Jeremy's interest immediately, pushing all the right buttons. Then, when Jeremy needs help, Lowell's kindness turns interest into something more.

But trouble comes knocking when Jeremy's place is bugged. Maybe Lowell's past is catching up to him, or maybe the danger centers on Jeremy's roommate Tristan's mysterious boyfriend. Whatever the source of the problem, the future Lowell and Jeremy hope for doesn't stand a chance unless they can find a way to protect themselves.

www.dreamspinnerpress.com

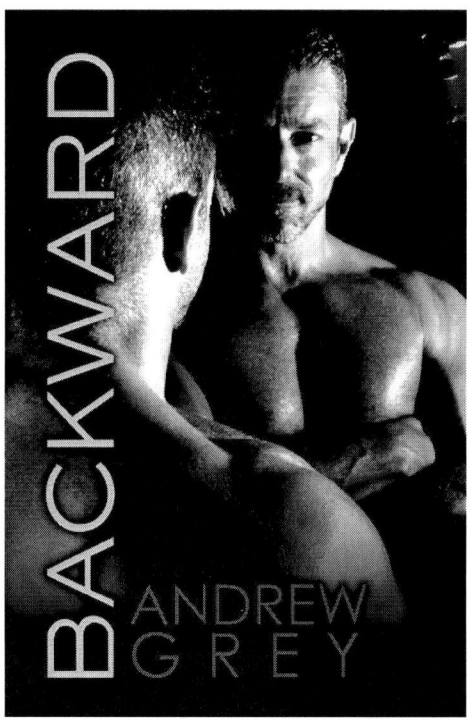

Sequel to *Upside Down*
Bronco's Boys: Book Three

Club owner Harry Klinger has had his eye on Tristan Martin for months, but never had the nerve to approach him. He's watched as Tristan dated Eddie and then reluctantly sat on the sidelines during the emotional breakup when Tristan discovered Eddie was dealing drugs. Now that Tristan seems to be healing, Harry hopes to get his chance.

When Eddie sends his men into Harry's club to harass Tristan, Harry steps in to help. Tristan is reluctant at first since he admittedly has terrible taste in men, but Harry seems genuine, and Tristan can't help but think Harry's sexy as well and begins to hope for happiness for both of them.

Unfortunately, Eddie isn't behaving rationally, sampling too much of his own product. With his determination to take Tristan back, it'll take more than Harry's help to keep Tristan safe as Eddie ratchets up his attempts to get what he wants.

www.dreamspinnerpress.com

ANDREW GREY grew up in western Michigan with a father who loved to tell stories and a mother who loved to read them. Since then he has lived all over the country and traveled throughout the world. He has a master's degree from the University of Wisconsin-Milwaukee and now works full-time on his writing. Andrew's hobbies include collecting antiques, gardening, and leaving his dirty dishes anywhere but in the sink (particularly when writing). He considers himself blessed with an accepting family, fantastic friends, and the world's most supportive and loving husband. Andrew currently lives in beautiful historic Carlisle, Pennsylvania.

E-mail: andrewgrey@comcast.net
Website: www.andrewgreybooks.com

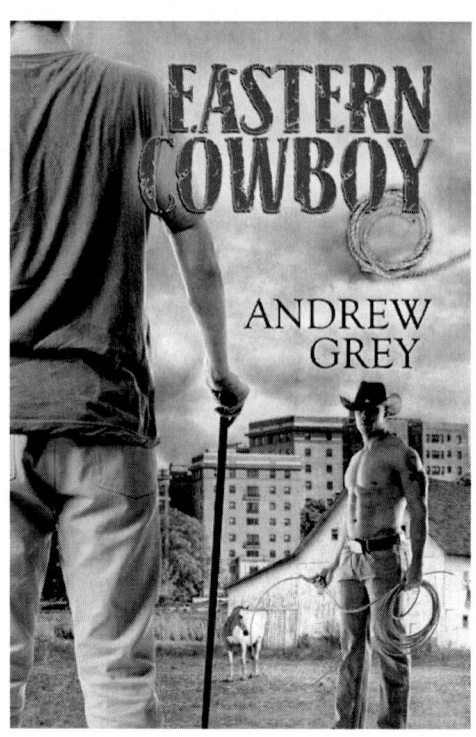

Brighton McKenzie inherited one of the last pieces of farmland in suburban Baltimore. It has been in his family since Maryland was a colony, though it has lain fallow for years. Selling it for development would be easy, but Brighton wants to honor his grandfather's wishes and work it again. Unfortunately, an accident left him relying on a cane, so he'll need help. Tanner Houghton used to work on a ranch in Montana until a vengeful ex got him fired because of his sexuality. He comes to Maryland at the invitation of his cousin and is thrilled to have a chance to get back to the kind of work he loves.

Brighton is instantly drawn to the intensely handsome and huge Tanner—he's everything Brighton likes in a man, though he holds back because Tanner is an employee, and because he can't understand why a man as virile as Tanner would be interested in him. But that isn't the worst of their problems. They have to face the machinations of Brighton's aunt, Tanner's ex suddenly wanting him back, and the need to find a way to make the farm financially viable before they lose Brighton's family legacy.

www.dreamspinnerpress.com

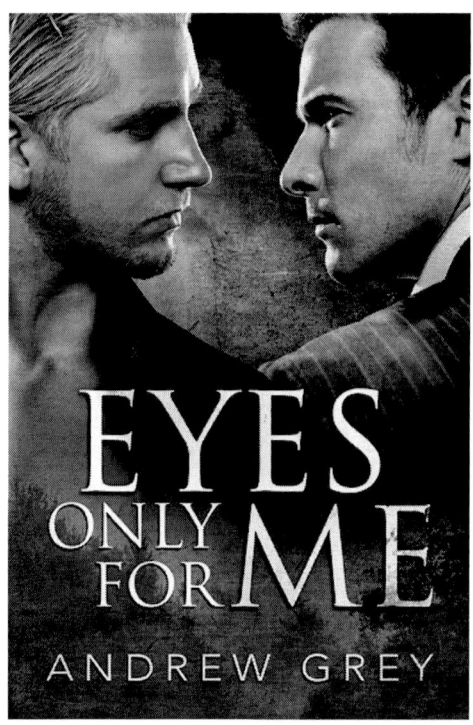

For years, Clayton Potter's been friends and workout partners with Ronnie. Though Clay is attracted, he's never come on to Ronnie because, let's face it, Ronnie only dates women.

When Clay's father suffers a heart attack, Ronnie, having recently lost his dad, springs into action, driving Clay to the hospital over a hundred miles away. To stay close to Clay's father, the men share a hotel room near the hospital, but after an emotional day, one thing leads to another, and straight-as-an-arrow Ronnie make a proposal that knocks Clay's socks off! Just a little something to take the edge off.

Clay responds in a way he's never considered. After an amazing night together, Clay expects Ronnie to ignore what happened between them and go back to his old life. Ronnie surprises him and seems interested in additional exploration. Though they're friends, Clay suddenly finds it hard to accept the new Ronnie and suspects that Ronnie will return to his old ways. Maybe they both have a thing or two to learn.

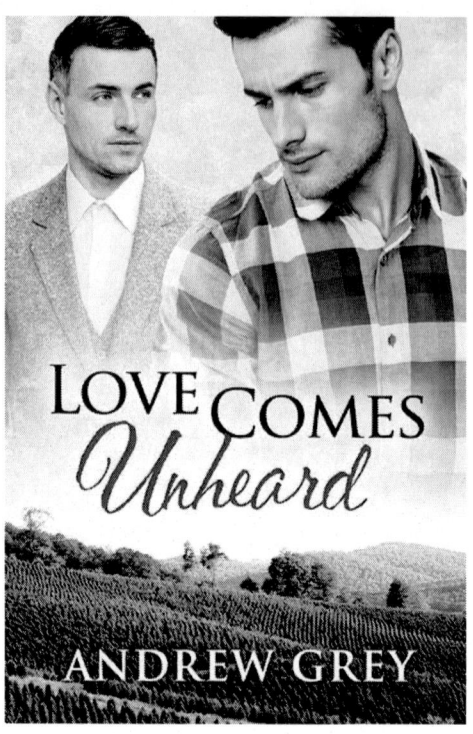

A Senses Series Story

Garrett Bowman is shocked that fate has brought him to a family who can sign. He's spent much of his life on the outside looking in, even within his biological family, and to be accepted and employed is more than he could have hoped for. With Connor, who's included him in his family, Garrett has found a true friend, but with the distant Brit Wilson Haskins, Garrett may have found something more. In no time, Garrett gets under Wilson's skin and finds his way into Wilson's heart, and over shared turbulent family histories, Wilson and Garrett form a strong bond.

Wilson's especially impressed with the way Garrett's so helpful to Janey, Connor and Dan's daughter, who is also deaf. When Wilson's past shows up in the form of his brother Reggie, bringing unscrupulous people to whom Reggie owes money, life begins to unravel. These thugs don't care how they get their money, what they have to do, or who they might hurt. Without the strength of love and the bonds of family and friends, Garrett and Wilson could pay the ultimate price.

www.dreamspinnerpress.com

On the train from Lancaster to Philadelphia, Trent runs into Brit, his first love and the first man to break his heart. They've both been through a lot in the years since they parted ways, and as they talk, the old connection tenuously strengthens. Trent finally works up the nerve to call Brit, and their rekindled friendship slowly grows into the possibility for more. But both men are shadowed by their pasts as they explore the path they didn't take the first time. If they can move beyond loss and painful memories, they might find their road leads to a second chance at happiness.

A story from the Dreamspinner Press 2015 Daily Dose package "Never Too Late."

www.dreamspinnerpress.com

SAVING
FAITHLESS
CREEK

ANDREW GREY

Blair Montague is sent to Newton, Montana, to purchase a ranch and some land for his father. It's a trip he doesn't want to make. But his father paid for his college education in exchange for Blair working for him in his casinos, so Blair has no choice. When he finds out he'll be dealing with Royal Masters, the man who bullied him in high school, he is shocked. Then Blair is surprised when he finds that Royal's time in the Marines has changed him to the point where Blair could be attracted to him… if he's willing to take that chance.

Royal's life hasn't been a bed of roses. He saw combat in the military that left him scarred, and not just on the outside. When he inherits his father's ranch, he discovers his father wasn't a good manager and the ranch is in trouble. The sale of land would put them back on good footing, but he is suspicious of Blair's father's motives, and with good reason. The attraction between them is hard for either to ignore, but it could all evaporate once the land deal is sealed.

www.dreamspinnerpress.com

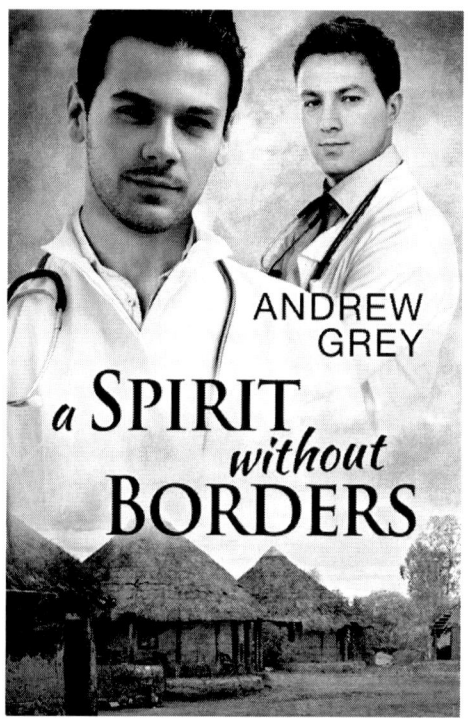

ANDREW
GREY

a SPIRIT
without
BORDERS

Sequel to *A Heart Without Borders*
Without Borders: Book Two

Dillon McDowell, an infectious disease specialist, jumps at the opportunity to work with Doctors Without Borders in Liberia. But when he arrives, things are very different than he expected, and he's out of his depth. Will Scarlet takes him under his wing and helps him adjust. A hint of normalcy comes when a group of local boys invite Dillon to play soccer.

Will's family rejected him for being gay, and he's closed off his heart. Even though meeting Dillon opens him to the possibility of love, he's wary. They come from different worlds, and Will plans to volunteer for another stint overseas. But Will realizes what Dillon means to him when Dillon becomes ill, and they can no longer deny their feelings.

When Dillon's soccer friends lose their parents and aunt to disease, Will and Dillon must work together to ensure that the boys aren't cast adrift in a society that's afraid they might be contagious. They must also decide if their feelings are real or just the result of proximity and hardship.

www.dreamspinnerpress.com

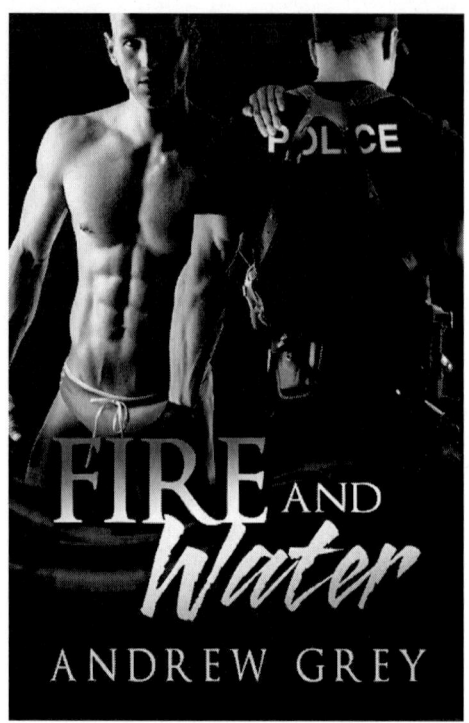

Carlisle Cops: Book One

Officer Red Markham knows about the ugly side of life after a car accident left him scarred and his parents dead. His job policing the streets of Carlisle, PA, only adds to the ugliness, and lately, drug overdoses have been on the rise. One afternoon, Red is dispatched to the local Y for a drowning accident involving a child. Arriving on site, he finds the boy rescued by lifeguard Terry Baumgartner. Of course, Red isn't surprised when gorgeous Terry won't give him and his ugly mug the time of day.

Overhearing one of the officers comment about him being shallow opens Terry's eyes. Maybe he isn't as kindhearted as he always thought. His friend Julie suggests he help those less fortunate by delivering food to the elderly. On his route he meets outspoken Margie, a woman who says what's on her mind. Turns out, she's Officer Red's aunt.

Red and Terry's worlds collide as Red tries to track the source of the drugs and protect Terry from an ex-boyfriend who won't take no for an answer. Together they might discover a chance for more than they expected—if they can see beyond what's on the surface.

www.dreamspinnerpress.com

Carlisle Cops: Book Two

Carter Schunk is a dedicated police officer with a difficult past and a big heart. When he's called to a domestic disturbance, he finds a fatally injured woman, and a child, Alex, who is in desperate need of care. Child Services is called, and the last man on earth Carter wants to see walks through the door. Carter had a fling with Donald a year ago and found him as cold as ice since it ended.

Donald (Ice) Ickle has had a hard life he shares with no one, and he's closed his heart to all. It's partly to keep himself from getting hurt and partly the way he deals with a job he's good at, because he does what needs to be done without getting emotionally involved. When he meets Carter again, he maintains his usual distance, but Carter gets under his skin, and against his better judgment, Donald lets Carter guilt him into taking Alex when there isn't other foster care available. Carter even offers to help care for the boy.

Donald has a past he doesn't want to discuss with anyone, least of all Carter, who has his own past he'd just as soon keep to himself. But it's Alex's secrets that could either pull them together or rip them apart—secrets the boy isn't able to tell them and yet could be the key to happiness for all of them.

www.dreamspinnerpress.com

Las Vegas Escorts: Book One

Hunter Wolf is a highly paid Las Vegas escort with a face and body that have men salivating and paying a great deal for him to fulfill their fantasies. He keeps his own fantasies to himself, not that they matter.

Grant is an elementary-school teacher who works miracles with his summer school students. He discovered his gift while in high school, tutoring Hunter, a fellow student. They meet again when Hunter rescues Grant in a club. Grant doesn't know Hunter is an escort or that they share similarly painful pasts involving family members' substance abuse.

After the meeting, Hunter invites Grant to one of the finest restaurants in Las Vegas. Hunter is charming, sexy, and gracious, and Grant is intrigued. With more in common than they realized, the two men decide to give a relationship a try. At first, Grant believes he can deal with Hunter's profession and accepts that Hunter will be faithful with his heart if not his body. Both men find their feelings run deeper than either imagined. For Grant, it's harder than he thought to accept Hunter's occupation, and Hunter's feelings for Grant now make work nearly impossible. But Hunter's choice of profession comes with a price, which could involve Grant's job and their hearts—a price that might be too high for either of them to pay.

www.dreamspinnerpress.com

Sequel to *The Price*
Las Vegas Escorts: Book Two

Ember is a drop-dead gorgeous Las Vegas escort. He notices Alejandro in some of the classes he teaches at his side business—a yoga studio. Then, color-blind Alejandro further captures Ember's attention when he's momentarily blinded by a quick change in light and needs Ember's help at a club. What Ember doesn't expect is the way Alejandro touches his heart.

Alejandro never intended to develop feelings for Ember. He's in Las Vegas for a year to sow some wild oats. But Alejandro quickly sees more in Ember when he sets out to make some of Alejandro's dreams come true—including a trip to the Grand Canyon and the beaches of LA. Alejandro's wild oats could turn into something memorable.

Ember knows keeping his escort job from Alejandro isn't the right thing to do, but he wants to be liked for who he is. Alejandro keeps his own secrets for the same reason. But Alejandro's family obligations, along with Ember's profession, could make it impossible for the two of them to stay together—unless they can figure out how to make the most of the gifts they've been given.

www.dreamspinnerpress.com

Manufactured by Amazon.ca
Acheson, AB

13081138R00111